HOPE

by dhtreichler

GOING TO SEED

Joshua tree seeds? Do I need to fly to LA and go hiking just to make this dish? What's the story X? Of course, Chef Xavier 'X' Francis isn't about to share his insight with me. After all, my job is to tell the world his secrets, among those of all the other chefs I cover for my blog site. As I watch his practiced preparation in his most recent release on his YouTube site it strikes me his usual stream of consciousness is not as gently offensive as usual. *Must be because he's not dissecting another chef's creation.*

"This is one of those stirring moments when you let your mind contemplate something arousing?" X adlibs. "And I know that's something different for each of you lovely ladies. For you guys it's something different. I know. Don't want anyone to think I'm not cognizant of the differences between us that make us all the same. Anyway. If you can get aroused stirring this dish call me. I just might be interested… in at least a conversation about how you did it. Now me? I get aroused by the most curious things. Something most of you all take for granted. Oops." X raises the pot off the burner. "You need to keep stirring it for a bit longer. Until the bubbles disappear. Like so. Do we have a close up here? That's a good camera person. Just in case any of you were wondering, the person responsible for capturing this glorious moment is not a guy. Makayla is my creative director." X turns to look around the camera as if he's trying to look into it from the other end. "Can you turn this thing on yourself so all those watching can see what a gorgeous woman you are?" X apparently gets the head shake rather than the nod he was expecting. He frowns. "Well. Guess I'll just have to keep your apparition to myself then." X shakes his head and returns to his pot and the maze of ingredients he previously apportioned to the right amounts to prepare this dish in near record time. "I learned the

3

Joshua tree seed trick from a Gabrielino-Tongva tribesman who happened to live across the street from a Somali restaurant owned by chef Dom Dualeh. Most of you will have to think back to that particular episode, where he demonstrated how he spiced his Sambusa meats to draw the fire out of the chili spices." He then looks away, and returns to camera uncharacteristically intense. "Unfortunately, Chef Dom is no longer with us. He lost hope of ever changing the world and left it last year."

X shakes the moment off, looks at Makayla, "What's that? Who are the Gabrielino-Tongva tribesmen?" X looks like: why is she asking me this question? Everyone should know the answer. "They're the Native Americans who were driven out of their tribal lands in and around what is now LA. Hairy still lives there. Who's Hairy? Well I certainly am." X looks at his arms. "Probably need hair nets for these suckers. Anyway, Hairy is this really nice guy who's generally chewing a peyote button he harvests from the deserts that are part of the national parks. Told me he figures that's part of the payments the government still owes his people for taking those lands from them in the first place. Now I don't think Hairy was hallucinating about the Joshua tree seeds, but anything's possible."

Typical episode, long on extraneous but interesting dialog and not so much on the particular dish he's preparing. At the end of the show probably not many could replicate what he prepared, or what was prepared by a chef he visits in the most remote kitchens in the world. But when you're no longer running the kitchen of a famous New York restaurant not many get to sample what you've prepared anyway. The fun is contemplating different food combinations than you find in most cook books or even websites. That's why he goes to such remote places. And then there are those in between episodes where he makes something that is vaguely familiar. Something you've either tried or heard of, but is made using ingredients you'd never have thought of. How that all tastes remain a mystery unless you go find those ingredients and try it yourself. X tries it and gives a verdict on air, but no one really knows if he's telling you the truth about how it tastes.

4

"You may be wondering why Hairy didn't suggest ground peyote buttons for this dish. And I have to admit Hairy told me peyote goes with everything. It's like chocolate for your mind. At least that's how he described it. But I'm not convinced peyote would improve the flavor combination I'm trying to achieve. I know the purpose of most dishes is to create a memorable experience. My biggest concern is whether someone eating a dish with peyote will remember the dish the next morning. There are definite advantages to forgetting a fast food experience, but we're not talking hamburgers here. We're talking slow food. Flavors that need time to work together. And only in time does the new flavor emerge, drawn out of the ingredients. Surprising your taste buds with something totally unexpected. Like pubic hair on a baby or a moustache on a teenage girl. Which reminds me. I need to trim my beard as it's getting a bit long and that's why I have this chin net on. Don't want to find course hair in the food. Or non-course or maybe intercourse hair as that would make it a three-course meal."

Like I said. X isn't as mildly offensive as usual because he only has himself to critique. But I am curious about what he's going to do to finish this dish. I wonder whether the Joshua tree seeds actually add anything or are they just an extravagance to get your attention. Just then I get a text from 'Z', the owner of my blogsite and budding media mogul. Z's real name is Zubair Ross.

J:

Need 300 words on Joshua tree seeds. X has them in his latest video and questions are coming fast and

Z is not patient. I need to respond now.

Z:

Working it. Actually watching the show now.

Okay, X. What are the rest of the ingredients? But I have to multitask now. Got to check the public sources, but not Wikipedia as everyone goes there first. What are the obscure sites? Something about the… what was the name of that Indian Tribe? Gabrielino-Tongva? What's there? I'm looking at different sites when I hear X continuing his dialog or was it diatribe?

"I know you're wondering where Hairy came up with Joshua tree seeds. That's an interesting discussion. Hairy said his people ate like a ton of acorns. But if you've ever tried to eat an acorn you know they're extremely hard nuts. So while the men went fishing and hunted to a lesser extent since they were right on the coast there, the women foraged for nuts. But they had to ground them up and cook them in a meal like mash which is how they ate their acorns. Interesting, hunh? Actually, Hairy only gave me half the story. I had to go research the rest myself."

No sense looking into that any more since X discussed it on his video. People want to know about Joshua tree seeds, not acorns. And the Indians who turned X onto the seeds didn't mention them in the things they wrote about. Just another seed they used to cook with. So why would X pick up on a seed that was of no particular significance to the people who mentioned them? Was it the fact they're different? That they're not commercially available? That they're something exotic and people will be wanting to know more about them and that will cause them to tune in to the next episode of his series? What people are looking for is the unusual, not the run of the mill stuff they find at Whole Foods. But X is canny. He knows Whole Foods will find a supplier if enough customers ask about it. Particularly if it has any kind of unusual health benefits.

I start my blog.

Joshua Tree Seeds

Joshua tree is a yucca plant, although this version is only known to grow in the Joshua Tree Park in southern California. Its spikey structure is instantly recognizable by many. The fruit and seeds of the plant have been used by the native peoples of the region for generations. However, the fruit is never eaten raw because the plant contains Siporin's, a toxic compound which is not easily absorbed by humans, but can still make you sick. Cooking or baking the fruit and or seeds remove the Siporin's making the resulting fruit or seeds harmless.

The Gabrielino-Tongva Indian tribes that inhabited the Joshua Tree Park area in pre-western eras often roasted and ground the seeds to add to other seeds they harvested to make breads and mashes. They also added the roasted seeds to herbal teas and coffees to drink on cold desert nights.

No reports of distinctive flavors or medicinal benefit have been identified. It appears Joshua tree seeds are simply a source of nutrition that seldom stood on their own. Rather, Joshua tree seeds were abundant and filled in the total harvest needed to feed the tribes.

This raises the question: why is a Joshua tree seed important in the creation of Chef Xavier Francis? Much like the other ingredients of the particular dish he created, this is one ingredient that does not stand alone. Rather it adds to the flavor flow that presents itself to you, either inspiring further consumption or repelling your tastes and interest in the dish. But that is not unusual. If you're a seed eater, you should like this addition to your repertoire. If not, it will not stimulate your interest to pursue opportunities to add it to dishes where it may change the flavor characteristics in only a slightly meaningful way.

I review the draft. I know 'O' and Chi will fact check and edit before it ever sees a set of eyes in the rest of the world. Who are O and Chi? Ophelia Jackson fact checks everything I write and the blogs of a stable of other writers. I just happen to be the food writer. Chi is Chi

Nguyen Giap, my editor. Not only do they make me better than I am, but both are among my best friends. We see the world in much the same way. Is that a problem? Should I be seeking out friends with different perspectives, so I don't think the world is one way only to find out it is not? I've already discovered the world is not perfect. The world is not even close to the one I'd like it to be. Is it becoming more like my ideal? In some ways and not in others. Is that something I should be worried about or is it just the general state of affairs that have been the way it is for as long as anyone can remember? I don't know.

I do another read through to make sure of my facts. O doesn't like it when I put in marginal facts she has to research and come back with alternatives for me. Chi doesn't like it when I write illiterately. He's crazy about punctuation and sentence structure. He sits on me since I have a tendency to write compound sentences. "One fact. One verb. Don't even think of using an 'and'." Chi has famously told me on so many occasions I can't begin to count them. But he has made me a better writer. A writer only gets better by writing. So that's what I do. Write. Every day. About food. About chefs. About ingredients like today. About how it all works to create a memorable experience for those who are interested in food and wine and conversation amongst good friends.

J:

You can do better. But I'll take it this time. Joshua tree seeds are hot. I don't have time or others will be out there before us.

Not happy.

I read the text. What does he want? The chemical compounds found in the Joshua tree seed? It's not like peyote and mescaline. And if it were, X wouldn't be putting it into the food. Maybe that's what Z was looking for. Something to start a controversy. Something along the lines of 'celebrity chef uses psychotropic ingredients to add a little something extra to his food'. You know he could probably get away with that. No one actually eats what he cooks except himself, and maybe Makayla or whoever else is supporting him on set or in his travels. If he used peyote buttons ground up the DEA and FDA would not have been stopping his next production and hauling his ass off to jail. What they might be doing is asking where he got that particular ingredient as they will want to put his supplier in jail.

I decide I need a little more insight into what Z is unhappy about.

Z:

What bug got up your ass? I mean this blog answers the question you were looking for. So why are you disappointed?

I have to be direct with Z. He's never direct with me. If I don't press him all I'll get is this vague comment that doesn't help me fix whatever it is he's unhappy about. Need specifics. Need direction if he wants a change. Otherwise I think all is well because my readership numbers have been growing.

Something draws me back to the video. "I'm not seeing the contribution." X is trying his concoction. Apparently, he's not happy with the result. "There's definitely a different texture, a different aftertaste. But not something I'd go pay extra to find the seeds in health food stores since they're not available in the mainstream markets where you probably shop every day. But it does give you something you can talk about over a meal with friends you're trying to impress. You know the type. They always got a bigger toy or have been some place exotic. Not the down to earth friends who just enjoy hearing about what you're doing and where you've been they haven't. Friends who don't try to say we've been places you'll never go. But friends who say I had a really good time at such and such restaurant. Meal was affordable and I had something that was unusual and really good. Worth what I paid for it. Those kind of friends. We all have them, but some of us are lucky enough to have more than others."

Why is he talking about friends? What does that have to do with his Joshua tree seed dish?

"You know I've had the best and the worst of what chefs around the world have put on a plate. I've had some meals I wouldn't trade for any memory I have. And I've had meals I'm still trying to forget. But that's just part of life. The good and the bad. I try to only bring you the good, so you know where to spend your time. The rest of it, if I don't tell you about it then you won't wonder is his taste just different than mine? Would I like it even though he didn't? I don't want to put you in the position of thinking you might find a gem where I found only coal. And it seems I've found a lot more coal recently than the gems I've shared with you. Until next time. X marks the palate pleasing opportunities for us all."

DISMISSED

O comes to my door. She's more than my fact checker, she's my best friend. Has been ever since she saved my butt in a bad bar scene. Some guy bought me a drink and thought he owned me. Started arguing and getting physical when I had listened long enough to know he wasn't someone I wanted to hang with or even have a conversation with. I pushed the drink back to him and thought that would be the end, since I hadn't even had a sip. Instead he threw it in my face and tried to grab me. I don't know what he had on his mind because I was trying to wipe the alcohol out of my eyes. I couldn't see what happened. By the time I got my eyes open the guy was on the floor. O and Ace were standing between him and me.

Who is Ace? Name is Harris Acevedo. I don't really know what he does. Z said he make deals which pay him real well. At least better than writing a blog. Don't know when I met him. Seems he's been around for a while. It's hard to read him as he doesn't say much. I should put him together with X. One never shuts up and one hardly ever says anything. One creates the universe you inhabit with his descriptions and non-stop discourse. The other seems to inhabit his own universe and occasionally spills over into mine. But curiously, on the few occasions when I couldn't take care of myself, he has always been there. He stepped in even though I never asked.

O wouldn't talk about what happened that night in the bar. But she must have realized I was pretty much alone in the world. I needed someone like her to be there for me. She was right. I'll be forever grateful she brought me into her circle of friends who are now my friends too.

"You on vacation or what?" O starts on me with her usual indignation that I seem to lead a wasted life.

"Cut me some slack." I throw right back. "I gave Z his three hundred words. He'll get his money's worth out of me this week."

"You have to understand that when you don't send in your blog, I'm sitting out here waiting on you. That makes me a whole lot less productive and the next thing I know Z is all over my ass about not pulling my weight, which as you know is considerably more than it should be."

"There's just more of you to love, girl."

"That's the challenge I got to address." She turns serious. "Most guys say there's too much of me to love."

"You want guys to work for your love and affection," I respond with a platitude, which I instantly regret.

"I have to do something because I'm finding I'm too much of a challenge for most guys I'd be interested in."

I've been down this road with her so many times I've lost count. No matter what I offer she always has a reason why that won't work in her case. I don't know what to say so I remain silent. O studies me, waiting for me to say something. She almost seems hurt I haven't responded, so now I know I have to say something. "You're at a fork in the road."

"What do you mean?" This is a different tactic and she's wondering what I'm doing.

"You can either continue waiting for someone with enough love or you can start working to reach your desired weight."

"That's bullshit," She protests. "There is no desired weight. I have no idea where a guy gets comfortable with me. How much do I need to skinny down? Where will it be enough? You know it's hard to figure out what to do when you don't know where you're trying to get to."

"That's bullshit," I push right back. "We've talked about this before. You're making excuses for not doing anything when you know you need to start and see where you can get to. I mean if you just kept losing until someone notices you, you'll never overshoot, if that's what you're concerned about. We both know that weight is not a fixed thing. You lose it today, it comes right back tomorrow unless you have a plan that keeps you there or close to there."

"Look who's talking. Miss size four. I don't think I've ever seen you eat a big meal. It's always salads and chickpeas. Eat a steak or chocolate cake? Do you have any idea what you're missing?"

I shake my head, "This isn't a contest. It's also not about a right. I know you enjoy your steaks and deserts. If you come to the realization they're the reason you're not a size four you can decide to find something else that meets your current needs with a great memory of what it was like to eat all those things. But for you, they're the enemy. The longer you enjoy those foods, the longer you wait for the relationship you're craving."

O shakes her head. "I'll never be a size four."

Wrong thing for me to say. Size sixteen or maybe twelve. I can see how hard it would be for her to get to my size. She'd probably have to stop eating all together and work out for six hours a day to ever get within sniffing distance of a four. "A woman your height would probably be less attractive at a four than you are now," I decide to respond, still not sure of how she will react.

"Glad we agree on something."

Okay, I got past that one, but where do I go from here? "You have to decide. Do you have the willpower to get to a better place or do you need something that will take you there despite your current eating and exercising habits?"

"Bariatric surgery?" She instantly conveys that's not something she's excited about.

"Works for some people and I've even heard of people who have their jaws wired shut so they can't eat anything. Something will work for you. But you'll have to decide what it is."

O drops herself on my couch. "This isn't your problem. I shouldn't expect you to solve it for me."

"I can't." I confirm. "In the end, only you can make it happen. But then again, only you will enjoy the relationship you're wanting to be the result. At least you have the right reason for wanting to do something. It's not like you're trying to be a fashion model where if you don't look like some male fantasy of a woman that you can't get work."

O looks at me like I've revealed some long held deep dark secret.

"You thinking you might be a model if you got down to a four?" I have to ask given that look.

"Options. We all need options," she responds with a grin. At least now I know she's not serious about wanting to be a fashion model. "I deal in words, just like you do. We go at guys through their brain and not so much their crotch. But you could, you know."

"Could what?" I have to verify what I think I hear her saying. "Go at a guy through his crotch?"

"If I were a guy, I could see doing you."

Not what I wanted to hear. Not where I want to go. How do I change the subject without it being obvious? But then again, why do I care if it is obvious I don't intend to sleep with O? "You do something about it, and you'll be beating the guys off with a stick. Mark my words. You have a great face, you're smart, and you've travelled all over. You can hold your own with anyone in a conversation. So there have to be hundreds if not thousands of guys who would want to hook up with you if you can just invest in yourself enough to cross the desirable threshold."

"What's that? The desirable threshold?"

"The point where you pass the first test."

"Looks?" she responds starting to see the logic of my argument.

I nod.

"You think I get past the looks test I'll breeze through the other tests," she tries to clarify what she thinks I'm saying.

"Depends on the guy and what he's looking for," I push back. "If it's a one night stand you could be a constitutional law professor and he wouldn't be excited. In fact, you'd probably intimidate him, and he'd never get it up. For some guys, you get past the looks test, if you're more than a nail technician you'll never get a second visit. But that's not who you're looking for. You want somebody of substance. Someone who would be fascinated if you were a constitutional law professor."

"But I'm not. I'm a freaking fact checker for a bunch of bloggers who don't want to get sued."

I shake my head. "You're not. You're someone who is dedicated to ensuring that the public gets facts and not fake news. That didn't used to be an issue. It was assumed that what we saw on television and read in the newspapers was factual. But one night when there was a new moon and no reflections of sunlight on the earth, something changed. Suddenly facts were a matter of perspective and belief. You're the guardian of our world view."

"That's all bullshit." O dismisses my argument.

I touch her arm, "It's not. You are the reason people reading my blogs. It's not what I write so much as is that I write the truth, absolute truth and not just someone's made up random thoughts to get us misdirected. Get us to not pay attention to what someone else is doing."

O looks at me and knows I'm not just blowing smoke. She's quiet for a long moment. Finally closes her eyes. She leans back to consider what I've shared with her today. I need to give her some time now, so I look back at my half-written blog. I read the last paragraph before she stirs.

"I've heard horror stories about bariatric," she offers, fear in her voice.

At least I know she's thinking willpower won't do the trick. "How many horror stories and how many successes?" I have to reframe her argument so she is looking at balanced perspectives.

She shakes her head and shrugs. I get the picture. She doesn't know.

"You're a fact checker. Go check it out." I point out the absurdity that she is expecting me to go find out the truth behind one simple statistic that will determine her future course of action

O grimaces. Not what she wants to do, but I can see she understands what I'm saying. "Yes mamma." A little sass to tell me it's not alright to point out certain things to her.

I change the subject. "What scuttlebutt have you picked up about X?"

"Xavier the man?" she engages my change of direction. "What are you looking for?"

"I don't know, but something changed in his last video. Maybe it was the tone, or maybe he was just having a bad day. I don't really know what I'm reacting to, but something was different."

O considers my observation. "I haven't watched it." A disclaimer to start out. Tells me she really doesn't have anything to share with me, but I shouldn't hold that against her. As a fact checker, she has incredible sources with all kinds of insights the general public doesn't have. "You're the first I heard to voice a concern."

"Probably nothing." I dismiss so she knows she doesn't have to spend any time on it. But knowing O that will make her all the more curious.

"So, are you going to say something about it in your blog? Of course, you know if you do, I'll have to check it out." She's telling me if I really think it's nothing, I shouldn't mention it.

"Already did." I admit. "Just giving you a heads up its coming."

O nods and looks out my window. The sun is shining. Fascinating that the air pollution has blown out so you can actually see something out the window. She gets up and approaches the glass pane. She glances up the street towards the Hudson River. Can't really see it all that well from here. If I'd paid the extra rent and taken a higher floor it would have made all the difference. But Z barely pays me enough to afford this floor. I can only dream of a room with a view of the Hudson. I watch as O strains to see the river through the tall buildings. There is one place where a patch of blue can be seen, but it's hard to tell whether it's the river or just someone drying blue jeans on a clothes line. More than one person who has visited has confirmed it is the river. But not until they've walked up the street to check it out.

"Someday." I respond to her implied thought.

"You'll have an apartment with a view of the river?" she wants to make sure she knows what I'm saying before she responds.

I nod.

"I know. We all have to have something we're working for. Something that will change our outlook on life. Make us more than we are today. Someone with a view is more important than someone who doesn't have it."

"Why do people think that?" I protest.

"Because people judge people not by who they are, but what they display, or talk about, or wear. And of the three only the second is at all real. What someone talks about reveals more about who they are than their clothes or where they live or even who they work for."

"Someone values someone else and pays them according to their contribution." I push back. "So, the clothes, the address, the company you work for tells people about you. Somehow you have convinced someone you are more valuable or less valuable than someone else. A third party takes that as a proxy for what they should think about you. Means they simply haven't taken the time to explore who you are and make an informed judgment."

"Isn't that the heart of the matter?" O challenges me. "That people are lazy and don't want to invest their own time to discover the truth about people?"

"And this brings us all the way back to our earlier discussion about your dilemma." I voice where I think she's leading me. "That people don't invest the time to get to know someone who is not of the shape, size, color or national origin they are used to?"

"Bridging the divide. Dive back into the familiar?" O responds. "You know I didn't think that for a long time. I thought people were open minded until something happened to make them wary of others. But what I've seen, most people come to meetings with their filters up. They're looking for reasons not to engage with you. Reasons to dismiss you. Reasons to say you don't matter because you're fat, or Muslim, or of a perverted sexual orientation. When we used to always meet in person it was easy to disqualify someone because you could see them. But now, with social media driving the train, and teleconferences and collaborative software systems, people work together who never see each other. And yet they come to these sessions looking for reasons to believe they are right."

HOPE

I hear the years and layers of pain from rejection and dismissal in her voice, see it in her eyes. "I still love you, O."

THE ANSWER

The knocking at the door and the ringing of the bell reveal impatience. What time is it? I look at the clock next to my bed in the dark room. Eleven. When did O leave? Around ten so I've been in bed maybe a half hour. If I actually got to sleep it wasn't more than a few minutes ago.

Pulling my carcass out of bed is always a chore in the morning. Now it's an impossible task. I'm in that limbo land between awake and asleep. There was that one time when the power went off and reset all the clocks. I went to bed at the usual time. The alarm went off and I was out the door to run my usual morning miles. When I got back in I realized it was only one am. The alarm had reset to midnight and I'd never checked the clock before going out the door. Of course, at that point I needed a shower, but after taking one I was back in bed for another five hours although it took a long time to get back to sleep because my body thought I should be getting to work. And then when the alarm went off for the second time, my body thought it'd not slept. That made for a very long day.

The knocking and the bell ringing continue, so I'm finally up, and on my feet. I shuffle across the room and look out the peep hole to see X is standing in front of my door shaking his head, probably wondering if I'm at home or out for the evening. I unlock the door and throw it open before realizing I'm standing there in my bedclothes.

X looks at me, "Is this what you wear when you write all those nasty things about me?"

"I don't..." X pushes on past me into my apartment. Do I want to let him in at this hour? Why is he even here?

X doesn't stop to look around but goes right to my kitchen. I'm kind of dazed, not sure what is going on or why he is here. Not yet being awake doesn't help. I finally get my act together and follow X who has his head into my frig.

"Don't you ever eat at home?" he seems mystified by what he finds in the frig.

"What?"

"I don't know how I can make anything with what you have here."

I look in over his shoulder. Three Styrofoam containers greet me. I vaguely remember the Chinese takeout I'd brought home. How long ago was that? At least a week. Would it be edible at this point? Probably only marginally. But then it clearly isn't something a famous chef like X would consider as a meal.

X closes the frig door, takes my hand and we are on our way.

"Where are we going?" I have to ask as I look at my bedclothes.

"Whole Foods over on 7th Avenue." X looks back at me and apparently realizes I have no idea where this particular grocery is. "Only about six blocks from here."

I'm still not happy I'm out on the street in my bedclothes, but what can I do now? X is one of those people you simply go along with because it's too hard to oppose his will. Besides, I'm the enemy. A blogger who is trying to create controversy about what he's doing so people will read my blog. Indirectly it helps him by creating interest in what he's doing. Drawing attention to his videos and broadcasts. But at the same time, he has to be guarded about me because if I get an insight the whole world is likely to have the same insight within twenty-four hours.

"I think I want a shrimp dish." X turns to glance over his shoulder at me. He is still holding my hand, but he has charged ahead and is bringing me along behind him. "I know you like shrimp. One of those containers was a shrimp curry. I could smell it. About a week old? Am I right?" X doesn't look back but just assumes I'm agreeing with him. "I knew I was. So, shrimp. Need green onions and garlic. A little olive oil, some feta and Italian parsley. That's a simple shrimp dish. But what do I want to serve it over? Any requests?" Again, he doesn't look to see what I might be getting ready to say. "Couscous. Israeli couscous. You know, the pearl kind. Cooked simply. In chicken broth with a little butter and salt. Simple but flavorful. Do you have any wine?" This time he glances back but can see I'm having trouble just keeping up let alone responding to his monologue. "No wine. Should have known. You look like someone who does edibles because you don't want to pollute your lungs. Yeah, I get that. Health conscious. That's why you only do take out rather than make it yourself. Do you even know how to cook? Of course, you don't. That's evident from what you write. Don't you think it's ironic that a food blogger doesn't know how to cook? I do. But I'm the subject of your uninformed criticism. Then again, I can see the logic of someone who relies only on taste to decide what's good. If you knew what went into a dish you'd probably not be as enthusiastic one way or the other because you'd be trying to understand why particular ingredients produce this or that flavor. Would a tweak of one ingredient make it more appealing? If you left something out would it blend differently such that some people might actually like it better? And pairing wine with food? Probably a foreign concept to you. Have you ever tried to pair a Soave or Torrontes with shrimp? Totally different flavor combinations but each highlights something different in the shrimp. Each refreshes you differently. Each suggests a terroir and culture that is very different from the other. Do you have any idea what I'm talking about?"

X stops in the middle of the sidewalk to confront me.

It takes me a moment to catch my breath and gather myself to be able to answer his question. "I've been to wine pairing events."

X shakes his head. "Do you remember anything about them?"

"White with seafood. Red with meat." I respond as if by rote.

"Nuance, contrast, absorbing heat, pulling flavors forward. Does any of this ring a bell?"

"I've written about them," is my defense because he's exposed how shallow my real understanding of food preparation and creation of food flavor combinations runs.

"Thought so," comes across not accusatory so much as a realization that explains why I've written what I have about him. "Lucky for you I'm about to provide you knowledge that will make you much more credible with your audience."

"Credible?" I'm not sure I'm following him.

"We are going to cook together and when we finish eating what we've made you will finally have the understandings you need to write something of substance instead of the drivel you've been putting out."

"I have the largest food audience among the major bloggers," I remind him.

"Shows how much ignorance there is out there." X shakes his head again as he leads us the last two blocks to Whole Foods. "I bet few if any of your followers has ever cooked a meal," he mutters more to himself than to me.

"Then why do they watch your show?" I challenge his understanding of his audience.

"Probably to see where I'll show up next," he offers without looking back. "What kind of crazy foods do people eat? The preparation is secondary. How they make what they make is only of general interest. They're more interested in seeing places they'll never go and learning a little about a culture they'll never experience so they can impress their friends at the next get together, whether in a bar or a blog."

"Like me." I push back. "Only I get paid to blog about you."

"Maybe I'm too close to things, but it's obvious to me that you don't know what you're talking about. For a long time I thought your audience could see that too, but you know what? I finally came to realize they didn't. They actually think what you're saying has merit. Something they should consider. And you know how I came to that conclusion? I started reading their responses to you. Not many challenged you. They are more willing to say I'm full of shit than you are. And that was when I realized you actually have more sway with my audience than I do. A blogger who doesn't understand me or what I'm trying to do has stolen influence over my audience."

"When did you come to this realization?" I stop him as we are about to go into Whole Foods.

He looks at me as if he's seeing me for the first time, looks puzzled. "Those your bedclothes?"

I nod.

He rolls his eyes. I'm not sure if he's embarrassed he brought me out like this or whether he thinks I'm to blame for coming out half dressed. "Last week. Makayla showed me your blog and the responses. I had to do the post production on that week's show before I could come find you."

"I was going to ask about that."

"How did I find you? Wasn't hard. You graduated from NYU school of Journalism. You mentioned that on your LinkedIn site. So, I checked with the alumni's office and they gave me your address."

"They wouldn't do that," I blurt out.

X gives me that famous smile he closes out his show with. "All I had to do was tell them who I am and that I was trying to track you down because I might have a job for you with my production company. Call was less than three minutes."

Realizing how easy it had been for him I suddenly feel very exposed. Anybody could find me. And if that is the case then I have to be concerned that someone who doesn't like what I have to say in my blogs could come looking for me. Not a happy thought. Do I ease up? If I do, I'll probably lose my audience. Can't do that, but maybe I need to call the alumni office and register a complaint and ask them to be sure not to release my address under any circumstances.

We head to the vegetables first. He picks out the green onions and garlic, having me smell them, feel how firm they are and describing what makes them ready but not past their prime. Olive oil. I see this shelf full of different kinds. I had no idea there were so many different brands and grades and those with fruit or herbs.

"How do you know which oil works best?" I ask totally lost.

"You want a first pressing of extra virgin. Tuscan is right for what we're preparing although there are some interesting oils from elsewhere than will create a different flavor combination that can be even more appealing. But I don't know your taste so Tuscan is safe. You'll like it." He picks up a green can of oil without any markings on it I can see. I have no idea why he chose that one but he's not about to slow down to explain it all to me. Just enough to make me realize how little I really understand how to prepare a gourmet meal.

We buzz through the shelves, he pulls down a container of pearl couscous, a box of chicken broth, a box of real butter sticks, salt, pepper and two pots. He looks around finds a wooden spoon and is off to the fish section. "A pound of large shrimp," he orders, and we watch the fishmonger bag and put them in a container with ice to keep them cold until we get back to my apartment.

A run past the wines. He apparently feels he needs to do more than just one bottle for this meal, he picks out an Argentine Torrontes, a California unoaked Chardonnay, an Italian Chianti and an Australian Shiraz. Two whites and two reds. Apparently, he wants me to taste wines so I can be more informed about how important they are in creating the overall taste experience of the meals he is preparing. Before we leave the wine section he points to a larger bottle of white.

"That's a Gruner Veltliner. Comes from Austria, like Vienna Austria, not Australia. Anyway, it's a great all-purpose white. Goes with so many dishes. You can even do spicy food like Indian or Thai. Cuts the heat. Since you like oriental..." he thinks about that for a moment and adds a bottle to the cart.

"Which one are we having with the shrimp?" I ask as we get into the checkout line.

"Torrontes and the Chardonnay. I want you to see how a different wine changes everything about the meal."

"We can't possibly drink two bottles..." I begin.

He shrugs. "This isn't about finishing everything you take. Did you have one of those kind of mothers? I did. Took me a long time to get over it. But now I realize I don't need to eat more than what established the flavor profile. The rest can go into the frig for another night. I see you already figured that out. And the wine. Often its better the next night after it's had time to breathe. Have you ever really done wine? Of course, you haven't. If you had it would have been evident in your blogs. But we're going to change that tonight. Immerse you in the experience. Bring you to a level of understanding that will inform what you write about. But we're not going to stop there. I'm going to arrange for you to get into a few working kitchens here in the city. Let you see first-hand what it takes to prepare and deliver a great meal."

My heart skips a beat. He's opening doors for me I'd never be able to enter on my own. Will give me access to people that will permit me to expand my blog to other chefs and kitchens. Grow my audience.

Maybe Z will have to give me a raise if I pull more eyes. I understand he's doing this so I'll be more informed about what I have to say about him. But why me? I'm not the only blogger commenting on him.

We scan the items, bag them and X looks at me, realizes I didn't bring my credit cards, so he automatically pays for the groceries with his. The woman who is overseeing the checkouts looks at me as we walk past her. "It's not Halloween," she comments, looks at X and acts surprised. "Aren't you what's his name? That guy. You know who I mean. The guy who has that show. Always talking about some place I've never heard of, eating stuff I'd never..."

X smiles at her but doesn't slow down.

"That happen often?" I ask.

X grimaces, "You have no idea how hard it is for people to remember your name," sounds like he is mystified why. "I got it down to a single letter. Thought that would be memorable. Nope. Not even close. And all they remember is I eat stuff they'd never, but haven't connected me to actually preparing an unforgettable meal."

"Is that what you want? To be known as someone who prepares unforgettable meals?"

I watch, fascinated as X tries to answer what I thought was a simple question. "I did that at Snob when I was the executive chef. Truly unique flavor combinations. And you know what? Nobody cared. The harder I worked to be that guy the more they just came to expect it of me. Put something unexpected in front of them each and every time they came in."

"Is that why you walked away?" I ask reacting more to the weariness in his voice than the words themselves. "You just got tired?"

We're only a block from my apartment but X stops to look at me, lowers his head and speaks softly. "I asked myself why I was doing it and you know I didn't have an answer."

OPENING UP

X puts me right to work in my kitchen. He has to show me how to use my cook top since I've never used it, although I don't admit that to him. He shows me how to cut the onions and garlic standing behind me and reaching around. I can't believe how quickly he chops. I'm petrified I'm going to cut my fingers off, but he just keeps chopping and using the blade of the knife to make neat piles of green onion and garlic particles. I guess that's a correct term for chopped food.

"Pour a little of the olive oil into the large pan, but don't turn the burner on just yet." He instructs me. "We need to get the couscous going first as it will take longer than the shrimp."

I pick up the can of oil and twist the top open, noting a plug in the neck. I point it out to X, who grins at me, takes the can and tips it over so I see the oil comes out, but just not in a rush. A small puddle forms in the middle of the pan and he screws the top back on and puts the oil aside. Next, he takes the shrimp from the container and looks around, "You do have a big bowl we can defrost these in?"

Big bowl. I have to think a moment. No, I don't have any bowls other than those I sometimes use for cereal when I can't find any take out of interest or am just in a hurry. This makes me realize I eat to live rather than the other way around which is apparently how X views life. I have to think for a moment. Where are those bowls? It comes to me and I open the cupboard. As I bring them down X shakes his head.

"That the biggest bowl you have?"

I nod, of course.

"Have to use the sink." He turns the water on hot and lets it run for a bit before he puts the stopper in. "This would defrost faster if we could put it directly in the warm water, but since we're using the sink, which probably isn't sanitary, we will leave the shrimp in the plastic bag and let the heat permeate and defrost them."

X fills the sink quite high and I can see steam coming from the water when he drops the bag of shrimp into the water. He turns on the heat for the oil and then goes to the other pot he bought for me, adds chicken broth and puts that on a burner he turns on. "We want this boiling hot, so we'll set it at seven until it starts boiling. Then we'll add the couscous to the boiling broth, turn it down and then start cooking the onions and garlic. We want the onions to turn translucent which should take three to four minutes and then we'll add the shrimp to cook for six to eight minutes until they turn white. By that time the couscous should be ready, and we'll take it off the heat and let it finish cooking in the pot. We add the parsley, which also needs to be chopped and some of the feta cheese and let that warm with the shrimp for two to three minutes."

I've been ticking off each of the ingredients as he ran through the recipe he has in his head. But then I notice, "What about the butter?"

"That goes on the couscous when you take it off the heat. When it melts, you'll stir it in. It coats the pearls and keeps them from sticking together."

I see the broth has begun to bubble. "How hot for the oil?"

"I set it on seven. Your lucky number. I'm here on the seventh of the month…"

"You were here on the seventh of the month, but it's past midnight now so it's the eighth."

X is checking the shrimp. Not quite fully defrosted, apparently. "Right. The eighth, which is when we will eat the meal, we're cooking even though it will technically be the morning and not the evening. I hope that won't upset your delicate digestive track. After all, most people are creatures of habit. I'm sure I'm completely destroying your routine by keeping you up all night just for a cooking lesson."

I'm pleased he's getting back into his running monologue. In fact, I was getting a bit worried that he wasn't going on and on as I expect him to. "No. I'm awake now, but I wasn't when you arrived."

That must remind him I'm still in my bedclothes. He glances over at me, one eyebrow raises barely perceptively, and he offers, "If you'd be more comfortable changing, I can start the onions and garlic."

I shake my head, "I'm good. It's not like you haven't seen me in this for the last hour or more."

X glances at me again, apparently thinking something he's not about to share, but I notice his face get a tinge redder, but only for a moment and then he's back into scraping up the onions and garlic, carrying them from the counter over to the pan, where he dumps them in, wipes the bits that cling to his hands and then goes to the sink to wash only to find the shrimp still there. He picks up the bag, feels the shrimp, apparently decides they are sufficiently defrosted and sets the bag on the counter. He reaches in, pulls the plug and lets the water run out as he soaps up his hands and washes them thoroughly before drying them on a towel I brought out from the bathroom.

"What next?" I inquire as I glance at the bubbling broth, the sizzling onions and garlic and not sure what I should be doing.

"Dump in the couscous pearls and cover the pot, dropping the temperature to five. If we're lucky we'll be done eating by five and you can get back to bed."

He would have continued that monologue if I hadn't cut him off, "It really take you that long to eat?"

He gives me a longer gaze before answering, "It's not good to eat in a hurry. The food should be savored, experimented with. What goes best with what? Somethings are best eaten in tiny bites. Just a taste. Others need some volume so more of your tongue, different parts of it maybe, can engage it. Chewing should be slow, measured, giving you more time to make contact with your tongue on the surface of the food. Think about it. Compare it to other similar food you have eaten. And then you can take a sip of wine. Mix it with the bit of food. See how it changes the impressions you have in your mouth. Swallow them together or swallow the wine first and then the food. Eating should be an experience with infinite variety. In fact, who you eat with can have as much impact on making the meal memorable as the food itself. What they discover as they eat, what they are experiencing in the moment. Giving you insights that you don't have from your approach to the food and wine as you engage it."

"You make it sound almost sexual." Slips out before I even realize what I've said. That stops X, who has been stirring the garlic and onions. He tries to cover his reaction by going over to the shrimp, pulling the bag open, picking out the shrimp and pulling off the tail, then tossing each one across the room to land perfectly in the pan. "Would you stir them, so the onions and garlic don't burn?"

I do as he requests, checking the couscous by lifting the top and peaking in.

"Don't stir it just yet," he instructs me. "Not until you take it off the heat and stir in the butter."

"How do you keep all this in your head?" I ask. "How many recipes do you have up there?"

"Never counted them, but lots."

"Do you have a favorite?" I inquire casually.

"They're like my children. So, no. No favorites, I love them all." His response is matter-of-fact.

"Really? I would have thought there were some recipes you don't care for personally.

He smiles at me. "I take it there are a lot of dishes you don't care for."

I nod noting that he hasn't answered my question. "But what about you?" I reemphasize.

"If you're only cooking for yourself, you should go live on the top of a mountain and become a monk. A chef, at least a good chef is trying to please, inspire, educate, and change the life of his or her customers. A chef is cooking for them, so what they like individually shouldn't come into the equation they are trying to solve. But to answer your question, since you returned to it, I can always find an interesting way to add something to a dish or substitute something that will change the entire flavor profile so I can turn it into something memorable, something I like, or something I'll play with to find a different way of presenting a dish so it will find a whole new audience."

"Like pork belly?" I respond. "Sounds awful, but I've had some that's been more than edible."

X comes around now that all the shrimp are in the pan and stands behind me, looking at the dish over my shoulder. "Inhale. Smell the blending of the garlic and onions and oil with the shrimp."

I do and it smells wonderful. X returns to the counter, pulls off some parsley sprigs and chops them up like a machine. I've never seen anyone who handles a knife the way he does. A glance over at the pan, "Turn them over so the shrimp cook on the other side."

I follow his instruction and turn them over one-by-one. He has opened the feta, cut a block and dried it on a paper towel. He brings the parsley and feta over to the cooktop on paper towels and once again stands behind me, inhaling the aroma and nodding, although I see the nod in the shadows on the cooktop more than see it.

"Spread the parsley on the shrimp."

I do as asked, picking up the paper towel and spreading the parsley across all of the shrimp.

"Now break up the feta, sprinkling it across the parsley covered shrimp."

I do as instructed as he checks under the lid of the couscous pot. He picks up the wooden spoon I've been using to stir the garlic and onions and turn the shrimp, stirs through the couscous, just once and slices off just one pad of butter, which he drops into the couscous and stirs through until the butter is melted and the couscous separated from the other pearls. He sets the pot down on the counter to let it continue cooking while the shrimp blends flavors with the other ingredients.

I turn to him, "Almost ready."

"Are you?" he smiles, but it is not his sign off smile that lights up a room. Almost a hint of sadness seems to be lurking there. "So which wine, miss food expert?"

"I thought we were going to have the two whites."

"And what are the two whites?" He catches me off guard, but I should have known it would turn into a quiz to see if I was paying attention to his lessons.

"We are not having the Austrian."

"What's it called?"

"Gruner eyeliner," I shoot back deadpan. He looks into my eyes and must see the twinkle I'm trying to hide.

"Veltliner." He is most definite in correcting me, but I can see he's pleased I remembered something he taught me. "Like the African Velt where all the big animals live. You're right we're not having that. But the absence of an incorrect response is not a correct response. So, what are we having with it?"

"The Argentinian…" I let that hang for a moment. "Something like Tonto Indian, like in the Lone Ranger."

"What do you know about the Lone Ranger?" X frowns at me now. "That was long before your time."

"It was, but I get into these trivia games and it come up once in a while." I defend myself.

"Torrontes, from the Salta region rather than the Mendoza where all the Malbecs come from. High desert gives it a distinctive character."

"How would you explain character in a wine?" I push him while I turn the heat off under the shrimp since they are all white now.

X picks up one of the plates I'd set out and begins to dish out the couscous. "It's a combination of things, starting with the bouquet. You put your nose into the glass, and you fill your senses with the aromas of the wine. You can begin to pick out fruit and other smells that separate this wine from all the others." He scoops out some of the shrimp and piles them gently across the couscous, arranging them so they are in a regular pattern. You spin the wine in the glass to ensure any alcohol that has separated blends back in and then you put your nose in again to see if it changes the bouquet, again looking for the fruit and spice layers." He sets the dish in front of me, then begins to arrange a second plate. "If the bouquet is pleasant then you take a sip, but don't swallow at this point. Roll it around your mouth, let the different taste receptors on your tongue experience it. Some people will then part their lips and inhale to bring air over the wine which releases additional flavors of a wine that has not had enough time to breathe properly."

"Wine breathes?" I ask, knowing the answer but acting dumb.

"Technically it mixes with the air and that releases more flavors. The longer it breathes the more flavors are released, at least in the better wines." He picks up the two dishes and carries them over to the table where I generally work. He waits for me to move my laptop out of the way so we can sit here to eat. I do, retrieve forks and glasses for the wine. Unfortunately, they are water glasses and not wine glasses.

"This is all I have." I offer showing him the green tinted glasses.

"Will have to do." He sounds resigned and not surprised in the least. "Do you mind sharing glasses since I want to put a touch of Torrontes in one and a touch of the Chardonnay in the other?"

"I knew that one." I kid him. "Unoaked chardonnay, no less."

He rolls his eyes as if there is no way he is going to win this discussion and fetches the two bottles of wine. "I hope you have a corkscrew."

I close one eye and squint, shaking my head.

"That's one thing about a good chef," X points out. "We always have a corkscrew with us." X removes a knife from his pocket and extracts the corkscrew which he uses to open the Torrontes, but the Chardonnay has a screw top. So, we were never in danger of not having wine with our meal.

X pours a bit of each of the wines and sets the glasses between the plates and we sit across the table from each other. He watches me pick up the fork and inhale the aromas.

"Smells good." I offer, but he doesn't react. "Aren't you going to join me?"

"A chef needs validation before he will offer his own judgment about what he has created."

Now I'm on the spot. I've been writing critically about what he prepares and what he discovers in kitchens around the world, but this is the first time I've actually sampled something he prepared. I think about his description of the experience one should have when the first forkful of the dish enters my mouth. I set no expectations but am almost instantly reacting to the array of flavors that have all come together in this dish. The shrimp is tender but firm. The couscous melts in my mouth in contrast to the shrimp. I move the shrimp and couscous around in my mouth, detecting a difference in sweetness in some places and less in others. I take a sip of the Torrontes, move it around my mouth with the shrimp dish. Very different. I swallow both together, take a second bite, follow the same ritual and now sip the Chardonnay. Way different than the Torrontes which seemed more acidic and more fruit flavor than the Chardonnay.

X turns around in his chair brings over the salt and pepper. "I deliberately didn't season the dish so you could get a sense of the basic flavors we are working with. But now, with a little salt and pepper you're going to find flavors that come to the fore you didn't pay much attention to the first time."

He pours a little salt on the palm of his left hand and pinches some between his right-hand thumb and index finger, spreading it on just a small section of my dish. He does the same with the pepper.

I mix the spices in and take another bite. He's absolutely right. I taste things and in parts of my mouth I didn't before. Particularly the salt comes through loud and clear from one section of my tongue. Each wine washes the saltiness away, but still, each leaves a somewhat different aftertaste than the first time.

"Which way do you prefer it?" He's eager for my opinion.

"Salt and pepper. No question. Adds layers to the flavor profile. Even the wine tastes better with them in the dish."

X nods, savors for a bit, apparently going through a similar examination of the melding flavors and washes it all down with the Torrontes. He takes a few more bites, apparently checking different aspects of the meal. He washes it all down with the Torrontes, which he must prefer.

He puts his fork down and looks at me. "Have you learned anything from cooking with me?"

I notice my nipples are taught and readily visible through my sleepwear. I don't want to call attention to them, but he has evidently noticed although he is looking into my eyes, which is refreshing. "So many things. I don't know where to begin."

"There's one more level I can introduce you to, but only if you won't regret it in the morning."

"Chocolate mocha mint pie?" I suggest with a twinkle in my eye.

"Chocolate molten lava explosion with caramel gelato and Reece's Pieces," he counters. But I know that's not what he's thinking from the look in his eye. He is appreciating me in a way he couldn't when he arrived because then I was just the enemy he was hoping to neutralize by giving me insight into what I write about. But he did more than that and now we are both drawn to the same idea.

X comes out of his chair and down on one knee to kiss me, once very gently on the lips and he pulls back to look into my eyes once again. He must see I'm wanting to continue and in only a moment his tongue is in my mouth, seeking out the hidden recesses. I push back and into his mouth, which he lets me do, lets me explore and invite him back into mine.

His hands gently caress me, and, in a moment, he has picked me up and is carrying me towards the bedroom. I feel the strength in him as he gently lays me out on top of the delicate oriental-designed image on my comforter. He comes up beside me and continues to caress me as he begins to kiss my neck and ears. I reach up to help him out of his clothes and he helps me out of mine.

A GOOD THING

Five am came and went. Somewhere along there X did too. When I stumbled out to the kitchen approaching nine, I found it clean and everything put away, including the uneaten food which is in a container in the frig. He must have emptied out and washed one of the containers that had been in the frig since I didn't have anything else in the house he could have used. The cork was back in the Torrontes and the screw top on the Chardonnay with a note. 'These will both be better today.'

What am I to make of X now that I've not only met the dude, but slept with him? He is like the food he prepares, just overwhelming in touch, look and feel. There's just so much more there and when he explains it all to you it just makes sense. But who other than a chef would take the time to savor every bite, to suggest you experiment with the food in your mouth? I'd never given it a thought. Will it all make me a better blogger? I don't know because I still have the same problem. I watch him make it, but I don't get a chance to put it into my mouth and understand what he has created. The simple shrimp dish we made together was incredible when I tasted it the way he taught me. Could I make it, now that he's shown me what to do? Probably not without a recipe. And even then, I'm not so sure.

I hear the 'ding' of a text coming in.

J:

Where's your blog? You're making me look bad as I'm sitting here waiting for you.

It's followed only a moment later by another, which I should have expected.

J:

You gonna sleep the day away? I need your blog now.

I respond to both of them together

Z&O:

Have a draft in an hour.

Now the problem is to get something down I can send them. But after last night I'm not quite sure what I should be writing about. And I only gave myself an hour to make it happen. I sit down and look at the blank screen. This is absolutely the worst time to try to write because I have mixed emotions about X. Can I still be detached? Can I offer something relevant without letting last night creep in? I don't know but I need to get some words down and then I can decide.

THE OTHER SIDE

I've been wondering. Who are these chefs who take us half a world away to show us something different than what we experience every day in the sameness that has become our lives? Are they great chefs who decided a larger audience for their creations could be had by those of us who watch and write about food and wine? Or are they not great chefs, but just entrepreneurs who decide an audience can be fooled into thinking something that isn't the case through the distance of social media?

What I've come to realize is there is no single answer to this question because both inhabit the world we live in. Some of those we watch are the real deal, as I've recently come to understand first hand. But there are others out there who aren't. Shock value is what they focus on. Repel your senses so you don't question whether what they are offering is real or not. Make you wonder why anyone would eat something so strange or disgusting. We all know the world is filled with people who have different tastes than our own. But that doesn't mean what they like and create is any less meaningful in their lives than the foods and beverages we consume as part of ours.

And in the course of coming to this realization I discovered that I have become one of those who have a fully kitted kitchen but rarely use it to express myself, feed my soul or experiment with the flavors that nourish my existence. What happened to us that we have become a nation of fast rather than slow food? Why is it all about eating to live rather than living to eat? These are the dichotomies of our life. We establish a fast track to success for ourselves, which doesn't leave room for the slow experience that regenerates our imagination, insights and spirituality. Why do I raise spirituality in the same sentence with food? Because someone recently taught me a very important lesson. Most of us are like ice skaters, skimming over the surface of our own existence at blazing speed, hoping if there is a soft spot on the ice ahead that our momentum will carry us across. This chef took the time to slow me down. Asked me to examine the structure of that ice upon which my life depends as I move from here to wherever I have chosen to go. Food plays in irreplaceable role in our transit across the sun in our cosmic journey. When we slow down and take notice of life's nourishment we better understand how we can achieve a different consciousness, a different outcome and a life that will have more rewards than we have come to expect, even if only small rewards every day as we put something that entices us in our mouths and contemplate the meaning of the flavor profiles we are experiencing.

So, the next time you put something into your mouth, ask

yourself, do I really like how this tastes? If not, what would make it better so I will enjoy the next meal and every meal thereafter for the rest of my life?

I go back and re-read what I wrote. Where did this come from? Not what I typically write at all. How will my audience take something where I've moved beyond the descriptive and into the directive? Worse yet, what will Z say? That I've sold out? Gone over to the other side? I haven't, at least I don't think I have. But I am more balanced in my perspective. No question about that. And I only ate two shrimp to get here. But I must have drank X's Kool-Aid. Is this the kind of change in my writing he was looking for or will this be as much of a revelation for him as it will be for my usual readers? But what happens if I lose my usual readers who are looking for the next clarifying analysis of the last show by X?

This is a gamble. Should I just delete it and start over? I have time because the hour isn't up. I could go back and write about X's recipe for Feta Shrimp and Couscous. That would be uncontroversial and I'm sure I'd get good feedback from my audience. Even Z couldn't fault me for writing that blog. But is that what I want to say? I don't know anymore.

I hit send and the blog is posted to O for fact checking. She won't have to do much because this is all opinion and not a bunch of facts. Generally, she's only checking with the chefs to make sure I have the recipe correct. But this one doesn't have a recipe, only advice and a challenge to my readers to get more out of their lives. Would I take my own advice this time? I already have, but only because X opened the door and led me into a different world of food and opportunity, to say nothing of incredible sex. It was slow. He'd already opened up my senses as we cooked together. Opened them further when we tasted the creation of our joint efforts. Made me contemplate differences and experimentation. Trying something new and different, realizing there is no wrong, or bad or regrets.

J:

What is this? Do I need to call you, or did something happen after I left?

O:

I had a visitor.

My only question as I send that text is how long before the call. I figure less than a minute and it turns out to be thirty-sight seconds.

"Who was it?" No hello, no how are you doing? O always goes to the heart of the matter and that's why she's not only a great fact checker but a fantastic friend who saves me a lot of time beating around a bush or whatever.

"X." Short and sweet on my part too.

"The chef?" a moment of silence and then, "Holy shit. How did you get together?"

"Long story."

"I got all morning," O responds annoyed I'm so cryptic. "I want details."

"He gave me a cooking class."

"What are you talking about?"

"You read what I learned."

O is quiet for a long moment, trying to decide something. "I don't think that's all. Did you sleep with him?"

"Would I do something like that?" I proclaim innocence, even though weakly.

"Not usually, but this blog ain't you."

"Is now." I inform her.

"You definitely slept with him if this is what I have to look forward to in your blogs."

"Will people read it?" I ask meekly.

"They'll read it, but the question is will this offend them? You're a bit over the top if you ask me."

"So, you think I should kill it before Z does," I voice my thoughts.

"Hell no. Z will love it. Create some controversy. You asked some questions that will call out some of the fake chefs who are out there trying to convince you that you missed out on the meal of a lifetime because you didn't come eat in their restaurant before they decided to change their whole lives around traipsing around the world in search of the ultimate food experience."

"And if they were such great chefs the ultimate food experience would have been found in their restaurant. Is that what you're suggesting?"

"That question doesn't deserve an answer," O dismisses my need to check the obvious conclusion with her. "If you're looking for a fact checker to check that fact, consider it done."

I'm quiet while I consider what I've walked into with this draft blog. O respects that silence but only for a moment.

"So, what am I supposed to do with your blog?" She finally asks since I'm not forthcoming.

Her question accentuates my indecision. If I pull it I need to write something less controversial, the same old stories that point out the obvious, because that's about the level of my understanding of cooking and food creation. But if I tell her to send it on, I risk losing what I've worked long and hard to establish. A loyal following that looks forward to my next blog and an opportunity to comment. And then where am I? Back at square one, looking to establish another career because Z will dump me faster than a day-old stinky tofu.

"You can't have it both ways," O points out. "Either pull it or push it on."

She's right. I blow up this blog no one is going to support me to write about something else.

"If you're not going to make a decision, I'm gonna make it for you." O warns me.

I close my eyes, shake my head and weakly respond, "Check it and push it forward."

"Going down with the ship," O pronounces. "At least you got guts."

"You wouldn't," I try to confirm.

"Not going there," O sidesteps. "So, when do you see your mystery chef again?"

"Don't know," is all I can think of to say. "He raised more questions than he answered."

"From reading your blog I would assume he called your bluff."

"What that I'm a food expert?"

"That you understand the role food and friends play in keeping us going."

I instantly think about X describing how he experiments with flavors in his mouth. Something I'd never considered. So, I decide to test a theory, "Tell me. Do you ever savor the food you eat?"

"Savor? What do you mean?"

"Do you take a bite, get an initial taste and then just finish the dish? Or do you continue to look for the taste with each bite?"

O doesn't instantly answer. "He really screwed you up, didn't he?"

"Answer the question." I'm impatient for a confirmation or not.

"First bite definitely sets my expectations," she acknowledges. "Generally, I don't pay much more attention to the flavor because I know what's coming. Should be the same as that first bite. Guess I only focus on the flavor again if something is sour or tastes bad part way through."

"In other words, you only notice the flavor if it changes," I seek confirmation. "In which case what I wrote is accurate and calling attention to it is probably a good thing."

O doesn't respond to my observation.

A UNIQUE COMBINATION

Of course, Z published the blog without a comment to me. And the response was immediate. Just a few of the thousands included:

Have you been on a spiritual journey somewhere? If so, please tell us where so I'll know where not to take my next vacation

Who are the fake chefs you refer to? Any chance we can get them all to post their credentials so we can go look up their old reviews and see who was what they would lead us to believe they were?

Would you talk more about the way we nourish our souls? I've not made that connection before.

Who was the chef who woke you up to the larger role food and friends play in our lives? I'd like to have a conversation with him like you did.

You trying to make me think? What's with this blog? I thought you were all about pointing out the shortcomings of certain recipes and why some foods just don't satisfy. That's all useful to me. But spirituality from food? Who are you kidding?

Hey Bozo. She's got a point. Don't dismiss the notion that food can do more than keep us alive. After all, a lot of foods are those we grow up with. They become comfort food because they remind us of the safe havens our homes were, generally, and the love and support we got from our family and friends growing up.

Who you calling a bozo? I got a right to my own opinion and just because you're hiding behind your mama's skirt doesn't mean some of us aren't willing to call something for with it is. And food is just food. Wasn't it Freud that said 'Sometimes a cigar is just a cigar?'

Glad to see your years of psychoanalysis has paid dividends. I for one look for the larger meaning in our lives. This blog has given me another place to look and for that I thank you.

The number responding is significantly higher than usual. Z must be pleased. He hasn't commented on it in any event. He only seems interested in the number of eyes I'm capturing, and this particular blog seems to have captured more than usual. So now I need to come up with another that is as controversial. Not an easy task. But then I get an unexpected text.

J:

Thank you.

Now how am I supposed to interpret that? Is he thanking me for not mentioning him in my blog? For taking on a difficult topic? For calling out those who are attempting to be his peers, but really aren't? Or is he thanking me for simply listening? For getting what he was trying to tell me, but not in so many words? For sleeping with him? For letting him escape into the night without a word? Maybe, just maybe he's thanking me for all of the above and that's how I'm choosing to interpret it.

Another text:

> *J:*
>
> *Looks like you made the right choice. It would be helpful if you'd include some facts for me to check or Z will probably lay me off.*
>
> ☺

Another day, another blog. Okay, what's it going to be today? I scan through several blogs and websites to see what others are talking about. I can either pile on or try to start a new conversation. My last blog was to start a new conversation, so it's much safer to pile on to someone else's topic. Then I see the perfect topic. A reference to a new video from X made in the mountains of Bolivia. This must be either where he was going when he left my apartment or what he had just finished before coming to see me. I wonder which.

The mountain vistas are breathtaking. Snow covered peaks and herds of llamas. The herders all wear blankets over their shoulders to keep warm in the high altitude.

And there's X. In the cramped kitchen of this tiny hilltop village restaurant. A wood burning fire warms the room and cooks the dishes in an adobe oven. The short of stature Bolivian chef is explaining the dish he is preparing.

"You would name this a stew. In Bolivia everyone eats soup. So, for us this is just soup."

X piles in, "So for you a soup is just a soup. The fact it's thick and spicy and has a lot of meat in it doesn't make it any different from a bowl of a thin broth with vegetables. Both are soups."

I wonder at X's reference to a soup being just a soup. Was that a reference to the blog responses I got, or was that blog response a nod to this video X had made before I released my blog, but I just hadn't seen it?

The Bolivian Chef nods his agreement. "Everyone cooks with what they have. If you are poor and do not have many animals, you may only eat the thin broth with vegetables you grow most of the year. But if you are prosperous... is that the word? My sister tells me Americans are prosperous. They have much money and can buy meat every day if they want."

X nods, "Prosperous is the right word."

"If you are a prosperous Bolivian, you may eat what you call a stew maybe once a week." The chef responds. "The rest of the time it's a thin broth." He wants us to know prosperous Bolivians still don't eat like Americans.

"What do you use to thicken the broth in this dish?"

"Ground wheat, same as you. A few root vegetables and the meat. Mostly it is chicken or beef, as they are what most people can find. But several of us have been using sheep and llama meat."

"Do you use baby sheep or adult sheep meat?" X presses. I know where he is going but the Bolivian chef seems unsure how to answer.

"In Bolivia we must raise our animals to be adult. It is the only way to get enough meat. A baby sheep would be a wasted opportunity to feed a family for a month or more."

"You have a secret ingredient you use in your stew. Could you tell us what Andean mountain secret could possibly alter the taste so radically that it has become almost as essential now as table salt among the people of your village? As I understand it, this is the only place in the world where this particular ingredient is used. Could also tell us why that is the case? Why only here do people use this particular ingredient to add spice to this dish which even you have described as a staple? But a staple only for the prosperous."

"It is used by everyone, now. Not just the prosperous. In fact, the prosperous are using it less than those who are looking to add flavor to their root vegetable broth."

"And you are the one who discovered this magical ingredient?"

The Bolivian chef shakes his head. "This ingredient has been available to the people of this village for as long as anyone can remember and even before that. But people did not use it, unsure about it."

"Why did you break the taboo, if that was what caused people not to use it?"

The Bolivian chef looks at X, unsure what he means. "Taboo? I don't know this word."

"A taboo is a commonly held belief that you shouldn't do something or use something without a law or government prohibition. You know the word superstition?"

The chef shakes his head again.

"A superstition is much the same thing. A belief about something that goes back long before anyone who is alive today. But a belief that your ancestors have handed down to you and therefore you feel obligated to follow their beliefs even though you have no practical explanation as to why you should."

"We might call that a tradition." The chef offers.

X nods and smiles, "That's close enough. Is that what we're dealing with here? A tradition that Bolivians don't use this ingredient in their food?"

The Bolivian chef sort of nods. He's not sure but realizes trying to get to a more precise definition of what he means will be an arduous task and probably not worth the effort. So, he concurs, although not enthusiastically. "I saw the need to introduce something new. This magical ingredient was something I hoped would change minds. Make something unacceptable acceptable. And it did."

"Why you?" X asks. "Why would you, a relatively unknown chef decide you could change the minds of your customers about what you have described as a long-held belief? Very few chefs take on such a daunting task. And in a place like Bolivia it must be even harder since people here cling to tradition. Cling to the way of life of their parents and grandparents and all those who have come before them. When I heard about what you had done, I knew I had to come here and meet you. Talk with you. Watch you prepare this dish and sample it for my audience. An audience I know will be fascinated by what you have done, the barrier you have successfully broken down, at least in your country. But as a result of this video you may actually begin to influence cuisine around the world. How do you feel about the fact that people in Paris, Rome, Tokyo and New York may be sampling your dish as a result of chefs and foodies around the world who will watch this video and take from it the essence of changing minds, changing perceptions, and changing expectations just as the Koreans did with Kim Chee? Of course, our audience knows the story of Sriracha, which is derived from Kim Chee, a dish of cabbage, buried in clay pots for a sometimes a year or more. The cabbage decomposes and ferments. It stinks almost as much as stinky tofu. Something that almost takes your breath away when you first smell it. But it adds flavor even though how it comes to add the flavor is something some people love and others can't stomach, so to speak. I think what you have discovered is much like Sriracha sauce. Something that adds a distinctive flavor, even though not many would want to bury and ferment cabbage in order to create that flavor."

The Bolivian chef is bleary eyed, obviously not following X, but nods. "Why me? If not me, who?"

"But you must have known of the way people thought of this particular ingredient. Why it hadn't been used in you don't even know how long. And yet you were willing to try it. See how people reacted to the flavor without knowing about the ingredient. You must have watched their faces. Studied their conversations. Tried to decipher whether what you had contributed to the recipe was a critical factor in what they thought about the dish or whether it did not make any difference at all. You decided that it added much to the desirability of the dish. And word of mouth brought people from the village you had never seen before coming in to try your new dish. It was a clear victory for your experiment. A clear vindication that you had brought something new, exciting and distinctive into the culinary experience of the people who live in your village. And by extension, into the culinary experience of diners around the world. This is a great distinction for you. Just the fact I am here, recording this conversation between us. Posting this, so chefs around the world will suddenly know the name Alejandro Suarez, a bold chef who dares to change social convention. To introduce us to a flavor fest no one else dared to open up to us. That is what will make you a renowned chef. One who will be considered one of the innovators of flavor, texture and culinary experience."

Okay X. What is this mystical ingredient? Peyote? Marijuana? LSD? Something that will cause all of us to rush to his restaurant just for the pleasure of a psychotropic experience? I'm getting a little anxious to get some words down on paper because I know I'll be hearing from Z shortly. And even though I know X is having just a wonderful time sitting beside the adobe oven fire, in the high Andes, I'm sitting in my Manhattan apartment expecting a flamer from Z in my text box any moment. I'm only as good as my last blog. My last blog raised expectations, apparently, although I thought it more likely it would do me in. Anyway, I need to know why this particular dish is so special so I can respond to it as I always have. So, what's the story here?"

The Bolivian chef pulls the pot out of the adobe oven.

"You're adding mutton. How much?"

"This soup should feed a dozen Bolivians. That means I would add about three pounds of sheep, or mutton as you describe it. We add about a quarter pound of meat per serving."

"That's about half of what we tend to serve in the US." X notes.

"That's about twice what we generally serve in Bolivia." The chef admits. "But I only mention that because if I served you what I serve my customers you probably would not eat it."

X nods, keeps moving. "What are the vegetables?"

The chef adds a double handful of diced vegetables to the pot. "Mostly root vegetables. Mashusa, Oca, Olluco, and Masa. Vegetables that are indigenous to my country and a staple for most of my dishes. Everyone eats these vegetables. That I put them into my soup is to be expected. Everyone will eat my soup as long as I have these four, or at least three of them."

"Which one is optional?" X asks.

The chef stirs the vegetables into the broth. "It depends on the person. Some love Masa. Have to have it every day. Others, not so much. If the other three are there they are still happy. That is the thing I have noticed about Bolivians. We are very independent, but we are also very interdependent. We all like the same flavors, the same texture, the same sweetness or sourness. But at the dinner time, if there are parts we recognize and something we expect is missing we are still happy. We still come back for seconds if they are available. You see Bolivians are seldom satiated. We can always eat a little more, drink a little more, talk a little longer. We make do. If we do not have what we want, we are happy we have something. We are happy we have a family. We are happy something has filled our bellies. Kept us warm on a cold winter night. For we know in the mountains there are others who have none of the things we have."

The chef adds spices from three packages, stirs them in.

"Tell me about the spices you added," X introduces almost nonchalantly.

"The spices." We are at the point of revealing the mystery magical ingredient that has transformed the dish into something almost mythical.

"It is dried and powered sheep dung, mixed with a few herbs from the highest reaches of the Andes such as powdered Maca, particularly when I've not added it directly as a vegetable. It's usually one or the other. Vegetable or spice. I prefer it as a vegetable, but at certain times of the year only the spice is available. It's thought to be an aphrodisiac, you know. That's why it generally ends up either as a root vegetable or herb in most every pot in Bolivia."

"But maca is not your magical ingredient since everyone has been cooking with it almost since the beginning of time. So, what is your magical ingredient?" X pushes having gotten lost in the discussion.

"The powder," the chef acknowledges. "From the sheep."

Suddenly X's face lights up as does some back-region cells of my brain. He said dried and powdered sheep dung. That's sheep excrement. *Holy shit he's using sheep shit in his dishes as a spice.*

The chef shoves the pot back into the fire to begin to cook as if there was nothing special about the mixture of ingredients he has produced to create this in-demand dish so revered by the Andean Bolivian peoples.

X must have known about the unusual spice for he doesn't miss a beat. "What is distinctive about the spices you use in this otherwise traditional soup dish so common in the Andes and even more common in the highlands of Bolivia?"

"It is not as profound as you adding chili peppers to a dish. But when the people of these mountains have come to expect that their stew, to use your term, will always taste the same, anything you add to it will change it from expected to unexpected. And that is why my restaurant is doing so well. I am serving the unexpected."

"But Sheep dung?" X asks, emphasizing the dung part to make clear that he is in fact talking about the excrement of a sheep. "I don't know anyone who would knowingly eat sheep dung. Why are the people of this village, high up in the Andes Mountains of Bolivia an exception to the rule?"

"First of all, it is only a spice," The chef responds. "There are many spices we add to a dish and dispose of because they are inedible as they are."

"Such as?"

"Cloves, bay leaves, cinnamon sticks to name only a few."

"That's true, but none of them have passed through the body of a living organism, with all kinds of digestive juices leaving something that is left behind and normally used as fertilizer rather than a flavor enhancement." X offers.

"What about that Sumatran coffee bean? The one that is digested by a kind of monkey and yet it is retrieved, dried, roasted and is one of the most desired coffees in the world?"

It's clear this chef has done considerable research to ensure a defensible position about the use of sheep dung as a spice. Still not something I would have normally considered, but he certainly has been persuasive, and X has done little to discredit his argument.

X must have been reading my mind, "The difference between a Sumatran coffee bean that survives a passage through a monkey's intestines and the product of all the food that has been digested by a sheep, generally grasses of one sort or another, is quite substantial. The monkey's digestive juices serve to break down the hard shell of the coffee bean such that it is more accessible during the roasting process and therefore more influenced by the extreme heat. It causes the flavors to emerge that otherwise would have been protected by that hard shell. Thus, the digestive process has served as an enhancement to the flavor release. But sheep dung? What has been released by this process? Grass has been reduced to its primary constituent parts. But what is there in grass that can possibly release flavors otherwise hidden from heat in a roasting or drying process? No, you cannot show me a significant flavor enhancement that comes from such a passage through a sheep's intestines. And in this case, I see nothing that will enhance the flavors in and of themselves. So, we are reduced to a theory that maybe, just maybe, when powdered sheep dung is mixed with powdered masa that a combination of flavors is in fact released in a unique and almost magical way."

AFRAID

Now it's time to write a blog about sheep dung as a spice. This ought to get a response from more than one of my audience.

SPICING IT UP

Chef X, in his most recent video, asked an important question: What makes a magical combination of flavors? Can something we would normally dismiss become a constituent part of something transformative? Can something we would normally never consider as a candidate for insertion into our mouth be acceptable in combination with something that makes magic of a meal?

In his most recent video Chef X visited a remote village high in the Bolivian Andes to interview a chef of unparalleled courage. A chef who would add something to a traditional meal none of his predecessors would consider. And in this process, he discovered a flavor combination unlike any other. For most of us, fashion wins out over flavor in almost every instance. What's fashionable? What is everyone else eating? What is trending today, what is the hot new ingredient we can't get enough of? Chef X has ripped away the social convention to show the puppet master behind the screen is not the arbiter of good taste.

How many people would willingly eat something spiced with dried and powdered sheep dung? Not many, if any I know. But in this Bolivian mountain village it is the attraction bringing those who would never have considered eating at a certain restaurant to experience the uncommon taste of sheep dung and masa spiced mutton stew. Mutton stew, in and of itself, is somewhat unusual in these villages. But when the dung-masa spices are added it becomes something different, something worthy of a special trip to a dining experience unlike any other they have enjoyed in recent memory.

Now will our restaurants follow suite? Will we have the opportunity to experience this different flavor combination? Will our social conventions permit us to sample something our minds would normally dismiss as unworthy of our attention? Chef Alejandro Suarez calculated that risk and found it has paid off handsomely for him and his small restaurant high in the Bolivian Andes Mountains.

It is a far cry from a mountain village to the restaurants of New York, London, Paris or Tokyo. It's an even further reach to Istanbul, Mecca or Santiago. But the one thing that is true for all restauranteurs around the globe is an opportunity to create a new flavor combination to engage the palates of patrons. What no one has been able to establish at this point is the effects of wine upon this flavor combination. The very remoteness of the Bolivian experience mitigates against a robust history of wine pairing. In fact, how many have even sampled a Bolivian wine? They exist. They take advantage of the traditional grapes of South America such as Cabernet Sauvignon, Syrah and Malbec. If you work at it you might even find Carmenere, the pride of Chile. And on the white site Sauvignon Blanc is widely available in country but almost never through export. Don't even bother looking for Bolivian wines in your Whole Food Market anytime soon. And yet Chef Suarez has made a practice of determining which wines have the most robust impact on his Mutton Stew with Sheep Dung and Masa spices.

If you find yourself in Bolivia, you won't find such an entry on the menu at Chef Suarez's restaurant. It is simply Sheep Soup with spices. One has to know what one is looking for, but Chef Suarez has said the Syrah is the one wine that best compliments his creation. So, try it on your next trip south. In the meantime, start a conversation.

I walk back through my draft blog. Pretty much sums up what I wanted to say about the video I watched, and the ground-breaking work Chef X is doing by challenging convention about the nature of spices and their influence on food flavor combinations. Even get a section in there about Bolivian wines which was kind of an extra, but the kind of thing Z really likes. Short a few words, but I suspect this will be one of those blogs where no one counts the words because the topic is so engaging for a foody, anyway.

Who would have thought I'd be extolling the virtues of sheep dung as a spice? Was never on my radar. But the more I reflect on the video, the more I have come to the conclusion that Chef X came to my apartment after making this particular video. Why do I think that? Because he was all about convincing me that traditional flavors create a wide range of experiences in the mouth. How they interact not only with your tongue and the receptors there, but the combination of wines seems to be an extrapolation of his discussions with Chef Alejandro, high up on that mountain, in a tiny Bolivian village on a cold winter's night.

It then occurs to me, how many will watch that video? How many foodies and chefs will care at all about a Bolivian food experience? I decide to check to stats. I'm amazed to find that after only forty-eight hours he has had over seven million visitors to his video website. Word travels fast. And, I wonder, how many of them are chefs who are looking for the next big thing? Will dried and powdered sheep dung blended with dried and powdered masa in a mutton stew be that next big thing, particularly when paired with a good Syrah? I doubt it. But chefs are inventive. I expect we will start seeing it showing up in combination with other foods besides mutton, since that particular meat is not often a primary source of protein in western diets outside of the UK. How do I know that? I can't tell you the last time I saw it on a menu in New York. And since that's where I live, and everyone tells me it's the center of the cultural universe, with the exception of my California friends who equally argue for LA and San Francisco, although the latter will tell you there's more going on in the valley than in the city, but I personally don't agree with that from a food point of view. Anyway, it will be fun to see how long it takes for powdered sheep dung and masa to show up on menus. Given the supposed aphrodisiac properties of the latter I expect it won't take long.

Time to send it along to O. A quick re-read to catch any spelling or grammar errors and off it goes. Given it's short of the six-hundred-word target, I give her an extra two minutes before looking to see what her response is.

> J:
>
> *Have you lost what's left of your poor depleted*
>
> *brain cells? Call me.*

I do as she asks.

"What's wrong with a dried and powdered sheep dung and masa spice combination?" I ask before she even responds.

"Nobody eats shit," is the response I expect to get from her, and I do.

"Obviously folks in Bolivia do." I push right back.

"Come on. I know you're playing the devil's advocate here, but do you really want to waste all these beautiful words going on and on about shit?"

"Would you have the same reaction if I was extolling the virtues of cloves?"

"Seems to me you did about eighteen months ago," she reminds me.

"That was all about the health benefits when used in combinations of certain meats and spicy beverages. But in many respects, it's similar. You don't eat cloves, you don't eat sheep dung either. You dry it and reduce it to powder. What you get is a flavor essence, not the stuff you would object to putting into your mouth or stomach. The bad stuff is gone. Burned up. Only a residue powder remains. With a clove, you insert it into a ham or piece of meat, let it float on a beverage, but you don't eat or drink it directly. In the case of sheep dung, you're even further removed from the bad aspects of it than you are in the case of spiced meat or a beverage where it has been removed prior to serving."

"You've made my point. You don't consume the clove. In the case you describe, you do consume the powdered remains. That's what I object to."

"Fine. Don't eat it." I hesitate to state what I'm thinking, fearful of offending my best friend, but I'm not smart enough to back off when I have something to say. "You're the one who will be running around a year from now trying to get into the restaurants that are serving it. You'll be the one trying to be like everyone else who has embraced this spice combination because of the aphrodisiac side effect everyone else is talking about and enjoying while you sit the wallflower watching and wondering why you're not in the thick of things."

"You're hitting below the belt, Missy." O observes.

"I know, but didn't we just have this conversation about how no one sees you?"

"I am invisible. Except when I'm wearing plaid, and then everyone thinks I'm just a moving billboard."

"I don't." I try to get her back into this conversation and not let her start feeling sorry for herself. I've seen her do that way too many times. "Look. I'm not telling you to go out and find someone who is doing this. I'm only suggesting you need to do your job and fact check me. Is there anything in this piece we can't substantiate, either through what Chef X says in his video or through other sources? Tell me what they are and I'll make the changes. Then send it on to Z so he can publish it and decide if this is the week that he fires me or the week he gives me a raise."

"When was the last time he gave anyone a raise?" O reminds me.

"Not since I've been here, but we have to maintain our hope for the future. That eventually we will do something that is worthy of a raise, or praise, or honorable mention in the blog writers hall of fame - or shame as the case may be."

"Why are you such a freaking optimist?" O can hardly conceal her frustration with me.

"Hope is all we have." I push back. "Tomorrow has to be better than today because tomorrow we will have the additional experience and wisdom we lack today."

"But what does that have to do with relationships?"

I have to give this a moment of thought. Don't want to riff and really send her into orbit. Temper what I would have said. "Look at us."

"Not the kind of relationship I'm talking about. Ours in an unnatural co-dependency based on unrealistic expectations about someone showing up who will look at either one of us."

I think for just a moment about Chef X and the one night we had together. Could O have an experience like that? Probably not given her current job as a fact checker. I experienced it because I'm the name on the blog. We all have to put ourselves into a position where we are recognized by someone for some reason, not even one we would have wanted if asked about it.

"I'm not going to argue perceptions. That's all we have at the moment. Neither of us know what will change our lives. Neither of us know what we're even looking for in a relationship, let alone who that other person might be or where to find him. If someone were to say you'll meet your future husband if you just go to Joe's Pizzeria over in Brooklyn near Citibank Park, I'm sure we would each check it out, if nothing more. But no one can tell us that. No one sees the future or knows what chemistry makes a relationship work while another ultimately fails. We've both been there. Trying to hold onto something that has no hope of succeeding. In those instances, we would be better off moving on and putting ourselves in a position to meet the next possibly Mr. Right. How long that will take no one knows, but that's where hope comes in. Belief that if we put ourselves out there, do what we can to make ourselves a better and more attractive person, eventually Mr. Right will appear."

"Here we are back to hope." O tries to temper my enthusiasm. "You have it and I don't. I know I'm never gonna look like you or a million other girls. So how does anyone get past all of you to find me? You know what I mean? I'm at the end of the desirability line so I'd be better off just eating a whole pint of gelato and gaining the next two pounds because it's not gonna make any difference in finding Mr. Right. In the meantime, at least I've had a nice pint of gelato to lift my mood."

"We've been here before." I use to shut down the pity party. "Can we get back to my blog?"

O seems to realize where we are and shifts gears. "Sure. You were talking about how shitty life becomes, so you might as well eat shit."

"That's not what I wrote." I defend my draft.

"That's what I got out of it."

"What facts do you need to check?" I'm again trying to get her back on topic.

"Does Syrah go with the Sheep Soup with Spices? But the problem

I have is finding anyone who has had multiple bowls of his concoction to see which wine, in fact, does go best with it."

"I'm sure Chef Suarez at the Bolivian restaurant could give you names and contact information," I reassure her.

"Yeah, I know how to do my job. Don't need pointers from you."

"Then what are you waiting for?" I'm somewhat mystified by her reluctance to get started on this one. Must have something to do with her love life which I know is in the pits at the moment.

"You remember Damien?" comes out of the blue. I have to stop and think for a moment.

"The IT guy?" is the only Damien I can think of.

"Yeah." She's quiet for a moment, apparently trying to decide what she should say. "We had a great conversation when he came by to set up new software and security on my laptop."

"Great. But where are you going with this?"

"He's someone I think I might like to spend some time with, you know what I mean?"

"But you're afraid of what he might think of you." I realize is the rest of that statement.

THE DECISION

Of course, O wants to have drinks with Damien, but she needs to have an excuse with others about, so it won't be obvious what she's up to. She also wants feedback from several of us as to whether he's the real thing or not. Somehow, she arranges it and a bunch of us are scheduled to meet at the Oak, a neighborhood club we have gone to forever. The staff know us by sight, even though not by name. What excuse O used to get Damien here I have no idea, but he came wandering in with Chi who is my editor. Chi Nguyen Giap is tiny in comparison to the rest of us. I'm not sure how much over five feet he stands, but whatever it is it's not much. And he clearly is less than a hundred pounds soaking wet. But what Chi lacks in stature, he makes up for by a powerful voice even if it isn't always matched by an equally powerful intellect. That's not to say Chi isn't a deep thinker. In reality he may be, but he has learned that superficial trends trump ideas for eyes of readers. So, Chi is all about eyes, getting them to our blogs and making sure we tone down our vocabularies to match that of most of our readers. Of that I'm generally his worst offender. And Chi lets me know what he thinks of words that don't simplify and illuminate the basic concepts we are trying to convey. They are either dispatched into lost computer memory or simply deleted. The latter tends to be his favorite approach to dealing with my alliteration. Generally, I'll plant at least one gem for him to ponder in each blog. I know it will never survive, but it's fun to watch him try to figure out how to edit to a simpler expression while still keeping my meaning.

Damien is tall in comparison to Chi. Over six feet he has the lean physique of an athlete and it's evident he frequents a gym. That fact alone would seem to doom O's budding infatuation to being one-way.

But Damien is nothing if not open and pleasant to everyone. Now that I see him again, I remember an encounter I had with him more than a year ago when my laptop wouldn't register with the network and I couldn't transfer my files without sending them by email. Damien was responsive, respectful and courteous. Answered every question and was encouraging even when it was determined I had reset something inadvertently causing the problem. He informed me I wasn't the first nor would he expect me to be the last to make this same mistake. Did Damien stand out in my mind as someone who might be interesting to get to know better? Not then. But now that O had developed interest, I had to look at him differently. Was he a good fit for her? What would it take for him to become interested in her? I was instantly concerned that she would have to lose a lot more weight than she would be comfortable addressing. It's not that O is fat. She really isn't. She just happens to be a large woman. Her frame makes it easy to carry a lot of weight. So, it's hard for her to maintain the diligence needed to avoid extra calories or exercise sufficiently to work off the excess she tends to add without realizing what's going on.

Damien is talking with Ace when Chi thinks to introduce him around. "Everyone. This is Damien. Mister IT wizard. He keeps us all on line when the gremlins decide to intervene in our systems."

Damien nods to everyone and then leans over to O.

"Your gremlins back in the woodshed?"

O almost seems panic-stricken trying to decide how to answer this simple query and keep the conversation going. "System's working fine. How are you doing? Settling in?"

Damien seems confused, "Settling in? Not sure I got your meaning."

"You seem to really understand our systems." O tries to keep the conversation going. "So, I assume you've worked IT elsewhere and brought your knowledge to our challenges."

Damien nods. "Kinda vanilla, really. Some of the changes coming will make things easier for you. Hopefully more challenging for me. That would be all good."

"All good?" O picks up on. "Where'd you grow up? I've not heard that expression before."

"South Carolina. Went to school at Clemson so I guess I didn't have much cause to change what I'd always said when I was sprouting."

"I love your expressions." O gushes.

"Got a bait bucket full of 'em."

The waiter brings the drinks. O looks at the glass with one ice cube and a golden liquid Damien receives.

"What's that?" she points to his glass as a goblet of red wine is placed before her.

"Eagle Rare Bourbon. Just what I'm working my way through this month."

"I don't understand." O responds gently, trying not to seem a pest.

Damien picks up the glass, passes it under his nose on the way to his mouth. A sip and the glass returns to the table. "Yup. Eagle Rare. I decided there are so many bourbons out there and so little time to try them all that I give myself a month on a brand. This month is Eagle Rare. Next month is Elijah Craig. I haven't decided after that. But I got lots of choices and hopefully lots of months to find the one great bourbon I'll settle down with."

O only hears 'settle down with' and dives right in. "So, you're on a quest?"

"That's one way of looking at it." Damien nods. "I don't think there's any such thing as perfection. We're all evolving to become

67

something other than what we are today. Bourbon's like that too. This year's Eagle Rare might come back in five years and suit my taste better than what I'm drinking then. Even though I've had it before, things seem to have a way of coming around on you. That opportunity you let get away? Just means you probably weren't ready for it when it came by the first time. When it comes back around, it might be as close to perfect for you as you're likely to find in this lifetime. But you just never know. It might not too. The trick is being open to everything. Don't take anything for granted. And never assume that what sits in front of you today will always be the same, because the odds are the next time you see something it's gonna be a whole different fish fry."

"Did you just share your philosophy of life?" Chi asks, fascinated by what he just heard.

Damien turns the glass in his hand. "Every one of us is a philosopher in his," Damien nods to O. "...Or her own right. We just share our philosophies in different ways. Where I grew up, we talk about the things we individually control and the things that control us, even though we don't necessarily realize it. So, the trick is figuring out how to move some of those things we don't control over on the other side of the smoker. It's like you can cook ribs, or steaks or salmon in your smoker and depending on the wood you use you'll get a whole different result. You over cook or you undercook the meat or fish and you please some folks and you don't others. Means you just got to know who you're trying to satisfy. To say you're just trying to satisfy yourself never works. 'Cause every one of us has a whole different look at things. We come at life with different wants, needs and perspectives. We sit down and share what we've come up with. Some folks appreciate it and others just can't make heads or tails of what we're saying to them. You know what I'm saying?"

"Ever think of writing a blog?" Chi asks, shifting the focus away from O.

"I don't wrestle with ideas very well. IT is simple. It's predictable. I can figure it out. If you follow the logic it takes you to the problem.

You ask me to start a conversation with someone I can hold my own. But to just sit down and tell you what I think about something without that feedback? Well I'm afraid I'd run out of words real quick. Then I'd be sitting out in the middle of the lake without a paddle, trying to guess where the waterfall might be hiding."

O looks at me as if she'd just lost the battle.

"What goes around comes around." I respond to her.

Damien hears my comment and looks curiously at O, then at me. I nod towards O and he winks at me before returning his attention to Chi. I'm not sure what the wink means, but I'm hopeful he understood what I was trying to communicate. That is all I can do for O at this point.

She starts to get up, distraught and I put my hand up to stop her. She looks at me as if I'm trying to stop her flight from disappointment, which I am. I nod towards the restroom and she nods in understanding.

Once inside she goes to the sink and lets her frustration out, "Why'd Chi have to steal him away from me?"

"Does he know what you're up to?" I come right back.

"No. I just said I'd met him, and he seems like he'd fit into our Friday group."

"Obviously Chi agrees with your assessment." I point out. "As I listened to the conversation it sounds like your friend Damien isn't closing any doors in his life. Now that can be good for you in that you're going to have more chances with him. But it could also be bad in that he doesn't settle down on one thing unless something changes his natural predispositions."

"What are you saying?" O is brimming with energy she doesn't know where to focus. "Chi needs to edit that speech, so I know what you're trying to tell me."

"Be patient."

"I don't want to be patient. I want to go home with him tonight."

"And I want to win the lottery, which reminds me I need to buy a ticket, or my chance remains zero." I inform her. "Do you hear me? Winning the lottery is a matter of patience. To win you got to keep playing. If you don't buy your tickets and your number comes up, you're not going to win even if you have the right number in your head."

"Not a good comparison." O responds sullenly.

"Wait a minute. I'm telling you any relationship requires patience, staying with it, meaning you've got to play every day. It means doing your part, which means making yourself look more appealing to him. You didn't say he's a body builder, but all the gym rats I know expect their ladies to be in the gym with them getting tight, getting fit and building endurance. You know why?"

O shakes her head clearly not wanting to hear this part.

"Not because they expect their ladies to win a body building contest, but because they're convinced that if you work out, you'll be able to do more and live longer."

O frowns. "Why live longer?" She's not thought about body building in these terms before.

"Because you have the endurance to work all day, go to the gym for an hour or more and still go out and dance for the evening. If Damien asked you to go out and dance after work what would you say?"

"I'd say yes and regret it the next day."

"In your condition you couldn't keep up with him. Maybe that's what he was saying about what's in front of him today may not be what he needs today but easily could be tomorrow or in five years. I know you heard that. You should consider it an invitation."

"I don't know where to begin." O finally admits.

"Ask Damien what gym he goes to and would he recommend someone to work you out. That should get his attention and let him know you seriously want to address your conditioning."

When we get back to our table, Ace is talking with Damien.

"Mind if we join your conversation?" I ask as O and I sit down.

Ace nods but keeps on talking. "I don't think anyone really has a clear direction on how to solve that problem. It's something we all have to deal with, and we will be dealing with it for as long as I can foresee."

"What are you talking about?" I interject.

"Cyber security." Damien explains.

O responds, "Didn't know you're working the security side as well."

"The whole gaggle of us work security issues." Damien responds. "Always dealing with folks being careless. So, as I go around, I hang about a bit to see how people work securely. Whether they're oblivious to things that let the bad guys in."

"So, you were observing me when you fixed my settings," O wants to confirm.

Damien nods, "Some folk are a lot more interesting than others. You have a particularly sensitive role. You're out on all kinds of sites, trying to decide what's fact and what's not. That takes you a whole bunch of places that can put you and your machine in jeopardy. So, it's real important I keep a close eye on you to keep you and the company safe."

"Did I pass the test?" O inquires.

Damien smiles. "You did. You're real careful. You double check things and walk away from sites when you should. So yeah. You passed. But I still have to keep my eye on you."

O nods, asks, "Since you're looking out for me, could you offer some advice?"

"Sure."

"I'm looking for someone to work me out. I'm trying to get into shape, but I've just not found anyone who was patient enough to take me at a pace that makes sense to me. Do you think you could recommend someone?"

"As a matter of fact," Damien brightens. "I know folks. You might get along with one or two of 'em."

At this point I nod to Ace to join me at the bar so O and Damien can talk.

"Where did that blog come from? Spirituality and food? It sounded more like me than you," Ace seeks to satisfy his curiosity.

"Let's just say someone took the time to show me a way to do my job better." I try to answer his question without arousing his protective instincts, which he's shown before.

"Sounded like it was a chef. Which one?" Just like Ace. He goes right to the heart of the matter.

I decide I have to make it seem like no big deal. "Doesn't matter. It just woke me up. I have a responsibility to not only my audience, but also the people, places and foods I write about. It was impressed on me there needs to be a balanced discussion and not just a food fight because I say something someone else doesn't agree with."

Ace evaluates my response with his eyes and some inner ear, then makes a decision. "Mind taking a short ride with me? I'd like to show you something."

He has never invited me out before, I don't know quite what to make of this invitation, but I want to give O an opportunity to cement a relationship with Damien. She'd followed my advice, so what the heck?

BLEEKER STREET

Ace lives uptown. I'm north of the village and in an area not nearly as affluent. His apartment is four times the size of my three rooms plus bath. I may almost have a view of the river. Ace seems to have a view of the whole world through his floor to ceiling glass windows on the 37th floor. He even has a deck with trees and vegetables growing at certain times of the year. Not now because winter is approaching. Z mentioned he'd heard Ace owns the building he lives in. Well, not exactly him alone. Ace and a whole bunch of investors. But he's the managing partner with the biggest stake.

I've only been here once before. Ace invited all of us up after one of our Friday get togethers. I think we were celebrating Z merging his business with a much larger media firm. Somehow Z had come out as the managing partner. Something like what Ace did with his apartment house. Z doesn't own it outright, but he calls the shots and gets rewarded well for managing things well.

The elevator opens directly into his apartment. I'm reminded that Ace must be a monk. He has all this great space, a phenomenal view and yet almost no furniture and absolutely no decorations or art. I've heard of minimalists, but Ace takes that notion to a whole different level. He has a stack of pillows to sit on, one table to serve food and drinks, a full kitchen, but not a single small appliance evident and a bedroom with a King size bed. All of his clothes are hung up in the massive walk-in closets or tucked away in built-in drawers and shelves. Neat or obsessive?

"Do you ever cook here?" I ask as I wander about his private domain. I can feel him watching me, letting me explore his space and therefore his psyche.

"Once."

"What did you make?" I turn to look at him to see not only what but how he answers.

"A seven-course dinner for sixteen."

I'm not sure if my jaw has dropped open, but I am more than surprised at his answer. "Seven courses." I seek confirmation.

"I started with a tiny Quiche Lorraine, about the size of a silver dollar. The accompaniment was a three-year-old white Burgundy. The Quiche was followed by a quarter ounce of lemon sorbet to cleanse the palate and frizzante water, Perrier if I remember correctly. I thought of San Pellegrino but since the wine was French, I was trying to be respectful of the terroir."

"Did you really?" I have to question this story because I can't imagine Ace cooking eggs for breakfast let alone an elaborate meal for a large party of guests.

"Actually, I did have a little help."

Now I get the picture, Ace watched as a chef prepared the meal and servers presented it to his guests. "And what was this chef's name?"

"Xavier Francis. Of course, this was back before he got his own restaurant and long before he became famous. Seems to me he was a sous chef or something when I met him. Just getting started. But even then, he knew what he was doing. My guests still remind me of that dinner."

"And what was the lovely lady's name?"

Ace drops his head just a bit, so his eyes recede and look much darker. "That was the night I closed the deal to buy this building."

So apparently Z was correct about one thing.

"The dinner was for my investors. I wanted them to see what they were buying into. Actually, had furniture brought in just for that night. X couldn't believe I didn't even have pots or pans in the apartment. He had to bring in everything from his restaurant. I guess that became a big deal as his head chef wasn't happy he was out working on the side. The last time I saw him he thanked me. Said that experience convinced him he was ready to go out on his own. Still took him more than a year to get his own place, but he eventually did and made a fortune."

"Probably not as much as you." I gesture to the room we are standing in so he knows I'm talking about the apartment house.

"He did all right." Hmm. Not willing to go there, talk about his wealth.

"And you haven't eaten here since," I push to confirm what I'm seeing.

"I have my celebratory dinners out now. That was to seal the deal for this building."

I wonder what he is willing to tell me about his work, "You're all about deals, or so I'm told."

"What would you like to know?" Ace is curious where I'm going. "I'm an open book."

"You obviously brought me here because you wanted to impress me." I grab a pillow and lay down over it like I'm swimming on an inner tube. Ace kicks off his shoes and sits into a lotus position. Didn't know he does Yoga. "You didn't need to, you know. I'm easily impressed living on Bank Street close to the West Side Highway."

"I grew up not so far from there, so you don't get any sympathy from me." Ace smiles ironically.

"What I'm saying is I'm nobody. Look at you. Thirty-seventh floor of a building you own in Manhattan. I'm sixth floor of a building that on a clear day lets me glimpse the Hudson. I constantly live in fear. Afraid of the rent going up or the utilities going up or losing my job. Any of those events and I'll be out in thirty days. Probably homeless for I don't even know how long. We may have come from the same neighborhood, but you escaped. I never did. Is that my fault? I don't know. I just never thought about anything other than writing. I think I do a credible job with my blog. But if you asked me to do what you do? I wouldn't have a single idea of where to even start."

Ace sits very still for a long moment, considering something. I don't know if it's the words, or the tone of hopelessness I use to describe my situation. And I realize I have never admitted to anyone that I actually have been running away from who I am. Not wanting to admit even to myself how the cards are stacked against me. Maybe I'm living in denial. Is that how I get through the day? Denying that things are as shaky as I've just described them. Denying that anything could change. Denying that tomorrow will be any different from today. And why did I admit this to Ace when I've never mentioned it to anyone else?

"We are each a product of our situation." Ace begins looking down but then engages my eyes. "We find ourselves faced with a never-ending series of choices. Talent only has a tangential effect on what we become. Of that I'm convinced. We make an uncommon choice we may find ourselves in a place where we can do remarkable things with whatever talents we possess or have developed. We make the safe choices and our opportunities are generally more limited. Our ability to rise above the common more difficult. I've heard people say they settle for the familiar because they're afraid of the unknown. And that's why you're such a conundrum to me."

I have no idea what he's talking about. "Tell me more."

"You clearly have talent. It's there for anyone to see who reads your blogs."

"Why do you read them?" I'm surprised someone who obviously has little or no interest in food, based on a cursory look around his apartment would read a food blog.

"Because they give me insight into your mind."

Now he's getting creepy. "My mind." I have to repeat to be sure I'm following him.

"How you see the world. How you see yourself. It's all there. In the words you chose. In the expressions you select. In how you describe things. Always with a sense of wonder and appreciation even of the things you don't understand or would never eat."

"So, am I like someone for you to play mind games with?" Just comes out and I wonder if I could have chosen better words. "What are you doing with me? You obviously could be with most anyone you want."

Ace reflects on my comment. I don't know if he's wrestling with its accuracy or something else, but he is wrestling. "You're the writer. What causes attraction between two people?"

"If anyone got that right there would be no further need for novels. Attraction is based on something other than the core magnetism pulling people into each other's orbits."

Ace smiles. "Exhibit number one. Listen to the words you chose to describe something that's abstract. Core magnetism. A great concept I've never heard anyone else use to describe why people see someone that others do not. It has to be something that resonates in another. You chose magnetism. An invisible force we all feel but can't predict the outcome of its effects on us."

"Now who's creating abstract imagery?" I observe. "Why is it you seldom discuss your thoughts in groups, like our Friday friends? It's always one-on-one, somewhere apart from others. At the bar, now at your apartment. Never in the give and take of a wide-ranging discussion."

"I like to control the flow. Have the time to choose my words rather than react and wonder afterwards why I didn't communicate more clearly. Wonder at how a bunch of people with different reference points will take my point."

"Do overs." I verbalize. "You're afraid you won't get a do over and you'll forever have to live with the words as spoken. I take it you said something that hurt someone, and you wish you could take those words back."

Ace immediately gets to his feet, "Would you like a San Pellegrino?" and he heads towards the kitchen. I wonder why he wouldn't respond to my observation as I scramble up to follow.

"You don't have any alcohol in your place?" I notice as I look around.

"No need," Ace confirms. "I'm the only one who ever comes here and all I really need is water."

He hands me a half liter bottle and brings out one for himself.

"Not the usual seduction, breaking down my resistance with alcohol to cloud my judgment."

"I don't want your judgment impaired." Ace lets that hang in the air for a long moment. "If we are to sleep together tonight or any other night, I want it to be because that's what you want with all your faculties telling you it's the right thing and what you want more than anything else."

"Who are you? No one acts this way." He's making it sound too good to be true, but that makes me even more suspicious. Why does it have to be his way? Why not a mutual desire in whatever state I'm in? If I want to sleep with him why do I have to wait until I meet his criteria?

"I'm someone who knows what he wants," Ace puts himself into perspective, at least as he sees thing. "Who has the experience to know getting what you want isn't always a good thing. Someone who has learned that patience is the most important thing when it comes to relationships and sex and life. If you rush into something it will inevitably come apart or disappoint you sometime in the future. If you go too slow it's likely to move away from you for something more immediate. So, patience is a finely balanced build-up of expectations with periodic payoffs along the way to validate you're on the right path."

"Were you a professor at NYU?" I accuse him. Ace is taken aback but lets me continue. "I'm sure I had you for introductory human psychology. There was something there in that analysis that is just so familiar. I got an A in your course, I'm sure, but only because I specialize in psychobabble."

Ace laughs. "Not guilty. "Never taught at NYU or any other school in the city. But I took that same course and I guess sometimes my penchant for psychobabble comes out."

I open the bottle of San Pellegrino and take a quick sip, expecting he probably doesn't have any glasses so out of the bottle is the best I'm going to do. "Where did you teach? You said not in the city, but you taught somewhere."

"Guilty," he takes a sip of water now to collect his thoughts. "That's where my life changed. I had this student. The names are a matter of public record. Came from a family of New York real estate developers. Why she was attending a public university upstate I have no idea, even to this day. Crazy. Anyway, she introduced me to her family and the rest, as they say, is history."

"I take it they needed a front man who could use psychobabble to close billion-dollar deals over a seven-course dinner on the thirty-seventh floor overlooking the whole world at sunset."

"It eventually came to that." He reflects. "And more."

"I take it she is your wife?" is a pure guess, but it makes sense.

"When the whole world opens up before you and there doesn't seem to be any limits on what you can do or who or what you can become the old Latin expression comes to mind. You obsess on it. Particularly if you were one of those people who sufficed rather than make the difficult choices."

"Seize the day." I guess.

Ace smiles an empty smile, "All the stories man has invented about the devil coming for your soul when you drive a bargain to achieve that which you were not destined to have by any other means? They're real. And they're not uncommon. Otherwise we wouldn't resonate with the story."

"With all your success, what are you regretting?"

"What it cost me to get here."

"What did you say to her when she left you?"

Ace first stares at me for a moment. "It's that obvious?" I hear deeply felt real pain.

"She clearly wounded you deeply." Another thought comes to me. "I would also guess I'm about as opposite to her as you've found. Tell me where I'm wrong. She was gorgeous."

Ace doesn't react. Not even a flinch. Apparently visualizing her or something about her.

"Society balls, clothes, parties all night and charity events." I go on.

A flinch.

"No charity events, I take it." Summarizing.

"When you have everything you need it's hard to sympathize with those who have nothing."

"But you do, coming from Bleeker Street."

Ace looks at me strange. "I didn't tell you that."

"Sure, you did, when you said you came from the neighborhood. We went to the same school, you just don't remember, but I do now. You stood out, I never did. Quarterbacks are seldom forgotten on city championship teams."

BOUILLABAISSE

The next thing I know Ace and I are in a car on the way to a restaurant. Of course, he did not ask where I'd like to go. He is probably not eager for an evening in the old neighborhood. And on my income, those are the only restaurants I know or can afford. Not much is said in the car as we both look outside the windows as a misty rain begins to hide the evening in reflective shadows.

When we arrive at Lagniappe, a French restaurant over on the East side Ace informs me. "The owner constantly has to remind people that he named this place from the French provincial use of the word, which is a little something extra." Ace holds the car door open for me. "Here most people think a lagniappe is a free gift a merchant gives away when you buy something. I can assure you nothing is free here. But he serves the most authentic French provincial I've found in the city."

"You've been to France?" I inquire, since he implied he's not only been there but likes it very much. I feel the mist on my face from the light rain and duck my head to step quickly towards the waiting restaurant door.

Ace merely nods and opens the restaurant door for me. As I step inside, I wipe the mist from my eyes and find a warm and cozy room, white linen tablecloths, sparking crystal glassware and a waiter holding an open bottle of white French wine to serve us as soon as we are seated. Ace holds my chair for me and seats himself with an expectant look.

"Are you expecting me to blog on this place?" I ask, wondering if that is the source of his expectation.

"I hope not to have to wait that long to learn what you think of a meal I look forward to."

"Why? Why here? I have no idea how many French provincial restaurants there are just in the city and the other boroughs. But there must be hundreds. I know I keep coming back to the same fundamental question. What is it about this restaurant that brings you back with so many you can choose from?"

At that moment a small white-haired man in a gray suit and purple tie approaches the table. His black leather shoes are highly polished so I can almost see my reflection in them. As he gets closer, I notice a pencil thin moustache which is salt and pepper gray indicating his hair had probably once been black. "Monsieur Ace. Is indeed a pleasure to have you dine with us tonight. And you have brought a lovely lady to dine with you. I am sure she will complement our meal with the conversation to make a very pleasant evening for you both. Will you be having your usual? I will have Jacques prepare it just the way you like it. Will you also be ordering for Madame or should I bring a menu?"

Ace glances at me and I shrug to let him know he may order for me if he would like.

"Gabriel, I would suggest you bring a sampling of your specialties for the lady. That way she might better understand the brilliance of your kitchen."

The man known as Gabriel nods to us both and withdraws. He steps back before turning so he is not turning his back on us. Interesting old-world manners.

"Does that answer your question about why here?" Ace raises his glass of wine and waits for me to do the same so we can toast. We clink glasses and his toast comes as, "To a culinary adventure for both of us."

"Tonight?" I ask confused since he is apparently having what he usually has here.

"Not just tonight." Ace replies before taking a sip.

"As to my question about why here." I return. "I may have a better understanding of what you like about this place after we eat, but for the moment, the question still stands. Apparently, this restaurant reminds you of someplace you ate at in Provence. What restaurant would that be and where is it?"

Ace considers my question, which I find curious. I expected he would have the name of a single restaurant in a very small village somewhere that changed his life. That is the story I've read others describe over and over. Some grandmother of a restaurant owner who comes only one day a week to cook because she's something like a hundred years old, but knows all the secrets to the classic dishes we love on this side of the pond. This is what I'm expecting.

"There really wasn't just one I can think of." Ace finally admits. "I would go to a small village and have just this incredible meal. You know what I'm saying? Better than anything I've had before."

I wait for him to continue and just about when I think he's not going to he picks up the thread. "And then I'd go to another village and have a meal that was indescribable. That's why I admire what you do. You find words to describe what can't be described, at least not in my mind. And the words you find are... they're just perfect. You capture the essence of a meal. The spirit of the people who create it and serve it to you for your appreciation. And what always amazes me is that those people don't think what they've made is all that special. It's just the way they've always made it."

"If you lived there it wouldn't be special." I point out. "Because it would be what you have all the time. You'd only discover how good it is when you can't have it any more, because the Nona dies and the recipe is lost, or you move away and there is no one who makes it quite that same way where you live now."

"Guess I've never really thought about that." Ace considers with an absent sip of his wine. I'm sure he's not tasting the wine, may not even know what he's drinking, but then I'm not sure other than a French white Bordeaux.

I get the impression he's comparing this evening to some other evening. I have no idea if it was last week or a decade ago. Did he bring his wife here? Must have been a place they both liked, or he would not keep coming back even now. But that is making a big assumption, which is that he went to Provence with his wife. That would seem logical as Provence just doesn't seem someplace a guy would go alone. But then again, maybe he went there to get over a failed marriage, hoping something so different would open him up to new experiences. But for someone who is so careful and patient, that just doesn't seem a likely response to a dramatic change in his life.

"When were you last in Provence?" I finally decide to ask, hoping it will get him talking about something he clearly relishes.

"I think it must have been five years ago, now. Yes. Five years last month. Harvest time. Workers in the vines picking the grapes, bringing them into the wineries. The leaves on the vines changing colors, the tractors in the fields, hauling the wagons loaded with the bins of grapes the workers used to pick and hold the harvest."

"So, you went right out into the fields?" I am again surprised by his answer, not seeing him as someone who would be particularly interested in the production of wines having grown up in the city and seldom getting close to fruit and vegetables anywhere other than a retail stall on a busy city street.

"I did. When I first went over, I knew absolutely nothing about how they grow grapes or how they produce the wines. I thought if you dumped enough grapes in a barrel and wait for a while eventually, you'll get fermented grape juice." Ace smiles at the recollection of how little he knew about this subject. "It's really a complex process. So many factors change the flavor, change the richness of layered flavors. So little makes the difference between a high rating that will fetch a higher price and a low rating that makes it table or cooking wine. It's incredibly difficult to produce consistently high-quality wines year after year."

"You could start your own wine blog." I suggest at least half-heartedly.

Ace leans back in his chair and looks at me. "Why did you suggest that?"

"My reaction to listening to you talk about wine." I respond. "You clearly have an interest and it's more than just trying to pick out one more flavor layer in a bottle or element of the bouquet."

"But don't critics decide if a wine is the best of the vintage or the worst? They assign the number of points to guide those who would buy the wines."

"You're getting into the business side of food. I'm not all that interested in how people make money. I'm more interested in piquing interest, convincing people to try something that maybe they've never heard of, visit a restaurant in a city they've never visited because there's something extraordinary coming out of that kitchen. I'm on the people side of the business, not the money side."

Ace smiles again, still leaning back in his chair. "An interesting perspective. We're all on the money side of whatever business we're involved with. Even you. When you suggest people should go to a restaurant to try something, you're driving sales to someone and away from others."

"Like here. A place you normally go to." I point out. "So, if I persuade you to go some other place, I'll be putting your money in someone else's pocket."

"True."

"But all I was saying is I'm not really interested in how much money I'm moving from one pocket to another. I'm more interested in sharing experiences."

"And the only reason anyone pays you to share your experiences is because you're moving money from one person's pocket to someone else's." Ace is clearly calling me on my perspective.

The soup comes. French onion. Presentation isn't remarkable, but the aroma hints at something uncommon. "What is that?" I ask Ace, who looks up at the waiter.

"The special ingredient, Madame?" the waiter glances at Gabriel, who is standing just outside the doors to the kitchen. Gabriel makes a very slight head nod. "Sour cream with a hint of fresh wild strawberries and Cognac," the waiter recites from memory.

"Where do you get wild strawberries this time of year?" I ask surprised. They're usually only available for like a week during the summer."

"I can't say, madam." The waiter can't wait to get out of the range of my questions and backs away from the table with a slight bow much as Gabriel had.

Ace watches me as I continue to let the aroma fill me, trying to pick apart anything else that is unusual about this particular dish. I notice, "You have the same dish. Aren't you going to try it before it gets cold?"

"I'm waiting for you. To see your reaction." Ace admits, daring me to at least sample it.

I do, blowing on it to cool before. The soup is flavorful in the extreme. A bowlful of tender onions, steeped in a thick broth revealing the hints of strawberries, cream and cognac with grated Gruyere cheese covered toast floating atop. The flavors blend nicely in my mouth even though, as most French onion soups, the toast and cheese has trapped the heat inside and made it very hot.

"Very nice," I admit to Ace. "But not yet worth a special trip."

"I doubt many appetizers are worth a special trip." Ace counters. I notice he's only had a few spoonfuls of the soup while I've put a major dent into the bowl. I'm instantly embarrassed that I ate too much and revealed that I don't get many meals out like this. Will he think less of me because I'm going to do more than sample the meal? That I will actually eat it? I decide I don't care. I don't know Ace all that well. If he makes his decisions about me based on a false set of impressions, then it will be hard for me to continue to be what he has come to expect of me. That just makes the whole relationship too hard. Take me as I am or don't take me at all. Do I really think that? No, I probably don't. Normally I wouldn't be dressed up because I would be in my apartment working on my next six hundred words for Z. But tonight, I'm out on the town, taking in new experiences I may not have again. Be me and be real. Anything else will end up taking me someplace I would probably rather not be.

But back to Ace. "So, what is worth the trip about Lagniappe? What's the something extra about this experience as you put it?"

Ace leans forward to be closer, so he can speak softer. "For me it's the Coquille St. Jacques. But I expect it will be something different for everyone who comes here. There are just so many different things. I've been told the bouillabaisse is exceptional. I've been meaning to try it. Seems like forever." Ace stops to remember something, then continues. "But then every time I come in, I hear the scallops calling me and I just can't resist."

"Maybe I should try the bouillabaisse and then you could try some of mine." I suggest.

Ace nods as if he'd not thought of doing so, motions for Gabriel. "Would you bring the lady your bouillabaisse? She would like to try it. And bring two soup spoons."

"Would she like a cup or bowl, Monsieur?"

"A cup should be sufficient." Ace responds for me. I'm not sure I like him ordering for me. This is a new experience. I know I've read where this behavior used to be the custom, but it just seems so formal. I'm not sure that's what he's trying to establish between us. But it's not worth bringing up now. If we go out in the future and go to some place I choose, I'll order for him and see what happens. I'll bet he won't like it. The question is will he understand why?

The cup of thin fisherman's soup comes almost immediately. It steams so again I have to blow on it as I inhale the fragrance of the sea, only hot and steaming. This time the flavor is from India Pale Ale, I recognize the flavor and don't have to ask. "The recipe must be authentic," I remark.

"Why is that?" Ace asks trying to understand the nature of my statement.

"Fisherman's soup was made up of the leftovers from the catch. Whatever was left in the nets after they sold off the desirable fish. The India Pale Ale was also something they took out on the ship because it didn't spoil in the heat. So, it's something the fisherman would probably use to make their soup. Something that had been out on the boat with them and left over when they got back. But not something you find in most fine restaurants."

"How did you know that?" Ace shakes his head since he clearly didn't.

"Researching my blog. My chefs make some strange dishes, but in order to understand why someone would put together certain flavors I often have to research the history of the country. What influenced what they ate. In most cases it's pretty clear why something that seems completely strange to you or me makes perfect sense to them."

Ace samples the bouillabaisse. I don't know what he's thinking about it, but he seems to either be trying to pick out the flavors of the seafood he finds there, or some remembrance of someone else who sampled this dish and told him it was excellent. Somehow, I think it more likely the latter.

TRULY INSPIRE

My phone rings as the waiter sets a decadent chocolate cake before me and a similar one before Ace. I know that ring. It's Z. "I need to take this call." I inform Ace.

"Tell Z he can wait." Ace responds, looking at the mountain of chocolate before him.

I retrieve the phone and head off towards the door so I can take the call and talk to him outside, even though it will be cold without a jacket.

"Don't try to convince me you have a life because I know you don't. What did I do wake you?"

"I'm finishing a late supper," is all I'll give him.

"Well I need three hundred words on the best wines to serve with Appertivo within the next thirty minutes."

"Why can't it wait an hour?"

"Deadline. Got to have the words J so you better get busy. You're down to twenty-eight."

"What if I'd been in the middle of something?" I protest.

"You're always in the middle of something. The most important thing is for you to do what you do best and not stop the flow around you. Get busy lady. You're down to twenty-seven minutes."

I hang up and start working his three hundred words on my

phone out on the cold street under a street light. I can see my nipples standing out again, only this time I'm not aroused or amused.

Appertivo Wines – Just So

Appertivo is a tradition in Italy. But the best wines served are not defined by that tradition. Generally Italian Prosecco is the go-to wine. Light, bubbly and refreshing with low alcohol it goes with almost everything. So a host without time to research tastes and food pairings can't go wrong with Prosecco.

The next most interesting option is generally an Italian white such as Soave, Pinot Grigio or Vernaccia di San Gimignano. Depending on the Appertivo small dishes, a white from Orvieto or even Sicily may be the perfect complement.

Reds provide a maze of options. Rossos from Montalcino or Montepulchiano provide a different twist on the traditional Chianti's or Tuscans. Borolos and Barbarescos tend to be a more expensive option, but also provide flavor combinations found nowhere else.

An interesting region to consider is the Maremma. This western region just below Pisa was long sparsely inhabited because it was mostly a swamp that harbored diseases and was inhospitable to growing much of anything. But in the late 1930s the Italian government decided to drain the swamp lands, eradicate the disease and turn it into agricultural land. It has taken many generations to reach its potential, but today many different grape varieties grown elsewhere in Italy are now producing excellent vintages rivaling the native regions for the range and expression of flavors.

So too, the Veneto, Umbrian and Puglian regions offer

interesting options to bring out the native flavors of a good Parma Ham, Emilia Romana cheese or homemade pasta from any Nona's kitchen from anywhere in Italy.

With over 18,000 wineries in Italy narrowing down the choice to just a handful of varieties is difficult. Each year new varieties are discovered. New producers pop up with an exciting new offering to make Appertivo an exciting proposition.

I push the send on the email to Z, rub my shoulders and return to the restaurant where I try to shake off the chill as I work my way back to the table where Ace waits patiently.

"This happen to you a lot?" he questions my behavior probably never having seen me get up and leave the Friday night get-togethers before. But probably only because Z is there and if he needs something, he asks me on the spot.

"I usually don't mind, except on nights like tonight."

Ace finally picks up his fork to attack the chocolate cake. "Since you've sent in your blog for tonight you shouldn't have any excuses not to come back with me."

"Oh, that wasn't tonight's blog. That was just a filler Z needed. Don't even have any idea where it will get published. Could be one of a dozen or more publications. Someone needed something to go with a story they'd already written, and they will pay a premium for something immediately that won't hold them up going to press. Z is all over those extra revenue opportunities and I seem to be his favorite quick turn artist."

Ace puts his fork down. "Quick turn artist? You wrote something from scratch just now?" He seems amazed.

"Z gave me the topic. It was general enough I didn't need to do any research, so it was just a matter of composing something that fit from my general knowledge."

"How many words?"

"Three hundred. What did it take? Ten, fifteen minutes? It wasn't supposed to win a Pulitzer. It was supposed to fill space and have something that is factual and relevant. That's all he was looking for."

My phone dings from the text Z just sent. "Oops, spoke too soon."

I retrieve the phone and glance at the text:

> J:
>
> *Would have been better if you had spent a little more time on fewer wines. I know I didn't give you much time, but a little research in the future would improve the overall piece. We'll go with this one, but I expect a little more effort in the future.*
>
> Z

I text back:

> Z:
>
> *Then stop with the fire drills and give me adequate notice.*
>
> *PS: Since you get paid more for these quick turns maybe I deserve a raise.*
>
> J

"That should put him to bed for tonight." I inform Ace as I click off my cell and drop it in my purse. Okay. Now on to the chocolate cake. I take a bite. Tastes every bit as good as it smells and looks.

I must have a content look on my face as Ace asks a question. "So, did I answer the question?"

"What?" I'm still thinking about Z and whether he actually would give me a raise.

"Why Lagniappe? Of all the French provincial or even any other restaurants in the city, why here?"

I have to think about the question for a moment while I linger over the chocolate taste in my mouth. "You told me why for you. It reminds you of all those country restaurants you visited. Excellent food, wine and real people who present outstanding meals simply and with little or no hype. That's something I don't see all that much. It seems every chef is into something that will attract attention. If you ask me, our society has gotten just too complicated. Too many choices without enough information in an age where we drown in meaningless words, but don't get information we want."

"Is that why you write what you do?" Ace pursues my comment, even though that wasn't what I was focused on. It just sort of came out.

"I don't want to add to the chaos. I want anyone who reads what I have to say to go right to the heart of a matter. To get real answers, get facts and enable their decisions. I don't want anyone lingering over my words one moment longer than they need to."

"Why not?" Ace challenges my assertion. "Why wouldn't you want people to read your blog, pass it on to others and then come back and read it again when they're looking for a place to go."

I shake my head. "I'm not a tour guide."

"Sure, you are." Ace puts his fork down again. Two bites of the cake. Now I'm really feeling guilty because I'm well past that. I put my fork down too. "I would love to visit anywhere in the world with you."

"I bet you say that to all the bloggers you bring up to your apartment," testing a theory.

"That would be correct since you're the only blogger I've ever brought up not in a whole group of people. And that was only once as I remember."

"If I come back up with you, what exactly is going to happen?" I push him to see what he really has in mind, because I still don't get his fascination with me.

"We slowly undress each other and take the time to appreciate what each of us are."

"Fat?" just comes out.

"You're hardly fat." He tries to put me at ease but I'm not sure that's possible. "You're an attractive woman. I'm sure you know that and I'm sure you've had lots of admirers over the years. In fact, if anything, it's a mystery to me why you're not married with a house full of kids."

"Is that what you want? An attractive wife who stays home and raises your kids?" again I'm testing theories out here since he's walking into more and more confusing descriptions.

"I'm not looking for anything. I've been around enough to know nothing is one-sided. A relationship is a series of compromises. What does each one want? How much is each willing to take less of in order to get the most important things? Kids? You don't seem to be in a hurry for them so I would suppose you have no interest in a house full of kids. One. Maybe two. But if you wanted more than that I'd be surprised. You want life to be there for you when the kids are grown and on their own and you don't want to be sixty when that happens. Am I right?"

I don't answer that question. "That apparently goes for you too."

Ace frowns at something he won't share. "If it's important to the person I get together with, I can adjust. I've come to the conclusion that life is not going to be this neat series of events I can select from to get the perfect life. That's already gone. And that's why I'm searching for something that probably doesn't exist. I realize that. I'm okay with that. I just want to be able to make someone happy. By doing so, hopefully I'll be happy as well. Does that make sense?"

"No." I'm the one who leans forward now. "None of what you say makes sense. You talk like someone who's been on the streets his whole life and has nothing to protect, nothing to build. You talk like someone who is taking what life has left him and is trying to make the best of it. And that is clearly not the case here. You have so much to give anyone and I'm not talking about your wealth. I'm talking about your love, fidelity, and hope for a future that is fulfilling for you and the family you will have together. Constantly making decisions, together. Not living alone. Not holed up on the 37th floor looking down on the world and wondering why are people down there happy and I'm not? Is that what this is all about? I'm one of those people down on the street you randomly picked out and want to know why am I happy when I have nothing and you aren't, even though you do?"

"Not even close." Ace squints at me, having apparently hit a sore spot.

"Then what is this all about? The dinner, the challenge, the tease of the apartment. Showing me bits but not telling me anything I need to understand you or what it is you're offering me. I need more from you to have any idea what this is all about. It's not an offer. It's a seduction from what I can see. All on your terms with no room for me, even though you say you're willing to compromise on everything. I just don't believe it."

Ace seems genuinely disoriented by my tirade. As if he has no idea why I'm upset. Like he's been here before but still does not recognize or understand why I am not willing to just accept what on the surface would seem to be a generous offer. Maybe I'm hearing all the things I expect him to say next. All the things that limit the seeming unlimited willingness to compromise in order to form a lasting relationship. For someone who has been married and been down this path before he just seems so naïve about what it will take to form a lasting relationship. I seem to have a better idea about it and I've never even been in a long-lasting relationship. But for whatever reason, I seem to have a better idea of what it will take to be with someone exclusively.

"Are you finished?" he asks simply.

"I don't know. Are you going to be honest with me and tell me what this is all about or are you going to continue whitewashing the fence in hopes I'll buy in without really understanding what you're trying to sell me?"

"I'm talking about dessert."

I look down at the half-eaten cake and the fork still in my hand. "Oh. No. I'm done."

"Do you need the powder room before we go?" Again, simple and straight forward.

"I'm good." I wipe my mouth with the napkin, and he rises. "Don't you need to pay the bill or something?"

"I have an open tab here." He comes around and helps me with my chair, waves to Gabriel and follows me out the door. Even though I haven't seen him order a car one arrives as we get to the curb. He opens my door and closes it behind me. The driver pulls away leaving him on the curb. I look back at him. A second car arrives for him almost immediately. The second car heads off in a different direction.

I don't understand what just happened, other than he wasn't happy I called him on what he was saying. Guess I wore out my welcome. But I must be right. He wouldn't have behaved as he did if I had it wrong. I'm just one of the little people down on the street he's trying to play mind games with. But again, I'm back to the same fundamental question: why me?

On the ride back to the upper village I try to retrace my steps. Where did he come from? When did I first meet him? It was with the group at the bar after work. He was just there. Who did he know among us? He invited us over to his place to celebrate Z's selling his company, but that's the first time I think I really noticed him, but only because he was hosting all of us in this spectacular but very odd place. I really didn't even know who he was. But he invited all of us. I wonder if O knows anything more about him. She was the other one who stood up for me that night in the bar. Ace and O. Did they know each other before or were they just trying to help each other protect me? I don't know. I can't answer that one fundamental question so when I get back to the apartment it's time to start working on my blog.

FRIENDS AND FOOD: THE PERFECT NIGHT

What do you remember more after a night out partying? The food or the friends you spent the evening with? You tend to go out with the same friends, so they don't change all that much. But the food? It changes as often as your underwear. But should it? If you think about families, generally the foods your mother made are the comfort foods you always remember. So, when you're out with friends, why aren't these foods your new comfort foods? The same foods you go back to with the same friends? You'll generally drink your favorite beverages multiple nights in a row. But not the food. So, what is it about the food that two nights of nachos is just too much?

I recently visited Lagniappe on the East Side around mid-town. Small place but excellent French provincial. Two dishes there to remember are the Coquille St. Jacques and the Bouillabaisse. Authentic preparation using what you would find in small French villages. Fish fresh from the sea and enough spices to wake up your palate, but not so much that the wine needs to drown your taste buds to put out the fire. Perfect pairings without asking, impeccable service and a friendly staff. So why hasn't the whole city heard of this hidden gem? Maybe because we go back to the places we know rather than the places that can truly inspire...

CORRECTOMUNDO

Of course, the initial responses I received from my Lagniappe blog were the usual:

What do you have against Nachos seven nights a week?

Lagniappe? Isn't that like some disease?

What makes the Coquille different than a hundred other restaurants in the city?

You asked a difficult question: Why do we change our socks and not our underwear? Of course, we're speaking metaphorically here. But the issue is the same. We cling to sameness at the same time we reject the familiar. But the real issue is that there is a lifetime of foods to explore while friends come and go with jobs and changing interests.

I have to ask a question here:

Do you dare be different in the face of a changeable future? To stand up? Bring a dish to the party that no one has ever heard of and looks like dog

poop? We all know looks can be deceiving, whether a person or a bowl of
some unknown beans. But that's the issue isn't it? If we want people to
look beyond the surface of us, don't we want to challenge them to look
beyond the surface of that which nourishes us and our soul?

Now that I got that off my chest, maybe I can wade through a few
more before I turn this over to Chi and let the response team parse the
replies and give me guidance on how to respond in my next blog. They
absolutely hate it when I do what I just did. Respond to just one without
identifying myself even though I think a lot of my audience can figure
out it's from me. If nothing else the color should be a dead giveaway.
But I'm always amazed at how few people actually pick up on what I'm
doing. It's like I'm fashion or something. They all know someone who
reads my blog so they do too just so they can comment on whatever I
said the next time they get together. And this time I've gone directly at
those people. The ones who only read to comment. The critic of the
critic if you will. So how long will it be before we have critics of the
critics of the critics? I guess to some extent we already do so all those
who comment on the responses to my blogs are in effect playing that
role. The only difference is they're not paid to comment.

A text comes in:

J:

You gonna let me do my job? I got my hands full just trying to
keep your blog straight. But when you start commenting on the
comments and I got to go look shit up and straighten you out with
a subsequent post from me that's still anonymous, well, that just
adds hours to my day I really would rather spend on something
else. So, if you want to express yourself other than in your blog,
call me first and let me talk you out of it.

This is the opportunity I've been waiting for to ping her:

O:

What do you know about Ace?

J

The response is almost immediate, although I half expect a call.

J:

He's out of your league.

O

O:

We need to chat.

J

Of course, the call doesn't come immediately. She's talking to some of the others to figure out why I'm asking about Ace before she calls me. Apparently didn't see us at the bar or leave together. I'm surprised, although she was up to her eyeballs in Damien, the IT guy so I guess I shouldn't blame her.

"What did you do?" O finally calls.

"I had dinner."

"With Ace?" She confirms.

"Haven't you had dinner with him?"

"Me? Never." O hesitates, puzzles. "If I think he's out of your league, I mean he and I don't even reside on the same planet. Do you know who he is?"

"How did he get mixed up in our little group?" a question I've been asking myself.

"I don't know. He was just there." O thinks some more. "You know I think he was at the bar several times when we all came in. Just sitting at the bar. Thought it was funny because he wasn't drinking anything except Perrier. Always Perrier. Didn't seem to be talking with anyone. Just sitting there drinking his Perrier. The next thing I know he's talking with everyone as if he knew us. All of us. Always seemed to spend the most time with Z. Think that's why he invited us over when Z sold the business. Don't know if they knew each other before that and Z invited him to join us? That could have been. Probably what happened, but I don't really know."

"So, he wasn't your friend," I clarify.

"Me? Nuh unh. I've talked with him a bunch of times. Seems real interested in how I check facts and how we make sure what we're reporting is real and all that. But he never says much about himself. About all I do know is that apartment he took us to. You remember that? Way up on one of the top floors somewhere. That told me all I needed to know about mister Ace. He's not hanging around me to propose. Never did figure out why he was hanging around, but I was sure glad he was there that one time when he stood up for you. Chi would have been no help unless he bit the guy's ankles. And Z? Not going to ruin his expensive suit just because some guy is getting rough with you. But Ace backed the guy down."

"Did you know he played football?" I offer to put some perspective on Ace.

"Who? That guy who wanted to beat you up?"

"No. Ace." I clarify.

"Him? He's kind of small, isn't he?"

"He was actually very good, but I've been wracking my brain about why he never played again after high school. There was something I remember reading about him. It was just so long ago I've lost it."

"I'll bet I could find out anything you want to know about him." O entices me, although that wasn't where I intended to go with this conversation. Besides, Ace is probably already working on the next lady he sees down on the sidewalk so many floors below his eagle nest apartment.

"You know…" O continues her thought. "I've been wondering about Mister Ace. Like you said we don't really know all that much about him or why he's hanging around us. I probably need to ask a few questions and see just who this guy really is. He might be a psycho killer or something. Maybe a terrorist who's been in deep cover for decades and is just now coming out of hiding to bring down our little blogosphere. Upset all the foodies so they'll vote for some right-wing socialist or something."

"I don't think right-wing and socialist can modify each other." I suggest.

"Ask Chi. He's Mister Grammar." O pushes back, but I know she's playing with me.

"Don't think it's a matter of grammar."

"Just the same. 'bout time someone asked some questions."

"I think you can hold off on that for now." I respond to her continuing desire to figure out who Ace is. "I don't think he's going to be hanging around us anymore."

"Back to my original question: what did you do besides dinner?"

"It's not what I did besides, it's what I did at dinner."

"So, he didn't have you for dessert?"

"Decadent dark chocolate cake instead." I admit.

"Don't tell me that." O protests loudly. "Damien just got me hooked up with a personal trainer. I can't afford him, but I can't afford not to have him. You know what I mean? Anyway, the trainer tells me no more sugar. We're done with that bad boy. He's out just to ruin me. Blow me up like a balloon and make me unattractive to anyone who doesn't have a seeing-eye dog. He apparently didn't have the heart to tell me I already look like that. But I got the message. So, no more sugar and that means no more chocolate and no more sugar in my coffee and no more sugar even in fruit. Do you have any idea how long it's been since I've had a day without fruit? I mean I count on my morning fruit and fiber to keep things moving. But Jake tells me I won't have to worry about that if I follow his advice. First, we're going to burn it off and what we don't burn we're gonna wash on out. Got to drink like four gallons or something of water every hour just to keep the tidal wave moving through my body. Can you imagine drinking like a liter of water at a time? I've never done that in my life. And now I'm gonna need a life raft just for my tonsils to hang out on. I'm gonna be doing all my searches as I sit on the pot. That noise you hear won't be Niagara Falls, it'll be me purging all the bad stuff I've been collecting since I was five."

"So, when do you start?" I ask suspecting I know the answer.

Her response is tentative, "Tomorrow. I promised Damien. I've got to keep my end of the bargain."

"So, when you went to see the trainer today that was like just setting expectations, but you haven't put the new diet and regime into effect yet?"

"Correctomundo."

"Meaning you told Damien you would start today, but you've already fallen off the wagon and had something you weren't supposed to, and you haven't been drinking the water you were instructed to."

"Correctomundo."

"So what changes that you'll get on board tomorrow?" I have to ask knowing she'll have another excuse tomorrow if someone doesn't hold her accountable.

"First of all, you have to come over and help me clean all the food out of here. And you have to do it today because Damien is coming over tomorrow before I go work out because he's coming with me to make sure Jake gets me started off right."

"That's good. Damien's going to help you through this. I just didn't see how you could do it by yourself. You've never shown that much will power."

"I resemble that." O tries to sound upset, but I know she's not. "I have lots of will power. I mean I can eat things when no one else has any room left. But that trap door opens and the next thing I know the second turkey has been swallowed up along with the rest of the chocolate cake. Isn't that how we got started on all this? You had chocolate cake and you didn't bring a piece home for me? I'm hurt. Where did you go by the way?"

"Lagniappe."

"I didn't ask what the dog said, where did you go for dinner?"

"Lagniappe. It's French provincial. East side. Some place he knew."

"I was going to say. Definitely not your taste. Do you even like French food besides French fries?"

"Never had the expense account necessary, so I thought it was great, but just not something I'm very familiar with."

"You know all about food." O can't believe we're having this conversation. "You're the damn food blogger. How can you not know all about French food?"

"I do know all about French food, I just very seldom eat it. So, while I can tell you the history of their cuisine, and the major dishes one finds in the various regional areas, I really only have a vague idea of what it tastes like. At least that was the case until last night."

"Is that true of just French food or are there other cuisines whose taste you couldn't describe without a Geiger counter?"

"That's not true of just French food. If it's not within two blocks of my apartment I've probably never tried it. But that's what's great about the city. Restaurants come and go so quickly I've tried all kinds of things for a month or two before they close up to be replaced by something even more unusual. That's another thing about the city. People like the unusual. There's a bunch of African or Asian cuisines I'd probably have never tried if someone hadn't opened up in my neighborhood."

"You're like this cosmopolitan food blogger. You write about the most exotic places on the planet and what the foods are like there. But at the same time, you rarely get more than two blocks from your apartment. Doesn't that sound a bit… parochial maybe?"

"Do you really think I'm all that unusual? I mean why do you need to get on an airplane to go somewhere to see something? You can see it any time you want on your computer or cell phone. People are going to these places every day. They take thousands of pictures they post. You can scroll through them at your convenience. So, what makes it so important for you to take your own pictures? You think someone's gonna give you a Pulitzer Prize or something for the picture of the year? No one cares about your pictures because there are so many others already out there. Who cares if you go there or not? In my experience the only one who cares where you go is your pet and that's because your pet is worried you may forget to come home and feed him or her. Speaking of pets, I need to make sure I don't throw out his food, but that's a problem because I've eaten his food on a couple occasions when I'd forgotten to buy food or something and it was all that was left in the house. I'm afraid with this new diet my dog just might die from starvation."

"You said Damien is coming to your place tomorrow." I remind her.

"Yeah?"

"Don't you need to clean it or something before he shows up?" I try to put this gently." I mean I've been there a few times and you're not exactly the neatest housekeeper."

"It's only a studio." O protests. "The problem I have is I have only one carpet to sweep the dirt under and no storage areas where I can hide things."

"My point exactly."

"So, you coming over now, before he gets here?"

REACTION

I'm watching X do his thing. And of course, his thing is interview a chef who has made a dish that sounds peculiar, but is actually representative of a cuisine indigenous to a region. And come to think of it, the basic dish is well known, just with a minor twist. Hardly X-ian.

"Today we are in Lima. Capital city of Peru. For those of you who are geographically challenged, that is on the left coast of South America just above Chile. An interesting fun fact for those of you who think you know all there is about the world. Peru is generally two time zones east of New York. But it faces the Pacific Ocean. Think about that for a moment. Doesn't that tell you most of the maps of the world you have seen are wrong? You need to go to an actual globe to see what I'm talking about."

Of course, X has a globe right there and he points the camera to come down and, "Waa lah. The Pacific Ocean two time zones east of New York. So, all you Californians who think you own the Pacific. I've got news for you. Anyway. Today we are with Chef Antonio Fernandez of The Hole in the Wall restaurant. This particular restaurant is unknown outside of Peru. Although Chef Antonio has been very influential. Those he has trained have carried the tradition of his restaurant to other cities around the world including New York, Mexico City, Tokyo and London."

At least X is back to his irreverent self. I thought he seemed subdued last time, but somehow, I'm curious why he went for a major city restaurant. He never does that. Almost like he's doing a safe session after the sheep dung.

We see X walking into the restaurant to be greeted by the short and dark-complexioned chef wearing the traditional white jacket and a hair net over his head.

"Chef, you said what makes Peruvian cuisine so distinctive is it's a blend of food from many different cultures that have incorporated local ingredients rarely found anywhere else."

"Exactly." The chef responds to X in heavily accented English. "The Aji pepper, for example. They grow here. In the Andes. I've found them in stores in other countries, but they always come from Peru."

"And what is it you are making for us?"

"Aji Gallina." The chef responds, checking his pans he has ready to use as he assembles his dish.

"So, this is an Aji pepper." X holds the green pepper up to the camera. "I thought they were supposed to be yellow?"

"They turn yellow when they are cooked," Chef informs X.

"Don't they have another name, something our viewers might recognize before Aji?"

Chef nods. "Yes. They also Amarillo chili and Ají escabeche."

"Aji is a chili then," X states but really asks.

"Technically. But we don't think of as chili. They have a different use than most chilis we find here."

"What's different?"

"Rather than garnish, the Aji we tend to blend into a sauce as a flavoring. That what we going to do here. Blend the Aji into creamy chicken sauce we pour over rice. We garnish with potatoes and black olives."

"So, the chicken is shredded and blended into the sauce," X adds to make the description complete. "I assume the sauce is spicy."

"Yes. The Aji is rated between 30,000 and 50,000 on the Scoville Heat Unit scale."

"Where would a jalapeno be on that scale?" X asks the question he knows his audience is wondering right about now. "Just as a comparison."

"About 3,500."

"So at least ten times hotter than a jalapeno."

"At least." Chef concurs.

"Doesn't this make the dish just too hot for mere mortals?" At last. A snarky question. Put the chef on the spot he's making a meal not many will eat.

"Peru mostly very high altitudes." Chef Antonio begins his explanation. "For your viewers only reference they have of Peru is Machu Picchu. That is ancient city built high in Andes. Is very remote even today. No trains or buses take you to steps of temple there. You must be fit to walk very steep trails to arrive at destination. That is Peru. Peruvians work very hard. We live what you consider simple life. But it very cold in high mountain villages. Most Peruvians live high villages. So spicy dish generally very welcome. It warms our stomachs even when not hot fire in fireplace."

"Is the Aji Gallina a traditional dish?" X leads him again. "One that I might find most nights in someone's home in any given village?"

"Yes. It very old recipe. Prepared basically this way by my Grandmother, her grandmother. While growing willingness try new dishes in Peru, at least in Lima and cities, still tendency most people to prepare traditional dishes in traditional way. But as you said in beginning. We incorporate styles of cooking from all those who come live in our country. Very inclusive. We welcome the new, but try find way bring into traditional. Make part of culture only with twist. Create harmony among new and old."

"Why would you be welcoming of people from different cultures when practically no one else in the world is at the moment?"

Here we go. Put the Chef on the defensive. Make him explain himself, I recognize the pattern.

"Peru is not densely populated country. People come here practice cultural differences without impacting many others. But we find we grow stronger when listen to people not like us. People who look things and world differently. People who question us, not tell us we wrong, but ask we have considered something different from way we always do things. Food is perfect venue, see results of philosophy. We enrich foods, open up tastes find new ways express harmonies previously escape us."

"That's the second time you've used the term harmony." X seems to be trying to bring something out that is eluding the discussion. "Peru has had a conflicted history with the Shining Path guerilla movement that sought to overthrow the government here for decades. Is the harmony angle new? Something you're just trying as a way of reconciling the conflict that has been pervasive in your society for so long?" *That's X back to his usual feisty self.*

Chef Antonio clearly would rather not go down this path. "Everyone lives conflict. Nature of conflict change day-to-day. I deal with conflict in kitchen, conflict with suppliers, or conflict in street among people come eat in my restaurant. Maybe fact we have conflict in lives that harmony in food is important. We need a place to go, something we eat will remind of shelter of youthful homes. Where we go bed, something warm in belly. Where parents comfort, wish good dreams. Harmony in food bring harmony in lives, eventually. Simply not give up trying create harmonious state because hard. Must persist. Keep working harmony.

X is quiet for a long moment with a puzzled look. A moment later the puzzled look vanishes, and he reengages. "What else is in the sauce?" X looks at the ingredients

"What just happened? He flipped. Normally he would have pursued that discussion further, but he just walked away from it. Why?

"You mentioned the shredded chicken"

Chef looks relieved and points to each ingredient which he had prepped before the show as he names it. "Also, white bread, evaporated milk, chicken stock, vegetable oil, walnuts, garlic, onion and parmesan cheese."

"I've talked before about how garlic and onions are the building blocks of most flavors regardless of where you come from in the world."

"Is true Peru. Many dishes they foundation. Bring flavors other ingredients. Generally, start them, then add other ingredients."

What's going on here? X is almost respectful of the chef. And this dish? Other than that really hot pepper, what's so special? I don't get it. Why is he here in the first place? He's been in and out of being himself, but it's not leading to a satisfying episode.

I watch as Chef Antonio prepares the Aji Gallina. There doesn't seem to be any special technique I couldn't do, and I barely cook. He plates the dish as X looks on without a word. He's never done that. He always has some comment at this point in his show. Ah, here it comes.

"Aji Gallina. Smells hot. Do I need to line my mouth with asbestos or something to protect it?"

Chef Antonio laughs, although it is a hollow laugh like he really is tired of the fear X is creating in his audience to try the dish. But then X picks up the fork and scoops a sample into his mouth.

"Spicy." X remarks before taking a sip of water. "But it's remarkable how the other ingredients balance it out. Cut the heat and bring the flavors into stark relief. Like you say. Into harmony in my mouth."

To show he really does like the dish, X takes another bite and smiles as he savors the flavors. He extends his hand to Chef. "I see why you have had such an influence among Peruvian chefs. Why your restaurant should be a must stop for anyone visiting Lima. Thank you very much for opening your kitchen and your food philosophy to our viewers."

X turns to the camera for his sign off. "Until next time. X marks the palate pleasing opportunities for us all."

I'm not sure what I want to say about this episode. There clearly is something going on with X. On one moment and then something completely knocks him off his trajectory. Rather than being the obnoxious X of old, he just shuts down. *Why?*

IT'S CHILI IN PERU

Chef Xavier Francis gave us a geography lesson in his latest episode. Visiting Lima Peru, he brought us into the kitchen of Chef Antonio who explained why a rare Peruvian chili known as an Aji helps to establish harmony in the mouth even though it's ten times hotter than a Jalapeno. What was curious is that the dish he featured is a rather simple and accessible chicken sauce over rice. Apart from the Aji chili, I would expect to find this same dish in many homes around the world. So why the fascination with what an unusual chili can do to a staple? If you are looking for the answer to this question, unfortunately you will not get it in this blog. I am as mystified as you. Perhaps X will post or tweet a response to this simple question, but I for one am not holding my breath for an answer.

I must admit I found his questioning of the importance of harmony in Peru to be interesting, but I'm not sure it was relevant to the specific dish that Chef Antonio was preparing. Perhaps in the larger context of Peruvian cuisine and the importance of cultural incorporation over the long history of that nation it provided insight. But there was no discussion about how that cultural incorporation and seeking of harmony pertained to this particular dish. It was a side conversation. From my vantage point I would have been more satisfied if Chef Antonio had prepared a dish that demonstrated the evolution that resulted from incorporation of another culture. How chop suey incorporates the purple sweet potatoes indigenous to Peru, perhaps. Or how a simple Peruvian stew incorporates Arabic spices and Japanese soy or fish sauce. Demonstrate this discussion you're having with Chef Antonio, or at least ask him to give us some examples rather than letting him off the hook as X did throughout the program.

I'm also curious as to the reason X took us to a major city to a mainstream restaurant. In searching my brain, I have failed to recollect another program where X was found in a major city. It has always been a backwater restaurant where the meal is authentic. Something handed down from ancestors. Using ingredients we either can't find at home, or simply aren't exported from the area where the chef we are visiting lives. It seems to be a badge of honor for X to show us something unattainable anywhere except where he happens to be at that time. So, what changed? Why did he ignore the show tradition? Is this the beginning of something new? Moving into range of those who travel? Hoping to make the show more relevant because the chefs and unusual meals he shows us are more accessible? In my view of the world, I have to admit I preferred the old format. Take me somewhere I'll never go. Show me something I'll never see. Make it inaccessible and so unique I'll want to watch the show for fear of missing out on something I'll never again have a chance to learn about. And that is what I'm all about. Learning. I want to learn something on this show I'll never see or hear about anywhere else. My two cents.

I went a little long, but Chi will cut something. He's a master of fitting seventeen sardines in a can regardless of the number of sardines he is presented with because he only has one size can. Six hundred

117

words is all Z allots in space. He has it timed. Down to the second a reader will stay with a story. Six hundred words. If you're not finished telling the story, the reader is finished reading. Time to read back through. Make my edits, my corrections. O will fact check, but I'm really making her job too easy since I'm venturing into reaction a lot more than I used to.

Just as X is changing the product he's putting out, so am I. Is it a reaction to what he's doing? Or are my changes a result of my reaction to him? He certainly knew how to break down my defenses and open me up to him and the experience of making love. Not something I would have thought went together, but X has been surprising in more than one way. And maybe I'm getting too close to him such that I'm wondering what's going on with him.

That's not the case. I've only made love with him one time. That's not such a big deal I'd change my whole perceptions of the guy built up over years of writing about him, what he used to prepare himself and now that he's a monster media personality how he engages his subjects and his audience. I'm sure to him, I'm just part of the audience. Not someone special other than if he's nice to me I'll be more likely to write nice things about him. Looking back over that blog, I wasn't particularly nice. I called him on his change of direction. Questioned whether it will be something that will increase or decrease his audience and following. But some would consider that trying to help him. Am I?

BETTER

The responses to my blog came hot and heavy. Guess I'd hit a nerve with some folks. Or maybe my calling out the obvious woke some folks up who'd just gone to sleep only to find a cold splash of water in the face from my blog. Pointing out the obvious sometimes puts people into a position where they can no longer ignore something they're invested in. And in this case, if they're not invested, they aren't following X anyway.

Am I supposed to travel all the way to Lima to have a dish I can have around the corner? All I have to do is have Amazon deliver the Aji tuna to my favorite restaurant and ask them to add it to the appropriate dish. Then I can have the meal X featured without the air miles.

It's not Aji TUNA moron. It's a pepper. You know, like a Jalapeno. But then I have to assume you weren't just stoned and not listening. You had to be listening because you knew your chef could make the Peruvian Chicken a la King with something extra to spice it up a bit. Hey. Even I could make that with the help of a certain canned version available at any grocery. But then you might be one of those gourmet types and get yours in the frozen food section.

That's the problem with you homestyle do-it-yourselfers. You actually want to eat this shit (no pun intended) that Chef X shows us. So why didn't you talk about making the sheep dung dish? You could make it

Chicago style with a deep-dish crust just so you could get more of the special ingredient.

Who's the little bitch who's trying to tell us to eat shit? I'll bet she'd be the first in line if Chef X were the one ladling it out for a take home. The only thing she's trying to cook up is how to get into the Chef's pants. So, keep your thoughts to yourself or we'll have to come take away your commenter's union card.

I have to resist making a comment about getting into X's pants. Wasn't appropriate since it kind of went the other way. He got into mine.

I skim through the other three hundred comments and let Chi worry about them. But there was one that caused me to stop and read the whole thing carefully.

Life is all about change and how we deal with it. Those who cling to the tried and true are certain to be swept away with the tidal wave of innovation, energy and drive some other individual brings to the party. Reinvention is as essential as breathing. And when someone who has been that innovator discovers he has lost the edge, then maybe breathing is no longer essential.

I re-read that one. The depression just leaps out at me. I wonder if I should respond and finally decide to even though I know I'm about to get another missive from O.

I would agree that life is all about how we handle change, but change is layered. There are big changes and small changes. Successful people handle both by concentrating on the small changes needed to avoid the big ones. That would appear to be what Chef X is trying to do with his change of venue and approachability of his subject. Only time will tell if he made the right choices and either his current audience follows, or he finds a new one.

I brace for what I think will be the immediate response from O, but strangely there is no immediate response. None from Chi either. Is no one paying attention or is my response so buried that they haven't seen it yet? While I'm waiting for one or both to upbraid me, I scroll through the other responses and suddenly realize why there was no response. I find a half dozen other responses written in the same vein as mine. Others, who apparently were not surprised or upset with the new format for the show. Very understanding and accepting. But would they continue as followers? That will be the test. Does X have the pulse of his audience or has he turned a deaf ear to their needs, wants and desires? About to go off into the wilderness of medialand never to be heard from again?

But curiously another response appears:

A forest that dries out from the draught, becomes brittle and a pale version of the majestic trees that grew to such heights. A fire emerges from a spark and rages for miles in all directions from that one point of ignition. No forest is immune to the weather. No forest can escape the inevitable destruction of the old that precedes the arrival of the new. Just as no good idea will continue to live on forever.

Sounds like the same person, same outlook. What can I do to help this person? First of all, I shouldn't be responding as I did. At least this person engaged, continuing the discussion rather than sitting on feelings of despair. Not solving the underlying problem. Not maintaining a winning attitude. But that's not my problem, is it? Because this person follows my blogs am I now responsible for them in some sense of the word? Responsible to try to engage them in a dialog that fundamentally changes attitudes? If I did that for all of my followers, I'd do nothing else. So, what is it about this conversation that I think I need to do more? Stay engaged with her or him. Help that person see there is hope for a better future even if things may seem bleak today? So, I respond and hold my breath.

Small controlled burns are often used to clear away the underbrush in a forest. Keep the fire small and contained. Keep it from burning more than is necessary. So controlled destruction is one means of preserving the core. Ensure that kindling is not present. Prevent a big and uncontrolled fire from coming through and sweeping away the dry majesty, the ancient lords who overlook their realm. So too we can change the narrative, deflect the winds of change, and shift the sunlight from blinding us to showing us the way to tomorrow.

She finally got to my response. Best defense is to plead ignorance.

But not for long.

J:

Do I have to come down there and slap you?

O

O:

What did I do?

J

J:

You've crossed over to the dark side. Trying to be one of them when you're a professional and should know better.

O

I could deny it and keep the conversation going, but what good would it do? She will never believe me. Besides she's right. I am a professional. I think. Sometimes I wonder if I am or I just think I am.

O:

What would you have me do? Sit on the sidelines and watch as my audience consumes itself in shared ignorance? Watch as my words are reshaped, reinterpreted, and reinvented to solve an internal dilemma brought about by the inconsistencies of life, liberty and the pursuit of one person's perception of what justice means? We live in an age when the common good no longer has meaning. It has become an age when what is good for me is all that matters. Shattering lives of innocents is a daily sport.

J

I don't know where that all came from. I hadn't been thinking it, but when I began to respond to O, it all just came tumbling out. Am I upset because X seems to be self-destructing? At least killing his series by not engaging his audience with what brought them to him in the first place. But maybe I'm wrong. Maybe he is smarter than I'm giving him credit for. Maybe the audience is ready for dishes they can create or a restaurant near them can duplicate upon request. Is that what he's up to? Wanting his audience to actually be able to taste what he tastes? Duplicate the experience even if not in the same environment. He shows the authentic source of inspiration. Introduces the chef who became inspired and produced this unusual combination of flavors. He contextualizes the meal so we can all understand why it evolved. Why it mixes with specific other ingredients to create something new, something different, but at the same time approachable by the vast range of palates that exist amongst his followers. I'm one of those followers. Am I planning to go find someone to make Chicken a la king with Aji peppers just so I can taste a hotter version than I am used to? No. I'm not. So as far as I'm concerned X has already flunked his 'move his audience' strategy. Will I keep watching? Yes. One show that doesn't meet my expectation will not cause me to turn away. I've been a fan too long. So how long will I hang in there if this is what the new normal will be? Probably not long, although he did pique my interest with his whole conversation about harmony being something Chef Antonio was trying to achieve. The way he tied it back to the disharmony in their society made me stop to think and wonder if that is something found in other societies? Is that something reflected in our foods? With the political polarization of our society do we find people only eating certain foods that represent their political perspectives? Do conservatives only eat what momma made and liberals won't touch comfort food? I don't know. But X is responsible for me even wondering about such a possibility. Has the open wound in their national psyche been healed with the reconciliation with the Shining Path rebels in Peru? It would seem that X is trying to tell us at least Chef Antonio is trying to bridge the gap and create a harmony in his dishes that will satisfy all segments of his national society. Satisfy their desires for both the comfort foods they recognize and the spices they recognize, just not in that particular comfort food dish. Chef Antonio is trying to bring the conservative and liberal palates together in something both can recognize bridge the political and palate divide of their nation.

Maybe there is more to X's change of approach than we are giving him credit for. But how many of his followers will look deep enough to see what I've ferreted out? I suspect not many because you really have to think about it to recognize what he's actually done.

J:

Give me a break.

O

O is not happy with my tirade, but that's because she doesn't understand where it came from. And I'm not going to take the time to walk her through it either.

O:

No breaks for you.

The Soup Nazi

I wonder how long it will take for her to call, but I shouldn't have.

"Soup Nazi? What is this a Seinfeld show?" She unloads first thing. No greeting like hi or any of that bullshit. Just dump expecting me to know who it is and why she's upset. She may be right in her assumptions, but still I have a right to push back.

"Who's calling?" I respond.

"Damn it. You know full well 'who's calling'. What are you up to besides getting us both fired? Do you think Z isn't monitoring what you're doing? I'll bet the next call you get will be from him if he didn't get to you before I did. I'm doing you a favor by giving you an opportunity to practice your plea to keep your job. I'm generally pretty good at critiquing such pleas. After all, I'm an expert at having to make them and I know which ones work and which ones don't."

"When did you ever have to make a plea to keep your job?" I know she's regarded as one of the best fact checkers in the business.

"All the time. Z seems to think I'm a luxury he doesn't really need. So he's always trying to find a reason to let me go. 'You didn't find out that so and so was doing such and such when she was sixteen and under the influence of not only cannabis but also a group of friends who encouraged wild behavior such as sleeping with a guy just because he had a ..." O stops short of giving me the whole picture, even though she has.

"Still bullshit. Z isn't going to fire you just as he's not going to call me about my blog and subsequent comments. He's looking for eyeballs. The more the better. The more controversy I create in a field that generally lacks much controversy is a good thing as far as he's concerned. I've elevated the art by focusing on people, famous chefs. People who create things the rest of us would never dream of, and yet we find them delightful."

"Don't drink your own bathwater." O warns.

I shake my head even though I know she can't see what I'm doing. "I'm not. Just as I'm not just telling you not to worry about your job. If you keep doing what you've been doing, questioning things before they appear on our sites, ensuring we're telling accurate stories you have nothing to worry about because you've given Z the defense he needs in court if anyone decides to come after him because of something I or the other bloggers write."

"Is there a castle in your fairyland?" O comes right back at me.

"No castles. No fairies. Just facts about life in the fast lane." I respond without thinking.

O seems to consider the full extent of our fast-paced conversation.

That's one thing about our relationship. No filters. Neither of us hold back. We give each other the unvarnished truth as we see it knowing there may be another truth we are unaware of and will discover at the right time. But that's just part of being a blogger. We know what we know. We discover things from the connections we have both virtual and in person. Although with the internet, the need for face-to-face has declined dramatically. But what I'm finding is that those face-to-face conversations are much more valuable than the mediated conversations by email and even webex. When you're sitting with someone and can look them in the eye, there is another whole dimension to the conversation. The body language. The unspoken cues in expression, a look, a tone of voice that is somewhat muffled by internet communications but is clear as a bell when you're sitting next to or across from that person.

"Fast lane. Do you really think we inhabit the fast lane?" O inquires skeptically.

"I do." I begin my answer. "We set the pace for a whole lot of people. We make people who are just doing what they like and want and find themselves good at, famous. Or at least we greatly increase the audience for what they do. In doing so, we shape society. Even if only in a very small corner of the universe. And you know what? That's okay. We don't need to shape all of society. We don't need to dictate what a vast majority of folks think. We can leave that to those who aspire to greatness and are willing to give up everything else to do so, because that is what it takes. Give up morality. Give up integrity. Give up originality. Give up caring about others before yourself. Give up all those things that make for good leaders because if you don't you will never achieve the levels where you can actually achieve influence."

"Influence?" O seems surprised at my comment. "Do you think you don't have influence in our industry?"

"Not the same. I'm talking everyone. Not just the small group of foodies who love Chef X and are willing to not only watch his show but comment on their reactions to share what they have learned from him."

"Just like you," O points out to me.

"And that's why your comment about going over to the dark side didn't make any sense to me. I may be paid for making my comments, but I'm more like them than I am like you. I just react to what he does, both intellectually and from the heart. You dispassionately dive in to make sure everything he says is true and then scrub what I've written to make sure I've not repeated something we can't verify as fact."

"Dispassionately?" O reacts to one word in an unexpected way. "I don't understand what you're trying to tell me. Are you saying I'm not passionate about my work, about what I do? Are you saying I'm somehow less of a person because I'm not reacting from the heart the way you do?"

I deflate knowing I've hurt my best friend in the whole world. "That's not what I'm saying. Should I have said objectively rather than dispassionately?"

"Objective's not an indictment. Dispassionate is," she clarifies her thinking for me.

"I'm sorry, O." I shake my head even though I know she can't see it. "I never meant to say you're dispassionate about anything. I was careless in my word choice."

"Nothing new." O informs me, hitting me back where it hurts me. I guess I have it coming. Since she changes so few of my words, I know it's more putting me in my place than how she really evaluates my work. I have it coming.

"You know you're the one person in the whole world who I count on more than anyone, and not just because you fact check me and make me better."

EXACTLY

Another Friday night. Of course, we all have to get together. Chi instigated the Friday get-togethers when he joined the company shortly after I did. Think it was his way of building relationships with those of us he works with since we don't sit together in an office and never have. And since he's responsible for editing what I write and several others, I think he just wanted to better understand us. Know what we see as important. Hear our voices rather than infer a voice from what we write. What do I mean by voice? It's the unique way I tell my stories. Each of us bloggers tell stores differently. I instantly know Delphinium's writing. Since she's the nature writer, she uses flowery expressions much more than I do. Maybe because she is usually describing something such language works in the context of her subject. I don't know. As a food blogger I'm much more likely to compare things. A dish tastes like something or a wine has a bouquet that suggests certain fruit or maybe leather or tar, depending on the tannins, soils and growing conditions the year that particular harvest was collected.

Anyway, Chi selected the place and we've been coming here ever since. Z is usually the first one here. He tried to convince us that he only wants the rest of us to be comfortable. If he is here when we get here, we know it's alright to have a drink or whatever. Actually, I've always thought he was ready for a drink by the end of the week. Most weeks we all are, but that's another story. It used to be that we would write several blogs early in the week and they would be published one each day through Friday. But then Z decided people wanted new content on the weekend as well. So, we suddenly had to produce two more blogs each week. Of course, Z didn't increase our pay, even though we were producing a lot more content. Told us it came with the job. So anyway, it takes a lot more research and time to draft two more blogs. We are seldom done until Friday. That's why I'm generally ready for a drink on Friday. Unwind. Get ideas for the next week from talking with the others. Let my brain cogitate on things for the weekend. When I start out on Monday, I'm generally able to get at least two done the first day. Just seems to be the pattern of how my week goes. Two stories on Monday, one on Tuesday, two on Wednesday and one each on Thursday and Friday. Generally, that last one is the hardest and takes the longest time. I don't know if it's because I've run out of ideas or the chefs I follow have run out of ideas for me to explore. Or maybe the chefs are preparing for their weekend busy time and have less bandwidth to be able to discuss something for my blogs. Whatever it is, by the end of the day on Friday I'm generally ready. Today is no exception.

"Is Damien coming by?" I ask O, since she is the one who first asked him to join us.

"Said he'd be by later. He's behind on his service tickets and Z doesn't want anyone to have an excuse on Monday morning that they can't get into their system. You know how he is."

I nod in concurrence about Z who I notice is watching us. "Z say anything to you about Ace?"

"Thought he'd be here." O looks around apparently just realizing Ace isn't with us. "Z." she calls out.

"And what can I do for our fact checker tonight?" Z has already finished a beer and is part-way into his next.

"You heard from Ace?" O makes sure everyone else can hear her question.

Z rises from his chair and comes over to sit next to us. Not sure why O's question prompted this behavior. Thought his response would be a simple no. But I'm constantly surprised by Z, so his strange behavior should be no surprise. "I was meaning to talk to you about X."

I was hoping he was going to talk about Ace, but no such luck. "What about him?"

"Did you ever eat at his restaurant?"

I'm not sure where Z is going with this question. "No."

"I think your readers know that." Z responds to my surprise.

"Why are you concerned about where I've eaten in the past?'

"I'm not, but your readers want to know you know what you're talking about. I think you need to research reviews. Dig in. Get to know more about what food trends are important to him. What he's likely to do next on his show so you can preview it. Do you know what I mean?"

"Nobody knows what X is going to do next." I point out. "Not even him, I would presume."

"Why do you say that?" Z is giving me the rope to hang myself.

"There doesn't seem to be a pattern. Sheep dung one week and Aji peppers another? What's the connection? How could anyone have predicted Aji peppers?"

"You should have. Should have alerted your readers what to expect next. That's why I say you need to get to know him better. Since you can't go eat at his restaurant, reviews are a place to start. I'll bet if you analyze the reviews, you'll find patterns. Something that will give you an idea of what follows whatever he's doing this week. What's the next logical leap for him? You might not get it exactly right, but if you know he's on a spice kick and he's taken spices from one region of the world to populate his dishes at the restaurant, you might be able to suggest he will do something similar on his show. Do you see what I mean?"

"Are you shitting me?" O goes after Z. "That's not a realistic expectation. If X decides to put out a program of his shows, what's coming up, then I think it makes sense to preview for her audience. But to speculate? All she can do is lose credibility because she's gonna be wrong more than she's right."

"That's not really what you're saying, is it?" I ask Z.

"What do you think I'm saying?" Z plays coy.

"That I need to do more research."

Z takes another sip of his beer with a satisfied glaze to his eyes. "What do you think it would take for you to get to the next level in your blogs?" His eyes suddenly get very clear.

"What makes you think there is another level?" O asks in my defense.

"She could always have a bigger audience." Z clarifies.

"For you next level is bigger revenues." I suggest.

"I'm convinced you're only just beginning to tap into the potential of your blog. You have a core group of followers who have given you the benefit of the doubt. They'll read what you write even if it isn't consistently great. But you're at least entertaining and you point out some things at least some people find interesting and informative. But I think you've got to educate more. Provide more facts they don't know. Give more background so the context is more meaningful. Your followers should say to themselves after every blog, 'Wow, I didn't know that.'"

"I get your point." I respond trying to understand. "But why now? Why haven't you said something before?"

"I have," Z informs me. "You just haven't been listening."

"Or you've not been this specific." I suggest.

"I prefer to tell stories and let you infer what you will." Z looks directly into my eyes in an unsettling way. I'm not sure what the look means but I don't seek to clarify, going off in a different direction.

"Are you suggesting we should learn from your example? Tell stories and let our followers infer what they will?"

Z seems to get a twinkle in his eyes, as if I've discovered what he wants me to know. Another sip of beer and he shakes his head. "To answer your original question, it seems Mr. Ace has simply disappeared."

"Meaning you haven't heard from him." I seek to clarify what I think he's trying to say.

But Z shakes his head. "No one's seen him this week."

"How would you know that?" I have to ask not thinking they were all that close.

"I talked with his assistant today." Z informs me, so now I at least know where he got his information, but still not the significance of it.

"You late paying the rent or something?" O asks. I wasn't going to say that, but the thought had just begun to occur to me that he must have had a reason to call her.

"No. He was supposed to send me a quote to do some updating on our offices. It didn't come when he promised it, which is unlike Ace. He's usually good to his word. So, I gave him a shout and he didn't answer his cell. That in and of itself is unusual for him, so I called his office. Now I know he's not there much, but usually his admin can get a message to him. She told me she hadn't heard from him all week and that he wasn't responding to text or email."

"Meaning she wasn't aware of why he wasn't responding."

Z nods and takes a reflective sip of his beer.

"This what got you thinking I need to get to know X better? That you thought you knew Ace and you're finding out you don't know him at all?"

Z stares at me for a long moment and then looks away without answering. But it's clear to me I've hit on the exact reason for his comments to me. And now I'm wondering about what may have happened to Ace. If he disappeared about a week ago, that would have been right after I went to his eagles nest apartment. Is there a connection? I quickly scan my memory of that night. Did he say anything about going somewhere? I can't think of anything.

O looks at me apparently wondering how I'm taking this news. Wondering if I have any ideas about Ace. I can see it in the way she looks at me. I'm uncomfortable, but really don't want Z to have any more insight into my love life than he already has. She then asks a question I've been wondering but also afraid to ask Z, "Why are you and Ace such good buds?"

"Not how I'd describe him." Z seems to reflect on something he's not ready or willing to share. "He's an interesting character. And he makes me think about things no one else seems to consider."

My frown precedes my question of him, "Like what?"

"Like the importance of dreams."

I'm not following him and have absolutely no idea where this came from. "Dreams?"

"Not the ones you have at night. Those could be wrapped up in it, but he talks about the dreams he has for a different world. One where happiness drives behavior rather than the pursuit of it."

Maybe my first glass of red wine has me off balance or something but I'm not following this discussion at all. "Hold on. Happiness drives behavior?'

Z looks at me that same way. Like he's trying to lead me to a revelation without telling me anything. "I believe that's what I said."

I have to think this through. "Are you saying Ace thinks we should make decisions because we are happy rather than to achieve some higher state of happiness?"

"Think about it." Z responds. "Would you make the same decisions if you're just trying to be happy rather than become happier?"

"What's wrong with aspirations?" I push back.

Z shrugs. "Everyone has them, but, think about it. Are you happy right now?"

Now it's my turn to shrug. "Yeah, I'm happy."

Z smiles as I've apparently walked into the trap he set. "Ace would say you're not."

"What does he know of my state?" I disagree, although thinking about our brief encounter in his apartment I'm not sure how much he does know of me.

"He would say he knows more than you do, because he observes your behavior and makes a judgment about your state. Objective. No delusions. You know? You, on the other hand, constantly delude yourself. You think you're happy even when you're miserable because you can't admit to yourself you've screwed up your life, your relationships and you're dependent on the wrong people for the feedback you need to make things better."

"We talking about Ace?" I respond not matching the description with the guy who took me to dinner. "The guy who hangs out with us here from time-to-time?"

Z nods.

"I don't know who's more screwed up here," I decide. "Him for suggesting he knows more about me than I do or you for believing him."

Z smiles as if he was expecting just such a response from me. "A little defensive, are we?"

"Hell no," I frown. "There's just no way he can know me better than I do."

Z rises and looks down at me, "And that's exactly what he said you'd say."

I'm caught off guard. "How did I get into the middle of this conversation?"

Z picks up his glass of beer, takes a long draw before answering. "He's obsessed with you."

"What are you talking about? I don't even know the guy."

"He's taken the time to study you." Z takes a sip of beer, looks around the bar. "I don't know if he's into food or what, but of all the writers in my stable for some reason he's picked up on you."

"Said something about his wife followed me." I mutter barely audibly, but Z hears it clearly.

"So, you have talked with him. I don't remember the two of you talking." Z notes.

"Hey. The dude's married. Why should I take any interest in him?"

Z comes right back after me. "See? You define a relationship as a sexual one. He's married therefore he has a monogamous relationship and there's no reason for you to get all that excited about getting to know him as a person." Z leans closer to me and I'm afraid he's going to spill his beer on me, but somehow, he avoids that catastrophe. "That's the problem with all of you estrogen-driven beasts. He has a lot to share and you're not interested because he's not mating material. Don't you ever get your head up out of your vagina long enough to see your true opportunities? Why does a relationship always have to end up in bed?"

"What the fuck are you doing? Trying to turn our narrative upside down? Blame us for the bedroom endgame of all you androgen-driven freaks? Get real, Z. None of us are going to fall into that trap. Your boy Ace thinks he has something to share with me besides his sperm, I'm all ears."

Z shows a smug smile and half-closed eyes, "Really?"

KEEPING HAPPY

My favorite chef is previewing his next program for the media, hoping folks like me will write about it and drive viewers. Well, that is my job. And at the moment he's also been the most compelling guy to share a bed with.

"Today we're in Dallas, Texas. Well, not really. We're in New York but visiting a typical Dallas Hot Spot that has moved east to find a new audience."

Why didn't he tell me he was in town?

"There are as many barbeque joints in Dallas as there are stars in a West Texas night sky. And just like that night sky, each and every place you visit is brighter and better and bolder than the last one you just visited. Today we are visiting Pecan Lodge, which just opened in New York."

I'm bringing up Dallas Barbeque on my laptop so I can hopefully stay at least one step ahead of Chef X in this discussion.

"Pecan Lodge is reputed by several Dallas sources as being the best of the best in that barbeque paradise. It started as a Farmer's Market stall. When the lines were longer there than for any of the farmers, the management of the market suggested Pecan Lodge find another location. They were keeping folks from buying what they came for. Namely fruits and vegetables from Texas regional farms. So, Pecan Lodge opened a second location in the Deep Ellem district of downtown Dallas. And the result is the lines are just as long at both locations. So now they are in New York."

The video footage shows the lines out the door at all three locations.

"What's the secret to your success?" X asks the chef who is turning the meats on his fire pit.

The chef gives X a look like are you really that dense? Then asks, "What do you see here you don't see at the other fire pits you've visited?"

"It looks to me like you've cut the fat away from the meat, but, put it back on top of the meat as it cooks. Is that the trick? Cook in the flavor but deliver a lean piece of brisket or beef so when they customer eats it they get the flavor but not the fat in their mouths?"

"I've noticed people don't want fat calories. So, this seems a good solution. Would you agree?" chef asks X.

"It just seems too obvious." X responds. "The flavor without having to eat the fat itself."

"Have you ever looked at what's still on a plate when it comes back from a customer? What is it they don't want to eat of what you've served them?" Chef asks X.

"I have." X responds almost immediately. "For exactly the reason you've suggested. What did I serve them they didn't like, didn't want, and didn't value?"

"Exactly," Chef responds finding a comrade in X.

"If it's just spices, I can understand why they didn't want to eat it, but if it's the tenderest parts of the main dish, well, that's a different proposition. And marbled fat in a prime rib or steak is exactly that kind of issue I need to look at. Why are they not willing to eat what delivers the flavor they value in the meal?"

"Exactly!" Chef is feeling like someone finally understands him.

"That's exactly why we've developed such a good reputation. We look at what gets thrown out. We study the patterns. We try to align our value with what the customer most values in the meats they buy from us. If we see customers aren't eating the beans, we change them until we find a vegetable that people seem to want with their brisket. Do you know what I'm saying?"

X nods. "I know exactly what you're saying. Never assume you know more than your clientele."

"And don't get all worked up when your clients say they want something other than what you want to offer them. You're the seller. Not the buyer and the buyer always knows best."

"Are you saying you're not the expert?" X seems to focus in on what the chef seems to be saying.

"Correct." Chef shakes his head. "I have to realize I don't know anything. My clients know much more about what they are willing to pay me to deliver for them than I ever will. And the fastest way for me to become irrelevant is to assume I know more about what they want than they do."

"Then how do you know what you should be introducing next at your restaurant?" X asks chef.

"I ask my patrons," chef responds. "I go out into the restaurant and talk with people who are there eating what I'm currently serving. You know? What brings them back? What do they like the most about the meal? What would make it better? And then I ask them the one question that is most important to me: What would you like to see on the menu the next time you come in that's not there today?"

"That's a hard question to answer." X responds seeming to consider it at length.

"Not so hard." Chef responds. "You know how most people respond?"

X shakes his head apparently trying to set up chef rather than distract from his answer.

"They almost always talk about some dish their mothers made."

"Do they have the recipe?" X has to ask.

"Never. But that gives me the freedom to go find a recipe that's similar. Put my spin on what they all remember was a favorite childhood dish. And they always forgive the license I've taken since they seldom can give me an exact recipe to follow. And when they do, know what I do instead?"

Again, X shakes his head.

"I look at the recipe and try to understand, does this add something unique that will make my version different. If it does, I try to incorporate aspects of that recipe into my version. But in every case, I can create a 'version' most people will rally around because it's similar to what they remember. Doesn't have to be exact. Just close. You know?"

"Is this something about the way you smoke the brisket?" X suddenly thinks to ask.

Chef shakes his head. "Almost always about a side. Different recipe for potato salad for example. Or someone has a different way to cook the beans so they're either more tender or have more bacon fat in there to add flavor. You know. Something to make them different from what you get at the run of the mill barbeque joint."

"So, at the end of the day, is there a typical anything or is everything regional cuisine?"

Chef stops to consider. "That's an interesting question." Chef continues to consider the answer and finally responds. "There are those who would like to establish a national norm, if you will. But the only place I've found that works is in burgers. A McDonalds, or Burger King or Wendy's is the same in Peoria as in Palestine, Texas. But anything that's not a chain? It's different. And there's a lot to be said about the standardization of food. If you travel a lot and don't care about where you are? Familiar food may be the best thing for you. No mystery about what you're eating. Tastes the same in Billings, Montana and Pensacola, Florida. But there are a lot of people who want to discover what is unique about a place. What makes Asheboro, North Carolina different from Sedona, Arizona? The food and the people are the big differences in my mind."

X seems to resonate with this answer. "Absolutely. You visit a restaurant in Asheboro and then one in Sedona you won't recognize the dishes on the menu, even if you're in an Italian, or Mexican, or Lebanese restaurant. Americans are incredibly resourceful at blending the recipes from the old country with the ingredients and flavors loved where they are. Something that would have been unimaginable in the old country suddenly becomes a rage in this country and a whole new food fashion. But it's regional. Something that makes Asheboro and Sedona different. Something about the tastes of the people in those places that are different. Something about willingness to try something new. Something that just wouldn't have been acceptable where the dish originated. There's something about tradition that's the enemy of innovation. The question is always the balance between the two."

An interesting question X has tee'd up. How will chef respond?

"I agree to an extent. But what I've seen is the tailoring for local tastes. In the south fried food is acceptable, but if you go to California or New York not so much. Where you have high immigrant populations you have a higher acceptance of Sriracha and Banh Mi sandwiches than you do where everyone has grown up in that small town and only have one food frame of reference."

"Is that what you saw in Dallas? That people only want the brisket the way their fathers and grandfathers made it?" X responds curiously.

"Actually not. What I've observed is that Dallas isn't Texan as you might define it. There are so many people who have moved there from somewhere else that there is really an openness to try something new. A desire for variety. A need for innovation that I've not seen in other parts of Texas, but that's not to say Dallas is unique or unusual. I think every large city has enough new blood coming in and old blood leaving that there's a healthy curiosity about foods, flavors and beverages to support a new food experience for the people living there."

X seems to consider this description for a long moment. "So that's why you've come to New York with Texas Barbeque. People here want something new, but they want something that's good and you have that. From what I've seen people crave the new. They want to have an opportunity to try something they haven't seen before. Will they adopt it as a standard for a period of time? That's hard to say. And I think their friends and neighbors have an impact on that. If not enough people embrace a new concept it will disappear even if there are those who really like it."

Chef nods in agreement. "Yeah. I'd agree with that. I've seen some great concepts just flop in my restaurants. People like what they like. You can give them bells and whistles. They'll still go for what they like. And it doesn't have to be what others like. I'm amazed at all the times I've introduced something that seems to be the hot thing in Austin and people in Dallas just shrug at it. I can't tell you why. It just doesn't translate, you know? I may think this is the perfect complement and nobody agrees. So, I take it off the menu and it seems no one misses it."

"But what about the ambience. I walk around Dallas and it seems all the barbeques have the same layout, the same assembly line, and the same pits you go up to and point to what you want. Doesn't anyone care for something that's a little less industrial? A little less the same?"

"Pecan Lodge is different. I'm not the same as the others, but it really comes down to how do you get people through your shop in the least amount of time? Do you know what I'm saying? The assembly line approach may seem industrial to you but it's really functional. I can serve more people in this layout than I can in a full-service waitress driven format. And people who are coming for barbeque? Well they're not expecting the white linen and plated service. They want what they want. They don't mind dishing it up themselves or taking a small bowl from a service tray. That's part of the ambience. If I tried the linen tablecloth no one would come in because they'd think they were paying too much for barbeque. This is like the back yard. This is something they can make at home and they love to make it at home. But they're in a hurry and don't have all day to smoke it or grill it in the backyard, but they still want it. So, they come in here, get what they want and they're off, on their way to the rest of their day."

"What makes Pecan Lodge so good?" X decides to ask.

Chef grins, "You'd have to ask my customers the answer to that question. I know what I do that's different than the other barbeques, but that's not to say what I'm doing is striking the note for folks, particularly here in New York. I don't really know. I just have to make what I like. If I'm happy with what I make, I hope the people coming in are as well. Now can I tell you what I do that will instantly make your barbeque the best in your neighborhood? No. The first thing that would happen is the guy next door would hear about my secret sauce and do the same. The next thing you know you're no longer the best in your neighborhood because your neighbor took what I do and changes it somehow. Adds something he or she likes. And that makes a whole new variation on my theme. Now you're no longer the best in the neighborhood. You're better than most but unless you come up with something that is your twist on that same theme? Well, you're just an imitation of a popular recipe. And that makes you no better than an imitation of Sonny Bryan or Spring Creek or any of the others in Dallas."

"Like the Chili cook-offs that are so popular." X observes.

Chef nods, "Exactly. Chili cook-offs are people taking a basic recipe and adding their twist. Something that makes it taste different than their neighbors, but still something that's true to the basics of the recipe. You go to a chili cook-off and you're gonna find a dozen variations on the same theme and all of them are great. But one stands above the rest. And why is that? Because the chef has found a different spice or a different ingredient that changes the flavor or the texture or just how all the flavors in there blend together. And that's what makes their variation stand out."

"Having mastered the barbeque scene in Dallas is national expansion in your plans now that you're in New York?" X redirects the chef.

"It's not so much where do I go from here as it is bringing in new people who can take what I've started in different directions. I'm teaching people how to get the most out of a fire pit. What different kinds of wood does for flavors, what different heats do to how juicy or dry the meats become. The subtleties of the process, the tricks I've learned, the variations I know I can get by changing different aspects of the whole process. But the idea isn't to make a dozen clones of me who can go out and open a dozen stores just like this one. The idea is to give them the basics, something they can then take in different directions. Experiment with. See what differences, what nuances they can coax from the meats that will delight their customers wherever they are. I don't want uniformity. If I did, I'd open a burger joint. Does that make sense?"

"It does." X responds. "But how do you identify someone who has that innovative spark in them versus the guy or gal who is only going to be able to replicate what you show them. May be great at keeping the tradition alive, but when it comes to taking it in a whole new direction? Well, that's just beyond them."

"I've seen what you're talking about. The sous chef who can make a great sauce, but you put them in charge of plating the whole dish, they just can't get there. They either don't have the eye appeal, or the sense of how much of the sauce to use to make it a delicate complement rather than the main attraction on the plate. But you know, I think there's room for all kinds of people in a kitchen. And while I'm looking for folks who will take us to another place, there's a whole bunch of restaurants that just want to keep their existing customers happy with their favorite dishes."

SAVING ONESELF

An interesting discussion about barbeque. But what do I say about their discussion that will interest my readers? And if X was in New York, why didn't I hear from him? At least contact me and let me know he was in town after he came and cooked for me and then... well.

I shoot off a note to X

> X
>
> *See you were in town.*
>
> *J*

Keep it simple. Let him know I'm not happy but without the histrionics. I don't know what else to say to him since I don't have any kind of relationship with him other than through what I write. I thought for a moment maybe I'd impress upon him that I'm more than words on a page. I'm a person worthy of his consideration. But that doesn't seem to be the truth of the matter. Probably just another one-night stand for him. Another vagina to visit, leave a few sperm and move on. But what if I wasn't taking precautions? He'd never know. He never asked. Didn't bring up the subject of what we were doing could lead to lingering consequences. It seems to me now that he was leaving all that up to me. Make sure he's not involved in a paternity suit. He's done me the honor of doing me. So, if anything comes of our moment of bliss? Well, that's my problem to deal with because he'll be somewhere else in the world and not able to deal with me and my problem.

To say I'm a little disoriented when my phone rings and I see it's X is an understatement.

"X?"

"When I came to New York I was really on my way somewhere else and the whole thing was kind of impromptu. I didn't have an extra moment. And I know this all sounds like an excuse and maybe it is although I don't want you to think that. The show was supposed to be filmed in Dallas, but we couldn't make it work. The show was filmed in three hours and I was on another airplane to Phnom Penh through I can't even begin to count how many cities we went through on the way here."

"You're in Cambodia." I finally catch up to him.

"Not exactly. I'm in a village. I came through Phnom Penh to get here but I really have no idea what country I'm in."

"And what are you doing there?" I have to ask.

"A show on Rice."

"Rice?" I'm not sure I'm following him.

"Water, rice and freshwater fish are the staples, if you will of the Cambodian diet." X explains to me. "The Mekong River, which most people associate with the long Vietnam War, cuts through Cambodia, but it has an unusual effect on the country. The Tonle Sap Lake is connected to the Mekong bringing in huge volumes of freshwater and an astonishing number of freshwater fish. The lake itself is believed to have more fish than any other in the world. During the monsoon season, Cambodia turns into a vast sea of rice-paddies. One French legacy is the baguette, known as *nom pang*. It may be stuffed with slices of ham or any number of grilled meats, with Kampot pepper, which is often found in the Vietnamese bahn mi sandwich. The French also introduced many different staples of the Cambodian cuisine such as potatoes, butter, onions, carrots, broccoli, pate as well as beer, coffee and chocolate which do not appear in the everyday meals of neighboring countries. Cambodians meals tend to include at least three or four dishes which will be either sweet, sour, salty or bitter in taste so that Cambodians ensure they get a bit of every flavor to satisfy their palates."

"I got it. You're already onto your next show. But after you cooked dinner for us…"

X seems at a loss for words. The silence hangs over us as he considers what he may have caused by simply doing what he does best. "You know…" the rest comes hard. "Cooking is all about the senses."

"You certainly opened me up to a lot of things I'd not considered before." I respond, although not entirely genuine. I'd considered such things before, but not realistically. That was the difference between then and now.

X seems confused, "What do you mean?"

"You invaded my privacy. You cooked me a phenomenal meal. And then you showed me there is much more to the senses than I'd ever considered."

"It wasn't just sex for you?" X seems surprised.

"No." I confirm. "It was special for me." I let that sit for a moment before continuing. "You have a way of opening up someone. You enabled me to let go and enjoy the experience. Not judge it. Accept it. Not many can do that. I attribute it to the meal we made and enjoyed together. It wasn't something you made for me. It wasn't something I made for you. It was something we made together. And the sex that came afterwards? It was the same. Something we created together. I can't tell you if that was what made it so special for me. Maybe it was. Probably. But I really don't know. All I can tell you is I've been waiting ever since for you to come back to the City so we could once again experience something that is greater than either of us alone. Do you know what I'm saying?"

X is quiet as he considers my version of the truth about our relationship. All I can cling to is the fact that he called immediately after I sent the text. And cling to it I do. Hoping he will tell me what I long so much to hear.

"I'm sorry if that's what you thought."

Not what I wanted to hear. "What did you think I'd think about you fucking me after a great meal we made together?"

"Fucking?" it's almost as if he didn't consider sex as fucking.

"What happened here?" I demand to know. "Was it just a means of buying me off? Get me thinking good things about you so I'd only write positive comments about you? Is that what you're doing? Going from city to city and fucking all of the food bloggers who have ever written about you? Make them think you actually care about us when you don't?"

"No," comes across as if he'd never considered that someone could consider him so callously. "What happened between us was an expression of the feelings of the moment. Isn't that how you see things? React to situations? Take things as they are at the moment?"

"Not at all." I push back. "I try to be open to things that are spontaneous. But for the most part I'm a creature of the expected. Someone who creates a whole understanding of my reality by the things that have happened before. When I sleep with someone it's because they have given me a whole set of signals that they're going to stay around for a while. That I'm important enough that they won't disappear with the sunrise. You're the one exception. You were gone before the sunrise. Never even got a chance to say good-bye and tell you how good it was for me."

"Was it?" X seems surprised. "I thought I'd turned you off completely because I wasn't at the top of my game."

I have a sudden understanding I'd missed. "Are you saying you thought you weren't worthy of me?"

"I wasn't," he admits. "I was so distracted by all the other things in my life that I kind of just went through the motions. You had to notice that. Had to know I wasn't really engaged with you. I thought you probably never wanted to see me again."

I hear the self-doubt I'd not considered. He didn't tell me he was in New York because he was ashamed of how he'd performed when we made love.

"You're wrong." I push back. "What we had that night was special for me. You opened me up to possibilities I'd never considered. And then you were gone." I hesitate to give it effect. "What was I supposed to think? You came, we had such a great time making dinner for each other and the love making was indescribable for me. And then you were gone. Now I find out you were in town and never even called. What would you think?"

X doesn't respond immediately. "I'm sorry I hurt you. I hear it in your voice. That's not what I intended."

"What did you intend?"

"To give you space." X sounds genuine, but I'm not quite sure. "To not create a sense of obligation. I didn't want you to think you needed to see me if I was so loathsome. Callous and not at all engaged with you."

"Why weren't you?" I challenge him.

"What? Engaged with you?" He seems clueless.

"Yes. You fucked me and left. What was I supposed to think? I'm just another conquest on your world tour? I want to be someone special. Someone important to you that you'd make a special trip just to spend some time with me. Instead you come to town and don't even tell me you're here."

"You're not the only one," X finally responds.

"The only one…that you're fucking? That you're leaving high and dry? That you're playing with to see how hard it is to drive us crazy?"

"That's not what I'm about." X responds. "But there are others who probably view me much the same way you do. I'm someone who is only concerned about his own dick. Where it's been. Whether it's happy regardless of how you feel about the situation. Does that describe the situation for you?"

"You're sending me in that direction." I confirm.

"That may be your perception but it's not accurate." X admits. "When we were together it was all new for me. Someone who was willing to share their essence with me. To not question what it was I had to give you. But an experience where we came together as equals. Came together seeking an experience that was as meaningful for one as for the other. And that's where I failed you. I wasn't fully there for you. I didn't hold up my end of the bargain. I went through the motions, but I didn't give you all I was capable of giving you."

What am I supposed to do with this admission? He was the best I'd ever had and he's telling me he was only partly there? Distracted by something else. I can't imagine how it could have been better but now that he's telling me it is something I should expect I have to recalibrate. "Then why don't you visit me and hold up your end of the bargain? I'll even cook with you again."

He seems surprised by my offer.

"After what I did to you, you'd invite me back to you bed?" The tone is one of complete surprise.

"What you did to me was open me up to a whole different level of expectations." I admit.

X seems to recalibrate how he should respond to me. "So, you're not angry."

I shake my head but then realize he can't see what I'm doing. I need to vocalize a response. "No."

"I don't deserve your forgiveness." X acknowledges.

"No, you don't." I wait to give the next comment more weight. "But I still want to see you."

X seems overwhelmed by my response, but then something must remind him of his work schedule as he responds, "I'm not scheduled to be back that way for the rest of the season."

I'm feeling my oats, "If I'm important enough to you and you're not just bullshitting me, you'll figure out a way to stop here even if it's a break between shows." I offer.

"That might be possible." X seems comfortable with this as an interim solution, but what I know is it's all in his court. He has to choose me over staying on the road. Will he do that? I can't tell, but it's at least worth the try.

"You know where to find me." I conclude the call and click off, to not give him another chance to rebut what I'd proposed. I know I don't understand the world he inhabits. My world is infinitely simpler. But if I want him to stand up for me, I have to make it clear what that would entail. And even with the discussion this afternoon, I'm not convinced he has it down. I could see him sailing off in a direction I'd not be willing to follow. But that will be his choice. And I hope to God I won't be required to have to make a similar choice to keep him.

The entire dialog runs through my mind so many times I can't discriminate how many times it may have actually been with him and how many times just with my imagination. I know there are those who would try to convince me X is just another figment of my imagination, but I know that's not the truth. He lives. He's an actual living person who has shown me a whole different side of life. One I need to pay attention to. One where men and women are equal, if only for that brief time where they are creating a new life, or simply creating a shared bond between them.

Maybe that is my problem. Maybe I'm looking for a shared bond only to find the man with whom I expect the bond is simply not up to the task. What can I do in such circumstance? I make a decision. I send him a text:

X:

You seem to be above the fray. Watching us who try to extract meaning from relationships. But you can join us if you will only decide to. And I will do everything I can to infuse meaning into our exchanges as I hope I did the last time we were together.

J

I wait for his text response, but it is not forthcoming. Have I crossed over some invisible line? Have I challenged him in some way that is threatening? I don't think so, but I've been wrong in getting to this point.

The silence from him is deafening. What do I do with the fact he's not engaging with me even though he has in essence apologized for his last visit being inadequate? I can't imagine how he would see it as being better unless he is indirectly telling me I am the one who is lacking in our whole lovemaking. I can see where he would get that impression. I'm not all that experienced, although I would think I'm at least adequate. His response has made me question things I've simply taken for granted. But then I realize I'm not the subject of this whole exchange. I may be a casualty, but the subject is my reader and his audience. We prepared a meal he pulled out of his head. The text response catches me off guard since I'm off in a whole other direction with my thoughts.

J:

*I will see you again. Not sure when or how with what's on my plate
at the moment. But somehow, I'll make it work. Don't give up on
me just yet.*

X

This message is out of the blue. What does this have to do with
our discussion?

X:

I'm counting on it.

J

I respond trying not to sound too needy. But I need him to
understand how important his touch, his kisses and just his mere
presence has become for me as a result of that one unexpected evening.
I've written about this guy for several years. I've watched him, listened
to him, and gotten to understand how he thinks. And yet I hardly can
guess what he thinks. Can't predict what he will do tomorrow, let alone
today. I want to believe him, but, know that's a fool's game. He isn't
responsible for his own behavior. He doesn't control his own schedule.
He isn't even sure where he will be tomorrow. How can I accept his
promise and expect him to honor it?

And yet that is exactly what I have now resolved. I'm his for as
long as it takes for him to convince me otherwise.

SPONTANEOUS

The next text brings me back from my wonderment about X.

> *J:*
>
> *Haven't seen your blog today. There some problem?*
>
> Z

I guess Z thinks I need to earn my paycheck today. But what do I write about? X's episode on Dallas Barbeque in New York is what Z is looking for, but the personal exchange between us still has me unsettled. What to do?

> *Z:*
>
> *Just eating barbeque here. Will have 600 words for you shortly.*
>
> *J*

I stare at my blank screen just long enough to answer my own question.

GOURMET BARBEQUE – NEW YORK STYLE

Who eats barbeque in New York? I admit I'm one of them. I eat barbeque when I'm in a hurry, because it's a quick meal. I eat barbeque when I'm in the mood for meat, which seems to be at least once a week. Probably my mostly fish diet forces a longing for something red once in a while. There's no meat like smoked meats and all the sides that remind me of the fourth of July. Why the fourth? Because it seems every year when I was growing up my parents would grill meats and make sides that were very close to what you find on a typical barbeque spread. Are the barbeque chefs trying to reproduce that summer picnic experience? I don't know. Chef X didn't ask that specific question of the Chef at one of the most prestigious barbeques from Dallas who has opened a New York outpost on a recent visit. But that seems to be about the only question of relevance that he missed.

It seems to me that one of the most relevant questions would be why would Texans, who are famed for grilling or smoking anything that isn't still moving be in love with someone else's barbeque? Isn't this a manhood kind of thing? The biggest buck in the backyard smoking scene is the one with the mobile smoker they pull behind their Ford F-550. You know the one. Has two rows of double wheels on the back and could probably pull a battleship out of the Gulf of Mexico if a hurricane was coming ashore. They're the same ones who tailgate. Cowboys game, or any college and increasingly high school football game in Texas. The parking lot could be a fast food court at any mall, you have so many smokers or grills. You smell the meat cooking from a mile away. Brisket, ribs, turkey, chicken, and sausage. I'm expecting someone to start grilling their tomahawk steak (at least 32 ounces of meat) and wrap it in bacon to get one more layer of fat related flavor in their mouths. Why is it no one seems to grill lamb? I've seen bacon wrapped scallops. Salmon. Even shrimp. But never lamb. That's good for the sheep herds, but I personally think it's a big hole in the cuisine of the die-hard fan. You know the one. Went to college but wasn't on the football or any other team. But since the football players were the ones idolized by all the women on campus, if they became a devout fan, they got to sit in the stands with all the beautiful chicks while the players had to sweat and run their asses off on the field below. Now that they've graduated, their trying to make sure they hold onto their beautaceous wife, girlfriend or consort by continuing their displays of super fan, even if they were never a super player. Now transplant all this to New York? Will anyone come?

So back to my question. If the backyard or mobile grill/smoker is the epitome of Texas manhood, why do Texans go to barbeques? I may have a limited perspective on this, but I think it's because barbeque takes time. Meat doesn't transform from a lump of animal flesh into a flavorful and aromatic steak, rib or whatever without time on a grill or in a smoker absorbing the heat and characteristics of the wood that enables the heat, time in a marinade absorbing the flavor and spices that enable the transformation. And it is that transformation, when paired with a dense wine, strong enough to mix as equals with the flavors of the meat that something truly unique in the world has been delivered to your palate for pleasure.

So, the answer to my question of will anyone in New York come? Join the long lines outside Pecan Lodge here in the City and get the answer for yourself.

I send this blog off to O for fact checking knowing she will send it along to Chi when she is done, and Chi will send to Z to get his blessing before it goes it out. I should have expected the fast turn-around from O.

J:

Beautaceous? Is that between the dinosaurs and the ice age?

O

Evidently Chi has a copy now too.

> J:
>
> *Beautaceous? Could you direct me to this word in Webster's?*
>
> Chi

I decide to answer them both at the same time.

> O and Chi:
>
> *Beautaceous is in the eye of the beholder.*
>
> J

Chi gets it, but he has a job to do and I understand that.

> J:
>
> *I actually like the term you have invented. It fits your narrative in a typically Texan sort of way. And since this blog is on Texas cuisine materializing out of the East River morning haze, I'm fine with what you're trying to convey. My question is will anyone outside of Texas get it?*
>
> Chi

This is a no-brainer response opportunity.

> Chi:
>
> *As a native New Yorker, you got it.*
>
> J

I thought that would carry the day, but I've been assuming way too much recently.

J:

Z just won't accept the fact we seldom need to be in the same place to do what we do. So, in that sense I'm no longer an insensitive boor, who lives through mediated spaces on the global info sphere. I'm a sophisticated man of the world who is able to detect nuances in culture and cuisine because I read everything you write. I'll accept this attempt to make me earn my paycheck this week, but please don't make a regular habit of it.

Chi

So now I just have to wait and see if Z has any comments. Generally, he is good with whatever Chi says is good, knowing his gate keepers have kept all us bloggers from going off the rails and suggesting something really radical. But Z knows me too well. I may call a bluff. I may miss something altogether that eventually becomes a trend reported on by someone else. But seldom if ever do I miss something of importance in a show I critique. But this column is different. I really only mentioned X once and that was to say he didn't do something in his latest show. Did I give my readers a reason to sit and watch that show? Only indirectly. But that's really what Z wants me to do. If all I'm doing is recounting the most salient facts from the broadcast, I have added very little value to anyone other than those who want to follow X, but don't have time to watch the entire show. They want the 30 second version of what's relevant. In this case I didn't deliver that. I talked concepts and referenced that X did a recent show on that topic. That in and of itself may be enough encouragement to get some folks to go watch it who missed it. I don't know anymore. There was a time when it was enough to give folks a reason to watch a show.

Expand the audience Z tells everyone. That's what we do. Expand the audience so the show will be rated more highly. That's what the backers of the show want. Bigger audience. Higher ratings. Each show seems to either perpetuate the assumptions behind the show or undercut them. And in the latter case, the show will likely be put on probation. If the ratings don't go up the show is likely to be cancelled. And maybe that's why we see so much experimentation on the shows. The chef-star is never convinced he has a sustainable recipe for more market share. Eyeballs on the screen. Ears listening to the blather he or she is spreading. And yet that is what makes the game so interesting. The audience is looking for something new. Something they can create and know their guests, who they intend to try this dish out on, will be amazed the host was able to create something so delicious and yet stimulating of different areas of their mouths.

Z doesn't disappoint.

J:

Good piece. I've missed you in your blogs recently. Glad to see you're back.

Z

I can't respond to this comment. I was driven to this kind of blog by the turmoil the call with X put me in emotionally and logically. I couldn't spend much time thinking back through that show. I'd been too consumed by my reaction to knowing he'd been in town and hadn't even tried to get in touch with me. And then his admission he'd not been really there through our whole night together. What was I supposed to think?

My phone rings, "What's the deal? X does a great show and you kind of ignore the whole thing to talk about the significance of barbeque. I don't get it."

O's voice in unmistakable. "Ever eat barbeque?" comes as my retort.

"Hell yes, but what does that have to do with you missing the story here?"

"And what was that?" I know what she's saying but want her to spell it out so I can disassemble her arguments.

"X is back." Is her simple summary. "He's not chasing sheep dung as a spice or toasted cheese sandwiches with a special sauce. He's doing mainstream. The kind of analysis of cuisine that got him notoriety to begin with. Been a while. And you just blow it off. Hardly even mention him even though you go off and invent a new word in the process. This blog is all about you and not him. But he's the chef. You're not. So, what's the deal?"

What do I say to my closest friend in the whole world? That X hurt me and insulted me by telling me that what was the best sex of my whole life was subpar for him? That he was too caught up by all the other stuff going on in his life to really give sex with me his all? I couldn't do that to someone. Even if it was the case, I'd never tell someone I was just going through the motions with you. "I'm opening a restaurant." I finally respond to really send her to the moon.

"Bullshit. You can't cook." O informs me as if I didn't know that.

"I've got a whole stable of chefs ready to cook for me. Different one each night if I want." I point out to her.

"I still say bullshit. So fucking answer my question."

"What do you really want to know? Why I didn't write the piece you expected after watching X's show? Why I'm not singing his praises for doing the show you wanted him to do? Why I'm not gushing over the fact that he went back to what worked for him and gave up this individualistic streak he was showing us? Tell me. What is it you're upset about?"

O is silent for longer than either of us are comfortable with, so I break the silence. "It's okay. We live in a world of the expected and yet each of us is yearning for something different. Something that will catch our attention because so much of what we deal with in any given day is the same old shit. It gets to the point that you walk past the Mona Lisa every day and you stop seeing her even though she's a remarkable work of art. We all want something to catch our attention. Something that will make today worthwhile. Do you know what I'm saying?"

"You think this blog gave me something that was worthwhile. Something that was so out of the ordinary that I'd take five minutes from my day to harass you about it?"

"You have." I point out but she knew this comment was coming.

"If that was your objective you accomplished your mission. But I'm still waiting for the blog on X. I want to see what you have to say about his interview. What insights he brought to us all. What he did to make me stop and think about barbeque differently."

"That's the problem with that show. He gave us a lot of insights about barbeque and how those who are making a living from it view it. Where they want to go with it, but nothing that would make me want to go there rather than the joint where I'm going this week. Nothing that makes me think about barbeque differently. He just reinforced what I already knew. Nothing broke new ground for me. I don't know about you, but are you running over to Pecan Lodge today after watching that show?"

"Not today, but I am more likely to try it at some point." Is her limp excuse.

"Don't hold your breath. Pecan Lodge is worth the trip, but I don't say that because of his interview. I say that from having waited in line for what at the time I thought was some of the best barbeque I've had. And I will go back there. But if I lived in LA or Chicago, would I make a special trip to Dallas or New York to try it after watching the show?"

O is quiet which means she knows I'm right. But at the same time, she's not confirming what I said. She's trying to justify her premise that I need to do another blog on that show. So, I ask the question that occurs to me, "Why?"

"Why what?" O comes right back.

"Why is it so important to you that I do another blog on Pecan Lodge?"

"I don't want you to," is her quiet response, which surprises me. Where is this going?

"Then why are you giving me all this shit?"

O assembles her response carefully. "X needs your praise."

I had never considered this aspect of my blogs. "What are you saying?"

"Do you want another sheep dung show?"

"It got its share of his audience. Those who are looking for the novel and really far out tastes." I point out to her even though I know where she's going now.

"What part of his audience is that?" She wants me to understand she thinks he has a problem and only I can help him address it. "Two percent?"

"You know I haven't looked at those demographics so I can't answer your question. At least I can't answer it with facts to back me up. But from the sample of texts I've gotten from his audience I think it's a whole lot bigger than that. Could be wrong, but that's my impression. His audience isn't you and me so much as it is folks who want to know more about the world in general. What do they eat in parts of the world they will probably never visit? Is it something they can find in a local restaurant or something they can try to make at home? I don't know for sure but from what I've seen of his audience they seem to be a lot more adventuresome than for most chefs."

"I've looked at those same emails." O informs me although I know she reads my email. "I don't see what you're telling me is there. The questions seem to be more incredulity, like is what he's talking about something that people actually eat?"

"For the sheep dung I think you're going to the folks who were asking whether they could actually buy it in the local grocery store. Not the same question. They were disbelieving that the show had any relevance to them because they didn't think they'd ever be able to reproduce it. Not that it wasn't relevant to them. They were more interested in knowing how they could reproduce it without going out and buying a sheep to make their own sheep dung."

"And your Chicken a la King with spicy sauce? Something that is available in a lot of stores and yet people had never considered using it."

"Because they didn't know about it." I point out. "What X did was inform his audience there is another option for spicing up the familiar and boring but routine meals that so many of us prepare. You don't have to be a world-famous chef to make something you already know how to make better. To add spices, you'd never considered. To look and see what's out there you've never tried. It may be just the ticket to make the old tried and true interesting again. Especially if you pair it with a different wine. Something you'd have never thought would go with that particular dish."

"Is that his only real value?" O asks. "To make us look at a dish differently?"

BOUPHA'S DELIGHT

What can you say about rice? Apparently, a lot as I'm finding out by watching the show X produced after leaving New York. Was it worth him not spending a night with me for him to produce this show? I may be biased, but in my view of the world I would say no. But then again, that's just me. Someone hurt by his inattention. Hurt by the fact he didn't even consider confirming his assumptions about our first night together. Hurt that I didn't get to experience what making love would be like when he was really engaged with me and not somewhere else in his mind.

The show is filmed in a rice patty somewhere in Southeast Asia, although X couldn't confirm it was really in Cambodia as the show is representing. So, what's so different about Cambodian rice? Apparently, it's one of the best in the world. In looking it up the first thing I find is that it was entered into the World Rice Conference competition which took place in Macau and finished third in the world. "Moul Sarith, the secretary-general of the Cambodia Rice Federation (CRF), congratulated Cambodian rice farmers for the great results, but lamented that the kingdom did not take home the accolade." According to the Khmer Times, a Cambodian newspaper. Cambodian Rice Federation? Didn't know such a thing existed. Sounds like something you'd find in Europe, but in Cambodia? Guess I need to adjust my thoughts about this part of the world. The farmers are banding together to enter international competitions. And that same article references that a Cambodian variety called Phka Rumduol, but often also called phka malis or Cambodia jasmine rice by millers and traders, won the competition from 2012 to 2014. The first question I have is what makes a world class rice?

"What makes this the best rice in the world for the billions who are sustained by it more than once a day?" X asks a rice farmer through an interpreter as they walk in ankle-deep water irrigating a rice patty.

"**Good rice** is transparent." The farmer responds to X's question. "Opaque spots indicate a chalky taste. You taste chalk in rice you throw it out as it is merde, to use a French term. The best rice has long, slender grains."

"And Cambodian rice is good rice?" X asks.

"Historically the rice federation has told us that it is one of the best in the world, but what do I know? Has that designation meant I sell more rice today than I did yesterday? No. I doubt many people go to the grocery and ask for Cambodian rice. They ask for rice. They don't stop to ask where it came from. They don't care if it is one of the best in the world as decided by some group of people who voted in a blind tasting. All I know is Cambodians like what I grow. As long as they have enough money from whatever it is they do for a living to buy my rice, I'm happy. Do I care what happens in markets in other countries? No. That doesn't affect me unless for some reason they are able to grow much more rice and they come to Cambodia and try to sell it cheaper than I can grow it. I must recover the money I spend to grow it, or I will go out of business."

"That would be the case anywhere." X informs this poor farmer. "No one can stay in business if they lose money every season and every crop they grow." X informs the farmer and his audience at the same time.

"You do not understand." The farmer raises rice grains to his nose to smell them. "It is not about money. I will grow rice here next year even if I don't sell a single grain."

X stops to look at the farmer, puzzled by this turn of the conversation.

"I am a small farmer. Not much land, but I own this land. If I don't sell my crop my family will eat it as that will be all we have to keep us alive. If I sell it, I can buy meats and cheese or milk. I can add things to my rice that will make my family healthier. But if I don't, my family will still not be hungry because we will have rice to eat. We will have full bellies until the next spring. We will not disappear. And next year the crop will be better or worse. We will sell more or less. It doesn't really matter. A good year, a bad year. One follows the other. In the long term we will survive. The markets will take care of themselves. What I'm saying to you is you have to understand Cambodian life to understand our rice, to understand our way of life. To understand what we eat and why. To understand us as a people."

X tries to interpret what he has just heard. "You're saying you don't care about your rice. Whether it is one of the best in the world."

The farmer shakes his head. "What matter does it make? As long as my family can eat it and survive until next year, that is what is important. Not what other people think about it. I don't care what you think about it. I just know my family is secure because of it. I have children. I will have grandchildren. We will all live here and grow rice. We will all live a life that is hard, but it is life and that is what matters. There is no life without family. There is nothing that is as important as making sure they each and every one has enough to eat. Would you agree?"

X has to think about this question for a moment. "Food is essential. But good food enriches life."

"Maybe in your world that is an important distinction. In Cambodia it is not."

"I would agree that we have to bring everyone up past subsistence." X tries to defend his position, but the farmer is having none of it.

"Bring up? To what?" the farmer demands. "In Cambodia this is as good as it gets. If I make money from selling my crops what do I do?

Do I buy more land and produce more rice?"

"In the west we would." X tries to respond, but the farmer is already one step beyond.

"This is not the west. This is Cambodia. In Cambodia if a farmer has money the government comes and asks for it. We are not permitted to make money as you are. We make money then we actually end up with less than if we had not. We are better off eating our own crops, selling a little and giving the rest to the government so they will leave us alone. Then we plant next year's seeds where we need them. It is all about getting through today. Not about tomorrow. Not about growing a business as you know it. We are just hoping to have enough to feed our families and leave them each enough that they can feed their own families. The worst thing we can do is have a big family. That means each of my children has less land than I did to raise their crops. In that case they may not be able to grow enough to feed their family. That is the worst outcome. Death from starvation. That is why we try to have one son or one son and a daughter. But the second child is always a risk. If you have two boys, then neither has enough. If you have two girls, they must divide up my lands when I pass on. But then they have a small parcel from their husband and small parcel somewhere else. That is not efficient, but it is the way of life in Cambodia."

X realizes he will not be able to recapture the narrative he wanted for his episode. "When you aren't eating your own rice where do you eat?"

"With family," The farmer responds. "My mother or my wife's mother cooks. We visit with them and all our family members. You have such family gatherings. At your holidays or weddings or funerals. Family wants to be together at points of change or points of remembrance."

"I agree." X is still struggling to get the farmer to focus on what he wants to talk about. "But if you aren't eating at home or eating with family where do you eat?"

"A restaurant?" the farmer confirms where he thinks X is going.

X nods and waits, hoping for the answer he is looking for. The one chef this farmer would seek out for a meal that doesn't come from his family.

"I will eat what someone else has cooked when I go to town. But that is only to sell crops that are more than what my family will need. That's is usually only once or twice a year. And I only eat there because it is too far to get home to eat."

"When you go to town, where do you eat?"

"My mother's sister's son has a restaurant. He cooks the traditional Cambodian dishes. I will eat what he cooks because he is family. He will ensure that what I eat is what I would eat if I were home."

"Does he cook with different spices? Different ingredients than you would get at home?" X pushes apparently hoping this will be the opening to a next part of this episode that people will want to know more.

The scene shifts and X is talking with a younger man who is sitting in a small kitchen. A hot plate and small dishes with spices and meats, fish and a bowl of rice ready to be put together to make the meal his patrons will want. "With us is Boupha, whose name means 'like a flower' in Cambodian. Boupha is the cousin of Kousa, the farmer who grows the best rice in Cambodia, the phka malis that was the best in the world until 2014."

Boupha smiles for the camera like a veteran of such events although this is the first time anyone has ever interviewed her. "Boupha, what is the most popular dish you serve your customers?"

"Chha Kh'hei." Boupha responds through the interpreter. "A spicy stir fry of meat, usually chicken, eel or frog flavored. We mix it with julienned gingerroot, black kampot pepper, garlic, soy and sometimes fresh peppers, for extra heat. Kousa like the extra heat because he never gets it at home."

"So Kousa likes to try something new." X pushes since Kousa seemed to minimize the importance of eating in a restaurant. That eating with family was the most important meal one could have, whether in Cambodia or anywhere in the world.

"Kousa is always challenging me to make something for him he has not tried before. Something spicy. Something that brings heat the way our Thailand cousins like to eat. We kid that Kousa's father must have been a Thai rather than Cambodian," Boupha responds to X's question.

"Cambodian's generally don't like spicy food?" X comes back trying to follow Boupha.

"We like to eat a balanced meal. Equal amounts of sweet, sour, salty or bitter in taste so there is a bit of every flavor. But spicy? No. That is not something Cambodian's look for in their meals."

"So sweet, sour, salty or bitter." X repeats to ensure he has it right. Tell us about your most popular dish. How does that stack up on your list of flavors commonly found in a Cambodian meal?"

"Gingeroot, pepper, garlic, soy and fresh peppers are the primary spices we add to the dish. Ginger would make the meat sweeter, although not sweet like you think of like chocolate or sugar. We think of flavors differently. Is pepper sour? It is not sweet and it's not salty. So how would you classify pepper, or garlic or soy? None fit the classification as you would think of them. But we classify tastes differently than you do. What is garlic? Is it sweet? Clearly not as you would think of sweet. Is it sour? Also, not as you would think of sour. It also is not salty or bitter, but it adds a tang to the meal that is essential for many dishes. So how would we think of garlic? For us garlic would be sour because it tones down the sweetness of fish or that found in many green leafy vegetables. It's not so much is it sweet or sour in itself, but how does it react to the other ingredients? How does it change the character of the dish as a whole? And that may result from how that ingredient interacts with just one other ingredient. The way we look at an ingredient is how it changes an aspect of the flavor, not necessarily the flavor of the entire dish. I know that may seem strange to you since western dishes tend to be loaded with ingredients that make the dish overwhelmingly spicy, sour, sweet or salty. But Cambodian food is subtle. We want to look for the different tastes that reside in the dish. And those tastes can oppose each other in the same dish. That's something we really appreciate. When opposing flavors coexist in the same dish. That is the mark of an accomplished chef."

"Who would you say is the most accomplished chef in Cambodia?" X is still looking for the person who will follow the story line he is hoping to get to.

"That is a very difficult question. We don't have restaurants like you do in the west. We are all local establishments. We serve our families first and then the public. So consequently, we make dishes that are favorites of our families. If you ask anyone in my family, they are likely to say that I am, for when they come to town they come and eat here. If you ask my neighbor, she will probably say her mother for that is who she goes to eat with when she doesn't eat at home."

"Does your neighbor ever come eat here?" X isn't sure how to follow this point.

"No." Boupha responds.

"You serve meals to complete strangers, but not your neighbor?" X doesn't believe her.

"Many Cambodians serve food to complete strangers, neighbors and people just visiting for a short time. But generally, they are serving rice balls and what you would call a snack. Not a major meal like we have once a day. Everyone has snacks, generally made of rice. Some are sweet and some are savory. I would say the savory are the most popular as Cambodians are not so interested in sweets. Cambodians want food that will sustain them when food is scarce. We have learned to be that way because in our memory when war comes to Cambodia, people starve to death. So everyone is very cautious about how much we eat and that we have stores of rice and what you would call staples. The spices we need to mix with our rice. The dried meats and vegetables we can mix in when fresh are not available. We have learned from our recent history that just because food is plentiful this year, it may not be next year. And even though we do not expect to be in a war this year or next, we never know when one of our neighbors will cause us to run and hide in the hills."

"A history of aggression by the countries that surround you." X suggests.

Cambodians are generally peaceful, but we have had some leaders who did not care about the people, leaders who only cared about making life better for themselves and their families. I cannot tell you what that has meant to the families of this country other than to make us very cautious that the peace of today is fragile and could change at almost any time."

"You're talking about Pol Pot and the Khmer Rouge." X understands but wants his audience to as well, although I wonder how many people really know who Pol Pot and the Khmer Rouge were.

Boupha nods and looks about uncomfortably as if she is wondering who might be listening to this conversation. I wonder if that means there are still people in Cambodia who remember the old days as the good old days and would like to see the Khmer Rouge return to power, even though they killed thousands of Cambodians during their bloody period of power.

"What are you serving us today?" X decides it's time to move beyond deprivation.

"This is Num Kom." Boupha shows us the prepared dish. "It is a glutinous rice dumpling made by steaming rice flower in banana leaves. As you can see it is round like a soda straw and fillings include ground pork flavored with oyster, fish and soy sauce."

"So, you would classify this as sweet from the banana leaves and salty from the oyster, fish and soy sauces blended together." X tries to understand the dish as Boupha would classify it.

Boupha nods, "This is a very popular dish." She offers one to X who bites into it and nods with a smile. When he finishes chewing, he takes another bite to Boupha's delight.

Hunting Incas

Since I'm expecting a text from Z at any moment now asking where my next blog is I better start coming up with something nice to say about Cambodian rice besides the fact that the Cambodian Rice Federation is unhappy they are no longer number one in the world according to some unknown and probably unknowable taste testing which said it once was. Okay, what to say?

THE CAMBODIAN TASTE TEST

I like rice. I think there are very few who don't. Even those who are gluten intolerant tend to like rice. So why did Chef X have such a difficult time in getting folks in Cambodia to tell him what he wanted to know, which was why is Cambodian rice so highly rated and yet few outside of Cambodia have heard about it? Their exports are ranked number nine in the world just behind Uruguay. That's right a South American nation exports more rice than Cambodia. But is that because so many more Cambodians eat rice than Uruguayans? That may well have something to do with it. Cambodia has 16.3 million people whereas Uruguay has only just under 3.5 million. A lot more mouths to feed in Cambodia, so if the truth were known, there is a lot more rice grown in Cambodia and that was probably one of the singular facts to come out of the X encounter with a Cambodian rice farmer. Where there hasn't been a war in Uruguay since 1870, the last Paraguayan War; the last war involving Cambodia ended in 1975. The atrocities that accompanied that war persisted well after that date. While neither Kousa nor Bhoupa, the two Cambodian cousins X interviewed were alive during the last war, it appears to be fresh in the minds of their families. Discussion of preparation for starvation and famine that results from armed conflicts. The visceral fears that Kousa described indirectly and Bhoupa acknowledged bespoke a country still adjusting to the effects of armed conflict on the citizenry within the lifetime of family and relatives. The stories that were handed down remain fresh in the consciousness and actions that Kousa and Bhoupa take as part of a normal day. Live for today, but, prepare for a very different tomorrow and not in a good way.

X also seemed surprised that Cambodians seek balance in their cuisine. He also discovered that the four flavors representing that balance mean very different things to Cambodians than to western chefs. The discussion of balancing flavors within a dish rather than flavors that overwhelm a dish was most interesting. It was evident that Cambodians have a very different understanding of western cuisine than may be the reality, other than that which is represented by so called 'fast food.' The whole slow food movement headquartered in Italy has sought to change the perception of food in the lives of everyday individuals. That meals from scratch, seeking to achieve harmony within the dish, just as Bhoupa described would probably be a revelation to her. Bringing about an understanding that food the world over is not so different. Individual tastes, how spices are combined and how flavor is balanced probably all vary greatly. But the underlying principles of balance and harmony are not different, only executed in very different ways for different purposes and different palates. A clear implication of X's discussions in Cambodia is that even in a nation of scarcity, there is a wide range of invention, seeking to create tastes that are new and different, even if not widely understood or demanded by people. The discussion of Kousa liking spicy foods because he doesn't get them at home is instructive. Something different is always desired even by those who have little in the way of choice. Spiciness is desired by those who have grown up with a bland diet, and those who live with sour foods, seek out a sweet treat to change that sameness in their lives.

I for one hope that Chef X continues his quest to inform us about rice. But the geopolitical reality of the rice bowl in Southeast Asia has to be taken into account in order to get to the underlying reality of how rice affects the palates of people around the world.

Off it goes to O and Chi. I wonder how this one will be greeted since the last one drew such strong comments. But in the end Z was pleased to see me try to be a little controversial without making anyone we are trying to groom mad at us. We want the restaurants to refer to our reviews and blogs. We want to attract new eyes just as we want the eyes we do deliver to wander over to a restaurant and try a dish we've described. It all makes for better business for everyone. At least that is what Z would say when I've delivered something that won't get people talking about either the chef I've reviewed or some dish they describe in their show or that shows up on their menu. My job is simple. Draw eyes. Get people talking about something other than the usual routine at work or at home. Make people look forward to trying something they never would have considered if they hadn't read my blog.

Here it comes. O first.

J:

WTF?

O

This one will require a phone call before it's done, but I give it one text try because I know O would rather not have to get into a verbal discussion when a mediated experience is so much less threatening even if it does tend to amp up the language she selects. Over the phone or face-to-face the language choice is much less confrontational.

O:

Didn't know I was a Political Science major did you.

J

The response is almost immediate. No thinking about it on her end.

J:

Are you writing for Foreign Affairs and someone forgot to tell me?

O

O:

Actually, I'm doing a guest gig for the Economist.

J

J:

I know I'm just a fact checker and I'm pleased you gave me a few facts to check and all that. But this piece has only a very limited appeal to the foodies who read your blog. They'll all soon start watching the Food Network while they play video games because the show is just way too slow for the modern millennial who wants instant information and gratification. That's what you're supposed to be delivering here. Six hundred words that represent 3600 seconds of airtime. You're supposed to be taking out the boring scenery shots and facial expressions and giving them just the easily

digestible facts. At least the facts as you know them and as
represented by the chef of the day. You know I love you and all that.
It just makes it hard for me to sit here knowing you're going to get
your ass fired if you keep sending along geopolitical analysis rather
than spice choices to foodies who would never think of actually
making one of these dishes. That's what restaurants are for. And
you're the color commentator who feeds them enough insights so
they can bullshit their friends and admirers over a twenty-five-
year-old Scotch that neither you nor I could ever afford.

O

Glad I didn't call her. She never would have been that direct with
me on the phone. Would have gone round and round about never
giving folks what they want, but never would have said she was afraid
for me.

O:

Controversy.

J

She'll know instantly what I'm talking about. No need to write
another six hundred words explaining myself when one will do. Not
sure I'll get away so easily once Chi sinks his intellect into this dilemma.
He's been much more straightforward with me in the past. Usually
when I get away from soups and spices, he gives me a little room to
explore. But what about this one? Zeroing in on culture of fear rather
than society of abundance? Will he see that as appropriate discussion
for this audience, even though that was most of what was discussed on
the show?

J:

Had to go back and watch the show to see where you were coming from. If that was your objective, you achieved it. Probably could have added a little more description into the spice section. You know, spice it up a little. Overall, I think I agree with O about this being out on the edge. Also understand your note about controversy. As I said you drove me to watch the show. Will let it go through today, but tomorrow's blog definitely needs to be less political.

Chi

Guess I'm right where I want to be. Warned and embraced in the same text. Guess I can't get any further out on the ledge that that. Then I get another text.

J:

Been thinking about you. Can we have dinner?

Ace

Now what am I supposed to do with this? He disappeared after I left him at the restaurant. Nobody seemed to know where he went or why. And now he just reappears wanting to pick up where we left off? Not going to happen.

Ace:

What's on your mind?

J

Do I really want to know? Then why did I ask? Why didn't I just ignore his text? I can still walk away. But I'm still trying to sort out what's going on with X and whether there's anything there or is it just in my mind and not his? That last conversation would surely make it seem like that's the situation. I'm a fool if I hold out any hope there. Nothing more is going to happen. I might as well get used to that idea. The fact he didn't come or even call when he was in the City was a pretty good indicator of where his head is at.

J:

I'm sorry for the way the evening ended the other day. I guess I was just trying to impress you and it backfired. I'm not that guy, living above everyone and just looking down on the world, despite what you must think. I'm really more that college professor than businessman. I got here by accident. Somewhere along the way I lost what I recognized as the simple man who wanted to just make a living helping others make sense of this world. Help them make a living, raise a family and do what is important to them and the community they inhabit. Does any of this make sense? And now I'm trying to establish relationships that aren't transactive. Relationships that last. Mean something to the other person as well. I'm hoping you will be an important person to me, and I can be the same for you. So, dinner? If not, coffee or a drink?

ACE

This is not what I would have expected from Ace. A confession of sorts. A plea from someone who sounds like he's hurting. I saw something in him when we were together that may have been behind this note. Something unsettling. Something that told me what I see is not real, not the person behind the façade, if that's what it was. Maybe that's why he sent me on my way when I asked him the hard questions he had no answer for. So why would I deliberately want to get together with him again? Because he's telling me what I saw was real, that everything I knew about him wasn't the real Ace? But what was it I knew about him? Not all that much. He's successful, generous and really smart from some of the conversations I've overheard. That would all be explained by the duality of his background. College professor who married one of his students and went to work at daddy's company where he made a fortune. But his wife's gone and now he's at loose ends, trying to reorient himself. Find the original self he walked away from. But when someone does that, walk away from what you know to become something else, don't you become that different person? And once you do that can you really ever go back to being what you were? I don't know, but that's the clear direction he seems to want to go in. Does that mean he's going home to wherever it was he came from? Leave New York behind? Leave all the trappings of his life here for someplace else? And if he's getting ready to leave why does he want new relationships or stronger relationships with people here? That doesn't make sense at all. But he did stand up for me that one time. I guess I owe him a chance to plead his case. Maybe all he's wanting is to have people here who he can lean on as he transitions to whatever person he is trying to become.

I look at his text once more, not reading it, but just staring at the words. They represent an opportunity he is offering me. But why me? I asked that question and I'm not sure I buy his explanation. What is it about Ace that throws up all kinds of caution flags for me? Makes me want to be with him and at the same time run away as fast as I can? O and Chi weren't much help when I went to them last time. Z was more insightful, but even he wasn't able to ease my concerns. He just gave me more information with no assurances of anything other than Ace seems to be reliable and straight up, whatever that means. Even I don't know why anyone would use that term to describe someone. Straight up. Does that mean he stands straight up and that makes him someone who embodies the traits of the military? Or does that mean someone who just deals the cards as they come? Someone who doesn't try to manipulate things for his benefit. I could probably play this definition game all day and still not have any more insight into Ace than I have right now.

I guess the only way I'm going to understand what Ace is offering me is to accept his invitation to get together, but I need to make it on my terms. So, dinner, coffee and drinks are out. But what does that leave me? He clearly wants to talk, but where can we meet, talk and I have no restrictions on my ability to get up and leave if I don't like where the conversation is going? Last time he was trying to impress me that he is someone of means. Okay. I got that. Knew it before we even went out. So why did he take that tact? He talked with O and Chi and Z about me before then. He must have had some idea about what would resonate with me. And yet his wealth is what he chose to impress me. Why not a conversation about what I do? Something that I would have instantly related to? He's been places I've written about but never been to. He could have started there. Read one of my blogs and talk to me about when he visited that place and give me some of the texture of the place. Nuance. Things I couldn't possibly know having never actually been there. But he didn't. He started with him. If he does that again I won't stay. But I'm making this all too hard. He will want to explain something about himself and why a relationship with me is important to him and why it could be important to me. Even if he's leaving.

The keyboard waits for my keystrokes. Waits for me to take the random letters available to me to create intelligence that another will recognize and be able to extract meaning from the letters selected and the order in which I select them. That's what I do. Select letters so another can comprehend the meaning I'm trying to convey. Maybe that's what Ace is trying to do, just verbally.

Ace:

Washington Square. I'll be on a bench near the monument. Plan for seven tonight. No dinner, no drinks or coffee. Just an exchange of meanings.

J

Now that I've committed myself and set the ground rules I need to figure out what are the meanings I want to exchange? What is it I want from Ace, if anything? Until I got his text, he had dropped off my radar. That would mean I didn't expect or want anything from him. So, this is bonus time. Kind of like the lottery. What would I do if I had a million dollars? Well, after tax I would only have about $650,000. And after I paid off my college debt, I'd have about half a million. Okay, so it's not so much as it sounds when you're up to your eyeballs trying to make enough to keep all the bills paid. And that's exactly where I am. Sweating each and every week that there will be enough in the bank to pay everyone who has a claim on me. Half a million in the bank. Okay, this is where it becomes fun, because now I know I've got things covered and I still have some to play with. Half a million. Would I move to a bigger place? One where I could actually see the Hudson even on the bad days? An apartment with even one more room would seem like heaven, like I've arrived because I can afford another room. But if I had the money that wouldn't work. I need a pay raise to get a bigger place. That's monthly income because it's a monthly expense that continues when the half million is gone.

Would I go someplace? One of those places that X has visited and I've written about? Cambodia? I don't think so. But someplace that's far away but someone there would have to speak the local language and English to keep me out of trouble. Where would I want to go? There are so many places I can't begin to even count them. How would I decide where to go first? Everyone goes to Mexico or Europe. I'd probably do them at some point, but they would be down on my list of places if I put it in priority order. The place not many people go is South America. Yeah, that's where I'd go. But maybe Argentina first. Go find Eva Peron's grave. I know a little about her. About how she and her husband plundered the country and sent it from the fourth largest economy in the world to one that barely registers when the global economy is discussed.

HOPE

The more I think about it I'm not sure I really want to visit Argentina. I've heard it's nice. Buenos Aires is supposed to be very European. They have the whole gaucho tradition. Cowboys of the pampas comes to mind but I'm not really sure what that means. Must be the gauchos are cowboys, riding horses and herding cattle in what is probably a wide-open plains area like we have in the western states where cowboys once rode. Someone said they raise a lot of grass-fed beef in Argentina. Supposed to be tender enough you don't need a knife to cut it. That might be interesting to try if I were someone who likes beef, but I'm really not. I'd rather have fish most days despite my barbeque fetish.

Still not coming up with a good enough reason to go to Argentina, but then again, I remember the Tango. Yes, that might be a reason to go to Argentina. Meet a tall dark stranger who will teach me how to Tango. That sounds romantic and forbidden. Something dangerous, not because something might happen to me, but because I might fall in love. Isn't that what they say in all the novels that take place in Argentina? The Tango is the dance of lovers? Thrilling for the dancers and the audience.

That might be the very reason to go to Argentina, but I wonder how long it would take me to learn the Tango. And nobody here does the Tango, so it would be one of those skills you rarely use. Someone has a party and you show up in a Tango dress daring the guys to dance with you. The problem with this scenario is I'd probably scare everyone to death if they thought they'd have to dance with me.

Scratch the Tango, scratch Argentina.

If I'm going to South America, I'm going to need to find someplace else. Rio maybe?

UNIQUE

Ace is waiting on a bench near the Washington Square monument when I arrive on foot having decided I need the exercise. Bloggers earn their money sitting around choosing words. Too much sitting. I need to get out more often. Once a day would probably be good. Ace is watching me approach him. A nice gray pinstripe suit with light purple shirt and no tie. Have I ever seen him when he wasn't in a suit? I don't know. His shoes give him away. I would expect wingtips or something classical. He's wearing brown penny loafers. High shine. I can't tell you the last time I saw anyone wearing them.

"Aren't you going to text me?" I inquire as I'm close enough to converse.

"What do you mean?" Ace isn't sure why he would want to text me when I'm right here.

"Just kidding you that everyone seems to communicate that way rather than face-to-face," I respond as I take a seat on the bench next to him, but don't look at him even though he is checking me out from head to toe.

"I prefer to be with someone when I'm trying to communicate." Ace informs me. "I miss fewer of the non-verbal things exchanged when you want someone to understand what you're trying to say."

"Sounds like you've had bad experiences with non-verbal communications," I remark although I'm not quite sure why.

Ace looks away from me and that movement causes me to look directly at him. Being this close I see the gray advance guards in his dark brown hair, the gathering lines under his eyes that would indicate he isn't sleeping enough, the tentative squint through which he perceives the world as if he is either in pain or reacting to bright light. The day is sunny for a change and that could explain the squint. Somehow, I don't think it's the reason. There's something behind that expression I hope he will share so maybe I'll no longer be cautious of him.

"You think we are friends," I start out since he is still reacting to my comment. "But you want to change the nature of our relationship. Why?"

Ace glances at me and then slowly turns to really look at me. I search his eyes trying to understand what he is thinking, feeling. What he's reacting to. And then he kisses me, not impulsively, not forcefully. It seems he barely touches my lips, but we are communicating without a word being spoken. That kiss is unexpected, not in that it happened, but in the tenderness he conveys and the fact that neither of us moves to end the kiss, but let it flow between us.

I don't know who moves away first. It may be me, but I must still be absorbing the meaning of that kiss when I see him looking deep into my eyes. I become embarrassed. I don't want him to see the confusion I'm feeling. The questions flooding my mind. See him comprehending that I am in fact open to him by the fact I didn't resist and fully participated in his gesture. So now I'm the one looking away. Seeing, but not really following those who are flowing through this green island in a sea of concrete and stone.

"You came out of hiding." Ace remarks to bring me back to this bench where we are attempting to exchange meaning.

"What are you talking about? I've not been hiding."

"You've been hiding from yourself and your readers," Ace is firm in his response.

"In what sense?" I finally catch a glimmer of where he is going.

"Your last two blogs." Ace points me in a direction so I can follow his thesis. "You were interpreting the world for all of us. Not just your readers. Not just yourself. You had stopped doing that. I don't know why, but it was almost as if you'd lost interest."

This is a dangerous line of discussion. It could get me fired if he convinces me to really get radical. "Didn't know you were reading my blogs wherever it was you went."

Ace looks at me for a long time, but his eyes seem hollow, as if his mind has gone elsewhere and left just the shell of his body and his intellect while his mind goes to save the world. And suddenly he is back, and he smiles at me in that way some people look at their dog when it has done something worthy of note. "I went home," he states simply. "To feel what it was like, to smell the flowers and trees and even the carbon monoxide coming out of tailpipes of cars that have been driving those streets for decades."

"Home?" He catches me off guard. This is probably the last place I would have thought to look for him. "Why home?"

"To see if what I'm feeling is real, or whether the old saying about you can never go home again is true."

"And what did you discover, both about yourself and the old saying?" I decide to play this out and see where he is trying to take me.

"I found that the answer to both is yes," comes across genuine but somehow tinged with regret.

I let his discovery settle in and think about the implications. It then becomes clear to me that I need to know a little more. "What are you feeling? That you really are just that professor who exceeded everyone's expectations including your own?"

Ace shows me a lopsided smile, one that accompanies an introspection in his eyes, "That I am most decidedly."

"And because you're not some ruthless developer tearing down paradise to put up a parking lot, as Joni Mitchell would have described you, that makes you a good person I should want to be better friends with?"

"Joni Mitchell?"

"You don't know her music?" I'm surprised. I thought everyone would know that reference.

Ace grimaces, "Of course I know it. But it seems everyone who has ever opposed one of my projects brings that up. I just didn't think you would."

I stare off across the park wondering why I'm here, why I'm letting him back me into being the bad guy who's hurting his feelings. I don't think I am and I'm not sure what game he's playing. The question I keep asking myself is what do I want from him?

I turn it around, "What do you want from me? Forgiveness for having been a rapacious real estate developer who turned people out of their homes so you could build a monument to money and success?"

Ace looks at me, apparently trying to figure out something about my reaction to him. "I told you what I want. Given that you came in response to my request I have to assume that you are at least open to the idea of a relationship with me in whatever form that might take."

"Such as?" I hear warnings in the words he is choosing."

"Friend." I wait for more, but none is forthcoming at least immediately. So, I just stare at him waiting for him to give me more.

"Conscience, maybe."

I still wait, now convinced his real objective is neither of these roles.

"Confidant then."

189

This is taking too long, "Why is now different than before. You could have asked me to be any of these things for you all the weeks you've been coming to the Friday night get togethers and yet you never have. I repeat, why now?"

"When I first encountered you and your friends at the bar, I didn't quite know what to make of you. It seemed to me that you all had these great relationships. Thought you were college friends or something. But when I realized you all work together, well then, I started listening differently to your discussions. You work together and yet you seem to be close in many ways. Not how anyone I work with would view their relationship with me or anyone else at the company where I work. I came to realize that you must be special people in that you really care about each other, and not just in a business setting."

"O is my best friend." I admit. "And I met her on the job."

"I graduated from High School with my best friend," Ace responds. We grew up together and we are friends because of the shared experiences we reflect on and wonder how either of us survived."

"That's probably more common than not." I acknowledge.

"That your best friend could be someone who hasn't shared major life experiences says a lot about you. It says you're willing and able to form close relationships with someone you haven't known your whole life. That you're open to changes, willing to discuss them and work things through because a relatively recent relationship is important to you."

"Is that what you're looking for?"

A momentary cloud passes over Ace's face, but he regains a positive expression, "Yes."

"Why not O, then? She's the same as me in that regard. Only she's funnier than I am."

"She seems pretty much into the IT guy." Ace raises an eyebrow. "Damien, I think is his name. You know if that's what she's looking for I must scare her to death."

I wonder if he used that last description of himself on purpose to see what reaction he gets from me. "I don't think you scare her. She'd only want you for your money because you certainly don't have Damien's most redeeming characteristic."

Ace apparently searches his memory to try to pull an answer out to explain the mystery I posed. "The ability to fix her laptop?" he finally guesses.

I hate to break the well-known secret about Damien the IT guy to Ace if he's not privy to the answer, but I wonder if it will shock him. "Damien is well known around town. I'm surprised you've never heard of him since even I have."

"This a secret only women share?"

"I'll have to think about that." I decide to play with him for a bit. To see how patient he is.

"I take it the secret has something to do with the size of his hands and feet." Ace comes up with a reputed indicator of the size of something else that would be of interest to a woman thinking about sleeping with someone.

"What do your hands and feet have to say about you?" I tease him now since his hands and feet appear to be of average size.

"That they aren't necessarily the indicator you might think." Again, Ace raises that same eyebrow, a characteristic I don't think I'd noticed before. "But in any event, if that's how O sizes a man up, then I'm probably not someone for her."

I let the silence grow for a moment, seeing him getting more uncomfortable about the discussion we'd just had. "Probably not, but I still wonder if there isn't something else that made you pick me out of the herd. As I said to you last time, there are so many women in New York, so many women just in Manhattan, so many women in the Village. What brought me to your attention and come to think of it, why have you started reading my blogs? Is there any relationship between those two?"

Ace seems to puzzle on how to answer this two-part question. "Let me answer your second question first. Yes, I did start reading your blog before I met you. Someone brought them to my attention, and I have to admit I didn't read them for a long time after that. Do you remember your blog about how and what food you prepare being a metaphor for how you live your life?"

"Of course. That was about a year ago." I respond without even thinking.

"That was the first one I read. I have to admit you made me stop to think about a lot of things I'd just stopped considering. That was the beginning of my self-examination. And I have you to thank for that."

"Well, you've thanked me, so why do we need to continue the conversation?" I don't want to sound rude, and I know I do, but I'm getting exasperated with him.

"Because I think I've just begun this voyage of self-exploration and you seem to be the key to opening me up to possibilities I've just not considered in a very long time."

"I'd suggest you just keep reading my blogs." I know I'm getting harsh, but I need to push him to get any answers. "After all, you called me out for hiding from myself and my readers."

"I did. And I hope you would let me be that mirror for you when you withdraw from your readers and go off on your voyages."

"You can text me."

"I'm going to have to have a conversation with O," Ace says more to himself than me.

This catches me off guard. "O? Why O?"

"To see if you make everyone you care about work this hard to get through your defenses."

I know he must think I'm a total nutcase because I start laughing, but I can't help it. He regards me with a look of total confusion. Since I'm looking down, he lowers his head to try to see my face. When I stop laughing, he seems to relax, although I can see he is very unhappy with me. "I'm sorry." I have to catch my breath for a moment before continuing. "She would agree with your observation, by the way."

Ace rises and looks down at me, I'm not sure what he's doing. Is he leaving me? Have I pushed him too far and he's now seeing me as not worth the work?

"I thought I'd walk you back to your apartment. Since you walked here, I would assume it's not too far to walk back."

I'm surprised he seems to be respecting my conditions of no dinner, drinks or coffee. I rise and nod in the direction we need to go. He steps closer and in one fluid motion our lips meet again. And just as before it is the most tender encounter I think I've ever had with someone else's lips. And just as before there is no push in or pull back. It's such a pleasant unique experience I want it to last forever. Ace gently touches my shoulders, they tingle. The next I realize I'm in his warm embrace.

LIFE

J:

Did you sleep with him?

Not even a how was your evening. Guess O thinks I have no will power. I decide if I ignore her question it will drive her crazy for the whole day. That ought to be fun to watch. The next text is not one I am expecting, although I probably should have been.

J:

Need you to do some research on X. Rumors are he's working on a special or something out of the ordinary. Very hush hush. No one seems to be willing to talk about it, but there are a lot of folks involved. We need to get a jump on it. Get out there first. You know what it means if you're not the lead dog, you're spending the rest of the trip staring at the other dog's asses. Don't mean to be crude so early in the morning after O tells me you've had a long night out. But this one simply can't get away from us. Might be the biggest story in your area this year.

Z

I have to admit I've not heard anything about this. Does it partially explain why X has been distant? Unwilling to engage with me? Maybe I was personalizing something that really didn't have anything to do with me. Maybe X is simply paddling as fast as he can to keep up with

194

his regular schedule of shows and fit in this special event. And now I'm conflicted since last night I was probably in some part of me reacting to the way X didn't seem to understand my feelings about our night together. And maybe that is part of the problem. I think of it as 'ours'. I've already crossed the line on that. The call made it clear he wasn't at that point at all. Just another night. Not even a particularly good night for him because he was preoccupied. Is this special program what he was preoccupied with? Highly likely given the timing of things. Probably was feeling guilty the whole time about taking time away from his project.

So how do I feel about that evening with this additional insight? What I should be feeling is happy, given all that is going on in his life, he was willing to come cook me dinner and share my bed for most of the night, if not all. That's what I should be feeling. But the more I think about it, and maybe this is influenced by the sudden reappearance of Ace, I probably was a distraction for him. Someone he regarded as ignorant about food and cuisine, but who was blogging about him and not in a constructive way. I was someone he needed to influence to not be quite so negative about his wilder inspirations. Turn an annoyance into a cheerleader, maybe?

If his stop by was professional and not personal I should be insulted he felt he needed to correct my perceptions of him. At the same time, I should be happy because he apparently thinks I'm influential enough to shape perceptions of his audience. My blog can drive eyes to his show. Isn't that what everything we do in this crazy business is all about? Eyeballs?

My phone rings, "Yes, O."

"So, you did sleep with him."

"I didn't say that, you did," is the first words to come out of my mouth, but probably because I'd already rehearsed them in my subconscious when I decided to ignore her text.

"So, how is he? As good as he looks?"

"Is Damien?"

Silence from O as she doesn't want to admit what I know already. "I don't know yet. I'm still working on that one."

"And neither do I because Ace's still working on me."

"Why? What's he up to?"

"It's not clear yet. Something about reinventing himself."

"Given what happened I can see where he might be doing some soul searching."

The warning bells are going off in my head. She's about to tell me something I probably don't want to know.

O gives me a moment to ask the question, but when I don't, she tells me anyway. "You know his wife committed suicide."

Suicide? Holy shit! I need to think about this. Ace alluded to his inability to save her, but he didn't say she died. "No, I didn't," comes out hoarsely.

"You need to read something other than sources for your blogs, girl."

I wonder how she knows so much about it. "Did you read about her death at the time or was this research on your part after Ace started showing up at our Friday soirees?"

"Hey. Somebody tall, dark and handsome starts hanging around with no clear objective I get kind of curious. I want to know if he's a pedophile, rapist, mass murder or just weird guy. You know there are a lot more in one or more of those categories than there are eligible bachelors in this world. Kind of scary when you think about the odds of ever finding someone who will hang around longer than a one or two night stand."

"Understandable," is my curt acknowledgment that she wasn't checking him out because he suddenly has shown interest in me, which she knows would not have been acceptable. "So, you've known about her suicide for a while."

"When did he start showing up? Couple of months ago? Yeah, that would have been about when I checked him out."

"But you didn't say anything when he took me out last time." I push on her.

"You said yourself it wasn't going anywhere and then he disappeared. Which reminds me, did he say why he disappeared? Where he went?"

"Home," is all I'll give her. Don't want this call to become a psychological examination of Ace.

"Family visit?" O probes.

I don't answer her question as I consider this insight about his wife's suicide. I guess it would be logical that when someone that close to you decides to end her life it would cause you to want to reexamine your own. Want to either do something different, or learn from whatever mistakes you made that may have contributed to the situation. Is his interest in me because I'm so different from his wife? From what little I know it would seem we are from different planets. She was the beautiful daughter of a rich real estate developer. No need for a career because she had Daddy's money to back her. When she married Ace, who also became successful in the family business, well she was set for life. But for whatever reason that wasn't enough for her. Most people would be willing to strike any bargain the devil wanted to be in that position. Would I? Need to validate the assumption I just made. Would I? My behavior towards Ace would say no. I wouldn't make any bargain to be in her position.

But then again if my preference is X, all based on one spectacular, at least for me, night, I'm hoping to make a bargain that isn't so different. X is well off in his media life. Clearly would be an upgrade from what I'm used to. Is X physically more attractive than Ace? That's really hard to tell because X is a personality. He's in the media. He's ruggedly recognizable, where Ace wouldn't stand out. People would think successful good-looking guy. But no one would walk up to Ace looking for an autograph or to talk about his real estate successes.

What is there about Ace that makes me so cautious, even more cautious than I am about making friends? He was right when he asked if I make everyone work so hard to get to know me. I'm not trusting of others. So, is the problem there's something about Ace, or is it really that there's something about me? And if it is me, do I need to back off? Let things happen naturally? Accept things at face value rather than have to validate everything? I wonder if O validates everything in her own life since validation is what she does for a living. She validated who Ace is.

"You back from wherever it was you went on me?" O brings me back.

"Yeah."

"So where was he now that you've had enough time to have visited there yourself if only in your mind?"

"Comparing."

"Uh oh." O lets me know she thinks whatever I'm thinking is a mistake. "You don't want to go there. Nothing good will come of it."

"Why? You don't even know who I'm comparing."

"Sometimes you make assumptions that are just dumb. You know that? I've known you for how many years now?"

"About three," I have to think back to that first meeting in Z's office, where she came bounding in and Z introduced her as the one person in the whole company who keeps everyone else out of jail and that I needed to be nice to her. At some point I will need her, Z predicted. He had no idea how right he was but for the wrong reason.

"And in three years how many guys have you talked about?"

I see the absurdity of my assumption. "Two."

"So, you don't want to go there. Neither one is in your class."

I laugh, "No. They're famous or rich and I'm just a blogger. Not even all that good a blogger if you listen to Z."

"No one listens to Z. He's just trying to keep you focused on your deliverables and making them controversial enough that people want to read them."

"You saying I'm a good blogger?" I test the waters since she raised the subject after telling me I'm likely to get fired if I stay on the political side of the cuisine experience.

"Good?" she apparently can't believe I'm asking the question. "You're the best in your domain. More people read you than anyone else. You make or break chefs with your reviews. Restaurants close if you're negative on them. And on the other side of that coin you help new restaurants get discovered. You have a little help on that with X leading you into some places you'd never find on your own. But that's part of what makes you successful. Your relationship with X. Now that's a professional relationship. Thinking it's anything more will just get you in trouble. He's never going to come in off the road, settle down and open a restaurant again. That's a tee shirt he already has. He's going to wander the globe, go to some of the most remote and in some instances disgusting places on earth just to make us consider something we would instantly dismiss as insane. Do you hear what I'm saying? X doesn't belong to you or any woman. He's a free spirit. Like the wind. Here today, gracing you with his delicate touch, stimulating your palate with his unusual talents and making you happy for one night by helping you experience something indescribable, according to you."

I'm almost afraid to ask, "And why is Ace wrong for me?"

"His wife didn't seem to thrive in that relationship," hits me full in the face almost knocking me over. I certainly didn't expect a summary judgment from her.

I don't hesitate in my response, not sure where the words are coming from because I'm not thinking them first, "Maybe he did everything he could to prevent what happened to her and it was her not him. That she was suicidal before they even married. Maybe he kept her from doing herself years ago. But just maybe whatever lead to her demise was bigger than his love for her, at least in her eyes. Did you think of that?"

"That his side of the story?" O pushes back, seeking validation as always.

"If it is, he hasn't shared it with me. We've not spoken of his wife other than in the past tense and without any detail. So, I don't know his side of the story. I probably don't have the right to ask him about it at this point."

"At this point." O hears what she is afraid of. "You're planning to see him again."

"Yes," I admit. "I haven't decided what I think about him. But I guess I've come to the conclusion it's worth the conversation even if it doesn't go anywhere."

"The backup plan if things don't work out with X." O tries to pin me down and expose for me what I'm doing even if I'm not thinking of them in this way.

"I don't have a plan, period." I disagree adamantly. "I'm just trying to get through the day. Figure out how to pay my bills, learn something I didn't know when the sun came up. You know. Just write my blog, have another conversation with you about what a fuck up I am in so many ways, and then I go to sleep wondering if I'll ever figure out life, what it means and what I want to be when I grow up."

"Why does your day sound so much like my day?" She's trying to get me to laugh, but I don't.

"Speaking of our day, did Z mention the rumors about X?"

"That he's developing some special or something?" O responds immediately. "No, we haven't talked about it but I've heard the rumor from a sound guy I know. Said he's got an open-ended ticket. Just doesn't know the departure date."

"And what's this ticket for?"

"Wouldn't tell me. Said he had to sign a non-disclosure on this one. Just said he was really looking forward to the trip."

"Think you can find out anything more specific? Like where the ticket is to? Might give us a clue."

"So, Z is expecting you to break this story." O guesses.

"And if I do, X will probably never sleep with me again," I realize as I say the words.

"That sucks." O sympathizes. "At least he may be helping make a decision about what it is that you really want. If X gets pissed and won't see you again, then you have to finally decide. Do you want to let Ace in or are you going to keep him out just like you do everyone else but me?"

"I don't have a choice." I plead.

"You always have a choice. The question is are you going to do what Z asked because you want the story and a side benefit is you keep your job, or are you going to let it go, so someone else will break the story so X won't be mad at you. Then in a happily ever after world, X marries you and helps you staff his bakery with your little ones."

"The story never ends that way." I point out.

"And neither does life, unless you make it end that way."

TWISTED ROOTS

I decide I need to go directly to X. No one else is going to give me enough to write the blog Z wants from me. This is a hedge. If X gives me the story, he won't be mad at me. If he doesn't, I'll have told him in advance I have parts of it and it may come out mangled, so has a chance to put it out there the way he wants it to come out.

> X:
>
> *Have confirmation from multiple sources you have a new project in the works. I'm working on the blog for tomorrow. Do you want to give me details and help me get it right or let the speculation drive what people think is coming?*
>
> J

Make it business-like. No emotion or asking for favors or any of that. Your project is out there. You only have until tomorrow to decide what you want the announcement to say. Just business.

> J:
>
> *What have you got on X's project?*
>
> Z

I'm not going to give him what he wants, but all I got is what I got.

Z:

Confirmation from multiple sources. Have gone to the horse's mouth.

J

This is only out there for a second when the response comes.

J:

Can't stop there. This has to be objective. No puff piece. No advocacy on your part. If he's changing directions and doing something totally radical I need you to call it. If It's a bad idea, say so. If it's brilliant, talk about the hard road he's going to have to walk to make it brilliant. Talk about elbow grease over inspiration. What's it going to take to make whatever it is work? Do you get the picture of what I'm expecting?

Z

I've not seen Z that direct before. Evidently, he's getting vibes that O didn't pick up from the sound guy who's going to be there, wherever there is. As I'm considering the task before me, I realize I need to acknowledge Z or he will be back in my face in another nanosecond.

J:

Can't stop there. This has to be objective. No puff piece. No advocacy on your part. If he's changing directions and doing something totally radical I need you to call it. If It's a bad idea, say so. If it's brilliant, talk about the hard road he's going to have to walk to make it brilliant. Talk about elbow grease over inspiration. What's it going to take to make whatever it is work? Do you get the picture of what I'm expecting?

Z

I at least have Z back in his box for a few minutes until he can't stand the thought that someone else may be first. I wouldn't be surprised he's drafting his own blog and will just post it on my site. Call it an editorial or something.

Now that I have the crisis of the moment under control, I let my mind wander again. What will X do with my text? Will he even get it anytime soon? He often goes places where he can't be reached and if he's in one of them now, like remote Cambodia or someplace near to Cambodia because he's not completely sure where he is, then I'll have to do the blog without his input. Can't help that. I really didn't have the twenty-four hours to give him, but maybe that was me walking the tight rope between getting fired and getting a raise since there are no promotions amongst bloggers. You're either one or you're not. No senior bloggers. No bloggers emeritus. Just us every day write me a 600-word piece and let the world know what you've learned or the questions you have about something.

I reflect on O's analysis of the situation. I've found in our short time together that she's right more often than I am about relationships. She can think about any two people for only a few seconds and be able to tell you whether there's a ghost of a chance of anything coming out of them getting together. And in fact, we've played a game once in a while, like every Friday, of the most unlikely pairs of people we both know. And invariably, when a pair do get together that we've previously seen as not working, invariably it doesn't. When a pair does get together, we instantly discuss whether he or she will initiate the breakup. Not a hard diagnosis since in ninety-five percent of the cases, the woman initiates the breakup. Either he's not good in bed, has bad manners, or is just too dull.

O has foreseen that I'm not going to get anywhere with X, so stop hoping for the impossible. Get on with my life and let him find his own destiny. From what I can tell, X has an active sex life, so he's not lacking for company when he goes to bed. And was that whole excuse he gave me about being preoccupied just his way of telling me that I wasn't that good so he wants me to think it was him so he can just walk away with no entanglements or regrets?

J:

Can we talk?

X

X doesn't wait for me to respond, the phone rings.

"You know I hate talking to you when I can't see you, be able to gage your reactions." X begins. "Make contact so you know what I'm saying is from the heart, just like with everything I do."

"Good morning." I respond as unemotionally as possible. X is waiting for me to ask the question, but I pretty much put it out there in the text, so I'm waiting for him to volunteer information.

"Are you mad at me?" X goes right to the emotional to see if he can rattle me.

"Not at all. Just doing my job, gathering facts before I wrap them in opinion to make them more digestible to my readers."

X considers my response and apparently tone of voice because his comes back more neutral as well. "What is it you think you know?"

"That you have people standing by to work on a special project everyone has had to sign a non-disclosure about. And no one has a return date. So open ended. Could be a day or could be a year. But everyone is really excited about the project."

"That's all you have?" X sounds relieved.

"No, but if I told you the rest, you'd probably be able to figure out who talked with me. I don't want them to get fired before you even get started."

"But that means you can't write about those parts because if you do, I'll figure things out." X reasons. "Do you really think I'm that cold? That I'd fire people for breach of non-disclosure? I wouldn't do that, but my business manager wouldn't hesitate a nanosecond." X lets that dichotomy come together in my mind. "I can't let you write about what I'm doing just yet. I can't even tell you why although if you do know what you represent you can probably guess why it's so important that things not get out."

What do I do with this? "Best I can do is write the column that you're in the preliminary stages of a whole new endeavor. Give some sketchy outlines without the specifics I have at the moment in case you were to greatly overhaul your idea and go in a different direction. But from what I do know, you're not likely to do that. If you change much it's not likely to succeed." Where are these words coming from? Recent conversations is about all I can think of. Sounds good even though I'm bullshitting a lot more than usual.

"You of all people know me. You must be able to see how important this will be for me. I have to do this, but I can't simply walk away from my current obligations and expect to still have a name in this industry. Just as you'd lose all credibility if you started writing about cars or home improvements."

"Those are definitely not me." I agree.

"I have to get back to my roots." X echoes a statement I've heard elsewhere in the last twenty-four hours.

"Seems to be a lot of that going around."

X has no idea what I'm talking about, "You're the reason. You and all the other bloggers who push all of us chefs to extremes. Something new and better. Help get each of us out of the ruts we inhabit. Move away from the tried and true for the novel, innovative and more stimulating taste combinations. Sheep dung? Do you really think that would make its way into a western restaurant? Even with my show on it, I don't see it on any menu anywhere I'm eating. So, what was the purpose of that? It was all about you wanting to write about how I'll go to any extreme to get a show people will talk about even if they won't eat what I show them."

"You're blaming me for your behavior?" I wasn't expecting to be the source of his inspiration.

"You and others, although you're my primary antagonist, if you want the truth. You push harder and criticize more than anyone else. But you do it in such a nice way that I can't get mad at you. And you couch it in cosmic references so I have to admit that on the larger scale of things what I think is momentous really may not be. My efforts at finding the novel and establishing a trend from it, no matter how short lived brings enjoyment to my audience and rewards to the restaurants I feature."

"If I'm the reason you're going off in this different direction, the least you can do is give me details so I don't have to imagine or speculate about it. That never works out well for the person I'm speculating about."

"If you have the detail you suggest, why would you speculate?" X circles around on me.

"To protect the innocent sources, I'll have to take it in a different direction, speculate in such a manner that there is room for interpretation. It could be this or that and one of the two or three possibilities will be right. Meanwhile those who are discussed in this way get upset about the fact you are supposedly discussing options with others, and those who you aren't in discussions with are upset because they're being mentioned but, know they won't be coming away with the prize."

"Are we even talking about the same thing?" X wonders aloud. I guess I've been too specific and missed the target somehow.

"Give me specifics and I'll tell you." I take the offensive to ensure he doesn't ask me to go first.

X considers my request and finally decides to give me something. "Yes, this is my last season for my current show. Two more episodes and it's in the can, so to speak."

"Speaking of the can, could you excuse me for just a minute while I visit…"

"Actually, I only have another minute to talk." X informs me. So, discomfort will have to go along with the rest of this discussion. I wonder if he's doing this to me deliberately to force a conclusion.

"Okay, so the last two shows." I frame the discussion. "Then your new project which will…"

"Take me back to my roots as I told you. And that's about all the time I have right now. As I said, I would prefer you not write anything just yet. I promise if you don't, I'll give you the whole story before I give it to anyone else."

"How many bloggers have you made that same promise to?" I accuse him thinking I'm getting played.

"You are the first today." I can hear him smiling. Not laughing at me, but close to it.

"I'm sorry," I respond hoping to put him off balance and give me at least one more piece of information.

"About what?"

"How I'm going to have to write this blog. It could have been the kind of announcement that people will be wanting to see act two. I'm going to have to write it such that people will probably wait for others to recommend it. Not the best outcome for you or your new project." I had to be so careful about how I phrased my challenge to him that I didn't preclude any possibility.

"Not so different from how my restaurant and show got started. Either the entertainment value will be there, or it won't. At the moment I don't honestly know which way it will go. But that's the truth about any new beginnings. Write what you will, and I'll let you know what I think."

"You could do that in person if you're coming through New York on either of your last two shows."

"As you know, I was just there."

"I'm painfully aware of that." I really didn't want to say that to him, but it just came out. I do want to see him, but he's reminding me what was ours never really was. It was mine and that was how he intended it. I just wasn't aware enough to realize it.

He is gone and now I have to write a blog that I know I'll just hate. No matter what I write it won't be accurate, complete or accomplish the objectives of anyone other than Z. But he owns my blog site and I really have no choice despite what O said.

TWISTED ROOTS

Ends lead to beginnings. Chef X is ending his long running series in favor of a return to his roots. Two more episodes and there will be a break while X establishes his new project. He will take the time to learn how to make it appealing to his audience and those he hopes will identify with something new that is really something old. And that's where the title comes from. X wants to intertwine the old with the new in such a way that you and I will become fascinated by the possibilities.

But what are those possibilities? Chef X won't say. In fact, he'd prefer that we don't talk about his new project at all. Give him more time to develop his concept, try out differing formats, approaches and research his content. But that's not what we are here to do. We are here to keep you informed of the latest events, happenings and trends in the culinary industry. While Chef X is not the kingpin of the industry, he is an important influence.

In a recent conversation Chef X pointed out that even though he recently filmed a program on the incorporation of sheep dung in certain foods for spiciness, he has still not encountered it in a western restaurant. He was trying to say that he is not able to dictate what people will eat, or what they will demand of restauranteurs. What he was pointing out indirectly is that we bloggers push chefs to try combinations that most would not consider because we need something to talk about that you as a devoted reader will consider to be novel or new. Something that will stimulate your palate in a new or different way. And that is our primary mission in life. However, since we bloggers are seldom chefs in our own right, we have a need to convince the popular and well-known chefs to reach for a higher standard.

Chef X seems to have grown weary of wandering the world in search of the perfect pinnacle of patience that many of the most spectacular sensual sensations will deliver. He is seeking a return to his roots as a means of challenging our thinking about the origins of gastronomy. Are we really getting bored with what we put into our mouths? What we mingle with assorted beverages to stimulate a new taste or reveal an aspect of something with which we are very familiar but haven't been aware of a particular flavor lurking in the background while hiding in plain sight?

And the bigger question is, will we be challenged, excited and engaged by the new format, the new look at what we see every day, take for granted while overlooking the opportunity to find the novel in the familiar? The very definition of innovation is taking something we see applied to solving a problem in one application and employ it with a modifying twist to solve an entirely different problem in a different domain. That would appear to be what Chef X is attempting with his new venture. There are indications he is setting his project in attractive surroundings. The crew that will accompany him is looking forward to the locale. While travel shows are popular for displaying the novel and traditional aspects of a foreign culture, a single locale for all shows would seem to be a risky approach to maintaining audience appeal. This is a major departure from what we have seen from Chef X to date and also from those who have developed similar programs for our entertainment and education. Stay tuned. Chef X is intending to deliver a twist to our expectations and thereby entertain.

There I have it. Six hundred words on Chef X's new venture without ever saying specifically what it is. Am I happy with this compromise? I need to reread it, but at least it will keep Z from jumping out the window of his office because we didn't break the story. I send it on to O for the fact check. I'm not sure how she's going to establish facts in this one since it is really mostly speculation and interpretation of conversations. I suddenly have the urge to send the draft on to X and get his reaction before Chi finishes the final edits. I don't have much time. I forward my email to O on to X and hold my breath. I shouldn't do that because I have no idea when X will get back or even if he will get back to me. Since he asked me not to write anything, he may just be angry enough to ignore it. If I don't hear from him so be it. I'll just let it go out in the normal course of releases and then see what reaction I get, if any.

J:

This all you got?

O

Guess she didn't think much of it. Particularly after she chased down the production assistant to get me a confirmation.

>O:
>
>*Send it on to Chi. I think Z has already broken the glass in his office window in preparation for the jump.*
>
>*J*

>J:
>
>*Already gone since there were no facts for me to check. Why is Z so wound up about this one? Got one more fact, but too late to insert now. You sort of hit at it on your ending anyway. It looks like Italy. My guy said something about crème Lemoncello.*
>
>*O*

SPECULATION

Of course, I would get a text from Ace in the middle of a conversation with Z.

"He's not going to give me anything more, of that I'm certain." I'm saying in response to Z's insistence that I have to have a follow-up blog ready tomorrow on X's new project. I only have one new fact and that's not enough, at least I don't think it's enough.

> J:
>
> *I need to explain something to you. Same park bench? Today at 4:00? I'll be nearby for a meeting and that would be a perfect time for me.*
>
> *Ace*

"You found at least one other source. You just need to work on your investigative skills. Dig up facts. Entice others to help you. Sell your soul if need be. Find a way to find out what he's doing." Z isn't happy with the blog but published it so he could be the first out there with the story. He wanted the whole thing laid out. What X is trying to do, where he's going to do it, what's novel or unique about his approach and then a cold-eyed assessment of whether it is likely to succeed and draw an audience? I kind of sort of got there with what I wrote, but it is all too loose for Z. Not enough facts, even though I specifically cited that I'd had at least one conversation with X recently, although I never said it was specifically about this project.

"Non-disclosures." I remind Z, because I'd already told him why the crew can't talk about it. "If anyone talks, they don't get to go and can be sued by X's lawyers for irreparable damages. You know I don't see how talking about what's coming does any damage, but I'm sure the lawyers have figured that all out."

"I'm with you on that." Z at least seems to be listening to me even though I'm more engaged at the moment about how to respond to Ace. "Should be a win win. This comes out people watch the last episodes because they're the last. Then they're waiting for the new format. There will be all this hype and discussion. No one will be able to avoid it. Like a presidential election. Everyone saying this and that. No facts. Just bullshit. But that's because everyone needs fifteen seconds. Everyone needs to get their say. That's why we had to be first. If we're not, we get drowned out by the fifteen seconders with no facts."

"But that's also why I wasn't concerned." I hesitate to see if Z is listening. If he is he will ask me about my statement. If he's not, he won't.

"How many words are in fifteen seconds?" Z asks.

"Hang on." I bring up my last blog and start the stopwatch on my phone as I read aloud the words. "About seventy-five." I inform him.

"Six hundred may be too many." Z seems to be considering something he's not sharing aloud. "See if you can come up with a seventy-five-word version of your next blog. I still want the six-hundred-word version which we will publish, but I'm going to see if I can syndicate the seventy-five-word version. See if we can drive folks who want more than the surface to our blog site. Might be a new way of boosting revenues. More eyes."

Great. Now I have to do two versions of everything I write and yet I'm sure there's no more money even though it's more work. If I even raise that question, I'll get the usual push back of 'you realize there are five thousand more just like you coming out of grad school every year. Won't take me a nanosecond to find your replacement amongst the hundred resumes hiding in my inbox.'

I let the silence grow on the call as I start to frame my response to Ace.

Ace:

Can make it work. Won't have much time as deep in a project for work.

J

"You don't think much of my seventy-five-word format." Z comes back.

"No, no. That's fine. You're the boss and all that. Will see what I can do on today's blog."

"Try it both ways. Write the seventy-five-word version first and then fill it out to reach the six-hundred-word version. Tomorrow write the long version first and try seeing what you can cut out to get to seventy-five. Let me know which way works better for you. You're the prototype in this case. What you learn is what I'll pass along to the other bloggers and see if they agree with you."

"And if they don't?" I have to call the bluff he's using. I know he'll get everyone else working in this format today. He's only saying I'll be the prototype because I'm the first he's launching it on. But no one will know what my preferred way is of doing things since he'll tell everyone to do what works best for them.

"I'll suggest they try your way again and if it doesn't work for them then I'll suggest they do whatever works best." Z sounds defensive, knowing I've seen through what he's doing. "Would rather everyone does it the same way, but it really doesn't make any difference unless one approach produces better blogs. Then I may have to insist that everyone does it the same."

>*J:*
>
>*Looking forward to seeing you again.*
>
>*Ace*

"You know, Z, we can continue this lovely discussion, or I can start looking for anything I can find that might be a new fact in X's project. Don't think I'm going to find anyone willing to talk to me, but as you said, until I get out there and start talking with folks, I'm not going to learn anything new. So, with your permission I'm going back to work."

"You don't see our conversations as contributing to your success?" Z tries to sound hurt, but I know he's not.

"Bye." And I look at the empty blog template:

AMALFI

Word has it that the new project to come from Chef X will be produced on the Amalfi coast of Italy. Sunshine, rocky coastal scenes, the Bay of Naples and Vesuvius looming in the distance, but too far away to have the devastating effects on this part of Italy that volcano wreaked upon Pompeii and Herculaneum near the beginnings of the modern era. Prepare for a treat for our visual senses and our palates.

Seventy-four words. What's wrong with it? Too much exposition about Vesuvius. Not enough about Chef X. But the good thing about this blog is it sets the scene. Not just in the modern era, but in history. Wasn't that one of the things X said to me? That I put what I write in cosmic context? Here I'm linking him with events that occurred in this part of the world two thousand years ago. A set of events that nearly everyone on the planet knows about. Is that a good thing? I'm not quite sure. But I need to get to the point a whole lot quicker if the seventy-five words are going to sell to other media outlets.

Okay. Now that I have seventy-five of my six hundred words, how do I make it fill in more information for the reader particularly since I only really have that one possible clue as to X's plans? I look up at the clock. Two pm. I have roughly an hour and a half to get the six-hundred-word version out before I go see Ace. That is if I walk. If I Uber it, I can get there in ten minutes. Just need to manage my time as O and Chi will want both versions today and so will Z.

AMALFI

Word has it that the new project to come from Chef X will be produced on the Amalfi coast of Italy. Sunshine, rocky coastal scenes, the Bay of Naples and Vesuvius looming in the distance, but too far away to have the devastating effects on this part of Italy that volcano wreaked upon Pompeii and Herculaneum near the beginnings of the modern era. Prepare for a treat for our visual senses and our palates.

The other clue we have in the continuing saga of Chef X's transition from wandering wayfarer in search of a winter's hot meal to wizard of the hidden habitats of taste is that he is seeking his roots. So, let's review where Chef X came from. He grew up in Cleveland, more interested in a future where he would be admitted to the Rock and Roll Hall of Fame than becoming an immortal in the world of cuisine. But the only way he could make enough money to support his dreams of becoming the drummer of Rock legends was by busing tables. As a curious lad, he soon found himself drawn to the kitchen, started asking the various characters he met about what they did that made their work distinctive. The Sous Chef at Ripley, an Aliens inspired restaurant near the Rock Hall of Fame gave him his first chance to make something memorable. That first Bordelaise sauce caught the attention of the head chef. Soon, he had not only replaced that Sous Chef, but found himself contributing twists and turns to the menu which led to the restaurant's highest period of popularity.

Is this where Chef X is going? Back to the basics of sauces? Since most of his early work was in French cuisine, that would not seem to square with Amalfi as the destination for his new project.

If we walk sauces to Italy, we are clearly talking red. Tomato based works of art that grace pastas of all shapes and sizes. Duram wheat and a little semolina. Mixed with a little water it is transformed into endless configurations. Add the sauce, generally augmented with pureed vegetables, fruit or a combination of both depending on whether one likes sweet or sour sauce. The result is a meal that not only satisfies, but warms the belly through the nights which in the Northern provinces can get cold. If it doesn't need to warm the belly, it at least fills the belly, so no one goes to sleep hungry regardless of their ability to pair the pasta with protein.

Italian food has been found to be universal. People the world over will eat Italian food even if they will not eat the local foods. What is there about Italian that Asians, Egyptians, Germans, Russians, and Bolivians will all eat it when the comfort foods from home aren't available to them? And maybe that is what we are seeing from Chef X. A recognition that Italy is our home from a cuisine perspective. That Italian is where we go for refuge in a storm, where we go when we are looking for something to warm us on a winter' night, or to have a conversation with family or friends, knowing they will be happy with the food irrespective of the nature of the conversation you're about to have.

So, by roots, are we seeing the classical experience Chef X wishes he had rather than the French sauce route he actually took to success? Getting a French sauce right and then being able to expand the envelope of acceptability is probably a more difficult life journey than rising through the Milanese rice fields to stardom. But Chef X may be on to something if he can show us what is right there in front of us every day, but we don't notice.

Okay. A little more than six hundred. But that's Chi's problem. I give him the words and he edits to get both the essential meanings in front of my readers, but within the six hundred word limitation. Thirty-seven words he needs to cut. Probably fifty by the time he figures out how to get to the optimal length. Only because he'll need to add a dozen key words here and there to make it all make sense. But then again, I've never been concerned about whether it all makes sense, knowing that O and Chi will fix that before it goes to Z for final release. They know what he wants better than I do because they have dialog with him almost every day. I get his anger about once a week. And it's never really anger. More dyspepsia. If he isn't in a constant state of heart burn, I don't know anyone who would be a better candidate. He has all those millions of dollars the new owners paid him to buy his business. He's got to deliver the revenues to support the money the new owners borrowed to buy the business. If he doesn't do that, he will be history and he knows that, O knows that, Chi knows that and most critically, I know that. Z has not kept the devil's bargain he struck a secret. But the overriding concern is not that he can't pay the bank loans from our revenues, but that they can't pay the bank loans and his huge salary each year. That's the real concern. Z could retire tomorrow and live comfortably on the money he got for the company. But that's not the choice he made. He wants to work. He wants to continue making that outsized salary. He wants to be the guy in charge, the one who cajoles and convinces the poor bloggers like me who provide the content he needs to derive revenues to give him something better or more timely than I did last week. I'm not at all concerned that Z will fire me. I've been almost a fixture at this company. I could easily take my blog elsewhere and get paid the same. Do they share information or something? Every time I've talked with someone else about moving the salary always seems to be the same as what I'm getting here. So, no incentive to go elsewhere. They must collude against the employees somehow. I just don't know how they do it legally.

I send the two blog formats to O. Her response tells me she's been talking to Z because she's not asking about the two formats.

> *J:*
>
> *Short form will need some more thought in the future. This one passes the smell test and is a good way of validating Z's concept. But somehow, I think you need to get to the subject quicker. Too much background about Vesuvius. Glad you put that reference in, but most of your readers could care about how long ago that was. This is shorthand. Seventy-five words. Punch, punch, punch and you're done. The long form asks some interesting questions. Z should love the dichotomy between the two.*
>
> *O*

That is absolutely about the most praise I've ever gotten from O, even though she is taking me to task that my first blog is weak for the format it inhabits. She must have been doing some research on that. Probably stimulated by a conversation with Z who was not too subtly telling her the same thing he said to me about 5,000 or so new grads who would love her job. Knowing Z, he probably said 10,000 fact checkers. No real skill. Just persistence to follow a question to the end of the line.

> *O:*
>
> *What am I supposed to do when I have no more facts? Everything is speculative. A few facts to hang a concept on and yet I'm still able to get over 600 words out. Not sure I've really enlightened the readers. I've raised some possibilities. Probably off by a country mile. But at least I'm taking a shot at what he might be doing given all we know about X. Your guy given you any more clues? I could sure use anything we can verify.*
>
> *Desperately, J*

O doesn't come back right away. I actually give up looking for anything. I re-read both blogs and decide I can't add anything. I've given my readers all I know at this point and probably more than I know. Speculation at best. I wonder how close I got. Time will tell.

YOUR SOUL

The park benches at Washington Square Park are all empty or have someone sitting there I don't recognize. No Ace. I find one near the arch and situate myself in the middle of the bench so if someone is passing by, they won't be tempted to try to sit down next to me. Not looking to be picked up by a weirdo. All too plausible in this part of the city.

I begin to review the stats on my blog. Readership is up by 28 percent. Evidently there are a lot of folks who don't read me regularly who are trying to find out what Chef X is up to. Probably the production folks from the other shows he competes with. Should have thought of that when I was writing the blogs. Who is the audience? I really didn't think about that at all. I thought about what did I know and what could I convey to people who are interested in what he's going to do next? I thought of them as the average Joe who is interested in what will be the next food trend. What restaurants are worthy of a visit? Which chefs are doing particularly interesting things? Things worthy of a special trip. And that's what it all comes down to isn't it? People wanting to know what is worthy of a special trip. Otherwise they would go back to the same place they always go. But if something is head and shoulders above the competition? That makes them worthy. If someone is trying something new that I might like? That's worthy of a visit. But if I were to go try every place available to me, I'd spend my whole life eating out and having a lot more awful or non-memorable meals than good ones. Few if any great meals I'll remember and come back for.

Z should be happy. More eyes. What else can I do for him this week? I'm sure he will tell me I have to come up with a way to keep that 28% increase coming back. I can do that by releasing more specifics about what X is doing. A drib here, a drab there. If I'd spelled the whole thing out the way Z wanted, I'd have never gotten the repeat visits. The eyeballs would have learned all they wanted to know and gone back to their usual sources. This way I've got their attention at least for a little while longer.

Deep into my stats, I'm not sure what causes me to look up, but I do. And of course, I see Ace coming across the square. Different suit, but same brown shoes. No tie. There's something different about his hair. More windblown today? Not as perfect as usual. His expression isn't as serene as usual either. Almost like he's trying to solve a math problem in his head and wishes he could write it down so he doesn't lose track of how he got to this point.

He hasn't seen me yet as he glances around to the benches as he gets closer. I set my phone aside in expectation of his arrival. Don't want to be trying to pull my attention away from something interesting when he does get here. Not that I haven't gotten to the most interesting parts yet, but I like to spend time with my numbers. I want to dive deeper. See what's going on behind them. What can I do to push them higher, if anything? Have I done something that has driven readers away? Generally, I've seen that eyeballs move based on the controversy. If there's no controversy, they tend to not come back. That tells me I have to raise a question each day that those who are interested will want to solve. If I don't do that, I lose some of those eyeballs. And I can't afford to do that, even though I often don't agree with the political position of those who have moved on. Probably why I don't reflect any political position in my blogs. Can't afford to antagonize or reward any one side. Got to find a neutral political stance. I can have those conversations one-on-one when the time is right, which isn't often since it seems that the media is on any designated person at any given designated moment. I don't want to piss off anyone. That's why I spend the extra time trying to fit between the pillars of belief without revealing a leaning in either direction. I need all those eyes and despite political leanings, my readers still need to eat and the better the food the better.

"Thank you for coming." Ace greets me when he finally gets close enough. I don't rise for the kiss he is apparently hoping I'll deliver. I see it in his expression. Hope denied. Been here way too many times.

Ace sits beside me, rubs my shoulders and back. Not sexual. Just a warm greeting and a means of establishing contact. Okay. "What do you need to explain?" I go right to the point of the meeting.

Ace looks uncomfortable. Finally looks away before returning his gaze to me. "I'm not a complicated guy. It may seem that way, but I'm really very straightforward. I'm not going to blow smoke at you to hide what I am. Anything you want to know? I'm an open book. Ask away. I want you to trust me. Without trust we won't go any further. I've come to realize that over the past few years. People won't give you the time of day if they don't trust you. I've apparently at least gotten to a presumption of trust with you or you'd not be here."

"I'm here because you said you needed to explain something to me. Trust hasn't been the defining characteristic yet. But if I don't get there soon? You're probably right. If you do anything to make me wonder about your character? And you have a lot to worry about given what you do for a living and the mysterious circumstances of your wife's death." I lay it right out there for him.

Ace nods. "That's what I thought. My wife is a wall between us, even though you haven't recognized it yet."

"I don't want to end up like her." I confirm. My response causes Ace to look inward. I've lost him for at least a while, so I give him space.

Ace thinks through my words, finally nods and looks at me once more. "Cindy."

"Cindy." I repeat. "And she..."

"Died very unexpectedly. Although the signs were there. None of us took them seriously. We... I... thought she was just looking for attention. Cindy had an identity crisis. She was trying to decide what her role should be. She had all she ever wanted. But she couldn't have children and that weighed upon her."

"She couldn't or you couldn't." I want to understand the situation.

Ace regards me coldly for a long moment, but it passes. He looks down and admits, "It was me. I'm the one who is sterile. If she'd made a different choice of husbands probably none of what happened would have."

"So being part of a family was important to her." I try to clarify.

Ace nods without looking at me. "She was an only child. So, the family flowed through her. No children, no family."

"You could have adopted." I offer.

Ace shakes his head. "Never would have worked. Anyone up for adoption probably isn't from the right kind of family. Doesn't have the right genes, the right heritage, the right sense of history, continuity and all that."

"Why does any of that matter?" I can't help but ask. However, the pain in Ace's face makes it clear he is the minority the family brought in, but only because their daughter loved him. They weren't about to get any further from the tree than Ace in looking to the future of the family. At that moment I understand he has been disappointing his wife's parents ever since it was established he was sterile.

I wonder if Cindy would have divorced him in order to have the children her parents were expecting. Was that a contributor to why she took the exit she did when she did? No way to please Mom and Dad and Ace. No way to position the family for the future as long as she stayed with the man she loved. What was she to do? Either way it would not end up with her and Ace together.

"Where do I fit into this whole sad set of circumstances?" I have to ask.

Ace looks away before answering. "You would have to agree to get pregnant. But I would not be the father since I can't be. You could either sleep with the sperm donor or go through artificial insemination." Ace puts it right out there. We're way past the introductory phase of this relationship. And it's no longer just a friendship. We're talking lineage now.

I shake my head, "Why me? There must be a lot of women from the right families who would be willing to have your kids even if you're not the father, just to be part of your family." I point out.

"Intellect." Ace responds. "The family needs heirs who are up to the rough and tumble of modern business. It's all changing faster than any of us can keep track of. But Cindy talked about you all the time. She read your blogs every day. Said you were the most insightful person she ever read."

Holy shit. I'm here because his dead wife read my blog? This is getting all too weird. "Who is the lucky farmer who gets to plant the seed representing the future of your dead wife's family?" I try to sensor my language, but it all just comes out. I wish I could get a handle on my impulsive responses. That's why I blog. I have an opportunity to edit before it goes out and I usually catch the ugly references.

"Her father." Not going to happen is my instant thought.

I shake my head. "This is all too…"

"Weird?" Ace asks. "I know it's a lot to take in all at one time. Particularly since we've just gotten to know each other. And it's only the beginning of our relationship."

"So, what's the plan? I'm a surrogate mother. The kid is borne smart because that's what I bring to the table, and then your mother and father-in-law come and take the baby away to raise it so it can be the next generation leading your real estate company? Is that what this is all about?"

Ace grimaces. "Not at all. You and I would get married. We would raise the child as if it were ours. That only makes sense as the child would be yours if not mine. It would be the next in line to take over the business when I get too old. It could be a great life. You wouldn't want for anything. You want to spend a month in Italy? Done. You want to sail around the world? Done. You want to become the CEO of the American Red Cross? That may take a little longer, but we could work towards that goal if that's what you want."

This whole opportunity just has me freaked out. His wife couldn't have kids, so she killed herself rather than disappoint her family and her husband, even though it was his fault. This doesn't ring true to me. Got to be more to it. But knowing how freaky the rich people become I can't rule it out completely. Family continuity? I understand that, although my family wasn't at all concerned about it since we had nothing of value to pass down other than a tradition as a family. I kinda walked away from the traditions when I moved to New York and decided to be on my own here. I talk with my parents, but I only go see them when there's some family event where I would embarrass them if I didn't come home. It's not that I'm not close to my parents and sister. But they have different lives. They stayed close to the family traditions even though they didn't mean much to me. Why is it that some people can only make sense of the world through the lens of family and others like me can't see the world through that lens?

Anyway, I'm a creature of the city, of crowds, of social media and loneliness. I'm not attached at the hip to a mass of humanity that can't seem to identify a singular direction forward in the world because each and every individual has a different perspective they have established for themselves. And by this I'm referring to a family. Sure, they want to see me at designated intervals which always seem to revolve around one or another holiday that is significant to them and the mass shoppers of the world. I'm only involved to the extent I am obligated to deliver a present to a small group of family members so they can affirm that I still remember they exist, and the token of holiday spirit is timed to address an existential crisis they are experiencing. Without whatever it is that I supply them on that particular occasion it is likely that they will not be able to continue on making a living and enjoying life to the fullest. If someone could provide me with a definition of fullest, I would be eternally grateful because I don't have a clue what that means. Enjoy life to the fullest. Are we talking about a state of eternal bliss that results from being perpetually stoned? I can help there. Just need to find a nearby dealer and that is never a problem. But if enjoying life to the fullest is supposed to be a reflection of a certain relationship one has with another. Well, if that's the case, then I would have to be considered a miserable failure. I've simply not been able to formulate a lasting relationship with a guy with a future. There are plenty of losers about who would willingly live off my meager income in exchange for occasional sexual relief. Or in some cases, frequent relief. Not because of anything I've said or implicated. But just because that is what certain individuals I've come across seem to believe is their sole purpose for being on this earth. And it has nothing to do with procreation. It's all about relief.

Is that what a relationship with Ace would become? Frequent sex, but only for the purposes of relief? Periodic insemination to add another heir to the family tree? Raising them as our own, even though after the first few years it will become evident that they don't look much like Ace. Couldn't if Grandpa is the real father. Going to look much more like their real mother if only she hadn't inconveniently ended the ordeal she was evidently living amongst these patrician property developers who are only concerned about the next generation's ability to preserve and protect the family fortune Grandpa and now Ace amassed.

"You've been quiet for a long time." Ace finally observes.

I nod, not sure yet what I want to say.

"I know it's a lot to take in all at once. You said you didn't have much time, so hopefully you can think of something else for a while and come back to consider the offer."

"You're making me an offer?"

"Of marriage, if you'll agree to this unusual approach to having a family."

"You hardly know me." I protest.

"Your blogs have revealed your soul to me and all your readers," Ace responds.

COINCIDENCES

It was a relief to get back to X's project and not have to think about Ace and insemination and all that comes with his too weird proposal. The more I think about it the one word I am looking for I never heard. Love. There is nothing in it other than a business transaction. I need a kid to take over the family business. Since I can't have one of my own, you'll marry me and raise it with me, but the real father will be my dead wife's father? I don't even have to think about how to say no to that proposal.

But somehow, I'm drawn to Ace as a person. Maybe that's why I was willing to keep on talking when he said he was looking for a friend. Why I was willing to keep on kissing him when he caressed my lips so tenderly. There is an attraction there, but this proposal just seems so beyond reason. Do I keep talking with him and hope he comes back to a more reasonable proposal or do I just forget I ever met him? And why is he willing to enter into this arrangement when it most certainly wasn't the one he had with his wife? Is he still on the rebound? Trying to get his feet beneath him after suddenly finding himself at sea? I've never been married or even cared for someone enough to get married so it's hard for me to imagine what he must be going through.

The more I try not to think about the situation, the more it invades my thoughts. I have to think his in-laws are the ones who came up with this whole idea of how to have an heir. It just doesn't make sense that Ace would on his own. It would seem to me that her parents were pressuring her to divorce Ace so she could remarry and have kids. But when she refused and took her own life, they were left to look for plan B. And this sounds like something someone who is not in the relationship would come up with. Not Ace, not his now dead wife. If that's the case, then maybe I ought to keep talking with him. Probe this more. Do the investigative journalism Z told me I need to do.

J:

Thanks for treating my mid-life crisis with dignity, even if you're not completely right.

X

Good to know I've not pissed X off with my blogs. I just wish he would give me a little more to work with. And the way he put it makes me feel good that I have more right than not.

X:

I'd still like to see you, in person if you're coming this way.

J

I've hardly sent the text when there is a strangely familiar knock on my door. I leap up in expectation, fling the door open without even checking to see who it is, which I always do since so few people I know have any idea where I live.

Ace is standing in the doorway holding bags of groceries. "Thought you might like to eat in tonight."

"I didn't know you cook." I stammer surprised and disappointed at the same time.

"The more you get to know me the more I hope to pleasantly

surprise you." I take a bag of groceries from him and follow him into my tiny kitchen. All the while I'm thinking the only other person who has cooked for me is probably half way around the world tonight and given a choice between the two, I'd rather have the other guy.

I don't respond to his statement, but set the bag of groceries down, pulling out cans and vegetables and a very nice bottle of red wine. "What made you think I might be ready for this? It's way past coffee, drinks or dinner out which I ruled out."

"Just a hunch that if I don't follow up after my proposal that I'll lose you entirely."

"Probably a good hunch," I confirm his worst fears. I catch the slight nod to himself.

Ace busies himself unloading the sacks, "Do you have a big pan? Something I can cook seafood in?"

I go to the cabinet where I keep the one pot that X used when he cooked for me. The big pot is still there, in the same place where X put it after he washed and dried it for me. Said he was a full-service chef. That was just before he slept with me.

Ace seems to know what he's doing. Finds my big knife and starts prepping the onions and garlic, heats a little olive oil in the pot. "Would you clean the shrimp? They're not frozen so all you need to do is remove the tail and wash them."

I nod, still observing his skills at prepping the food. He's much better with the knife than I would be. Must have had a lot more practice and yet I know nothing about him that would suggest this skill. "Did you work in a restaurant at some point?" I inquire as I pull the tails from the shrimp.

"High school. Started out busing tables and ended up in the kitchen by the end of my first summer. Worked there all four years until I went off to college. When I got to college, I ended up working my way through my undergraduate program as a prep chef in the college dining hall."

"So, do you like to cook, or is this something you had hoped you were past?"

"I enjoy a leisurely dinner once in a while. Would I want to cook every night either for myself or for others? Not anymore. But a special occasion like tonight… it's fun. I'll need some help as we go. Hope you don't mind."

"As you said. Once in a while."

"From reading your blogs you seem to like the simplest meals, with a twist. A spice or oil or different kind of accompaniment. Am I right?"

"Generally," I agree. "Simpler leaves the most room for improvisation. If a dish is real complex or layered in flavors it's real hard to deviate much. But to fundamentally change the flavor of a scampi or lobster tail? That's more of a challenge." I admit.

Ace smiles. "I hope you'll enjoy the shrimp tonight then. Just simple, straight forward with one addition. I look forward to your reaction."

He puts a second pot on the cooktop full of water to boil the grains he intends to serve with the shrimp. "Bulgur wheat?" I guess.

Again, Ace smiles, this time at my guess. I notice the tension I felt when he first arrived has lessened, but I'm still cautious of him. In only a moment the water is boiling, in goes the wheat with a little olive oil. He covers the now simmering wheat and drops the prepped garlic and onions into the hot oil in the big pot.

"Won't the shrimp cook much faster than the wheat?" I ask thinking that the wheat will take at least twenty minutes and the shrimp probably no more than five.

"Yes, but we want the shrimp to cool a bit before we eat them. That's part of the magic of this dish." Ace stirs the garlic and onions to keep them from burning, even though they are on relatively low heat. "Would you open the wine? I like to cook with wine and sometimes I even add it to what I'm cooking."

I find the corkscrew and wrestle with the foil, turning it around and around until it starts moving up the neck of the bottle. Ace looks at me like that's a strange way to open wine, but he says nothing. Soon I have the foil off and turn the screw into the cork, lever up and in a moment the cork is out of the bottle. I look for glasses, having no wine glasses, but Ace doesn't seem to mind.

"To beginnings." Ace proposes as a toast. I'm not sure I agree with his toast but clink the glass anyway. The bouquet is wonderful. "What is this?" I have to ask, going back to the label.

"Biondi Santi. Italian Brunello. Great with shrimp, particularly the way I'm fixing it tonight. Although I have to admit Italians would be aghast of what I've done with simple sea food."

That doesn't sound good, but now I'm thinking again of X and his apparent Amalfi adventure. Why do things keep intertwining between these two? It has to be sheer coincidence. But still I keep being reminded of something about the other from what one does or says. And the fact that Ace is now here cooking for me. Did they talk somewhere along the way? Did X tell Ace that cooking for me is one way to get me into bed? They know each other, but I don't think they have talked in years. Not since his dinner party where he convinced his partners to help him buy his apartment building. If he likes to cook, why didn't Ace cook that night? Was it too informal for what he wanted to achieve that night? Probably. But that's what I would do if I was a good cook and wanted to impress my guests. But then again, I'm sure that meal was spectacular since that was when X was on his way up. Before he had his own restaurant.

"Have you been to the vineyards?"

"For Biondi Santi?" Ace confirms my question. "Yes. In Montalcino and the Maremma. Did you know the best wines come from Montalcino, but they are nearly unaffordable for the average Italian, so Jacopo, who is the current owner left home when he was young and set up his own vineyards in the Maremma. He produced Brunello based wines, but they were affordable. His father didn't speak to him for years until just before his death. And then it was probably only because Jacopo was going to inherit the main vineyards and would now be responsible for producing the top of the line Brunello, he had walked away from when he was younger. From what I've been able to tell, Jacopo hasn't missed a beat. The wine is every bit as good as his father's vintages."

"Didn't know you knew so much about wine." I query him unsure of what he's trying to do. Impress me he's done research in something I might know, but could easily verify.

"Got the whole story from Tancredi, Jacopo's son who gave me the tour at the main Montalcino winery, Greppo I think is the name of it. Interesting place. Was actually the first winery to produce the Brunello varietal."

"You've travelled a lot, I take it." I guess. "Was any of it for work, or just because you could?"

"It's all been because I could, although I have mixed some business with the pleasure. In fact, that's usually the way we used to travel. I'd have an opportunity to meet someone who might become a business investor and we'd go meet them wherever they live."

"You and Cindy." I clarify.

"Sometimes her parents would come too, depending on who we were meeting with."

"I take it you're close to her parents." I think I'm stating the obvious, but I could be wrong and if I am that might deflate my theory about who is behind the strange proposal.

"They're more than in-laws. We're business partners on the biggest projects in the family portfolio. We each have some real estate outside our common holdings, but the major investments are all joint."

"Will that change now that Cindy is gone?" I have to ask.

Ace dumps the shrimp into the pot with the aromatic garlic and onions. "I offered to let them buy me out, but they said no. I will remain at the company and part of the family for as long as I chose to be. For now, I'm not changing anything in respect to the family, but they always have the option to buy me out if I displease them."

"Will I displease them?" Get right to it. I'm not getting answers that are reassuring so far so might as well put it right on the table.

Ace looks at me curiously. Stirs the shrimp, glances at the wheat and then takes another sip of wine before answering. "I haven't given that any thought."

"Replacing their daughter with an Asian blogger might be more than they're willing to accept."

"Why would you think they would have any say over who I marry now?"

"If her father is going to be the father of their grandchild. I mean that gets personal in a hurry."

Ace smiles and takes another sip of the wine. "He's not... going to be the father of the child. I was testing you. See how interested you were in me as a person, with me given the situation I find myself in."

"Testing me." I respond incredulously.

"I have to be careful. A lot of people would love to get their hands on my money but would divorce me as soon as the ink was dry on the marriage license. So, I have to find some means of knowing someone's heart."

"You think you know mine?" I'm still thinking there's something going on behind the scenes here he's not telling me. Either that or he's just having fun at my expense, trying to freak me out and see how long it takes to drive me away. But why would he do that? I don't get it.

"Actually, I think I do." Ace surprises me once again. "It comes through in your writing. You're concerned about the lives of the peoples in the strange and faraway places where your chefs visit. One of your recent blogs went a little overboard on the political front about life in Cambodia. If you didn't have a generous heart, one that cares for people, your column would have read very differently."

"Yeah. A bunch of people didn't care much for that column."

"Really?" Ace seems surprised, but I notice that same tiny nod to himself as if he's taking notes like I do for something I will be writing about in the future. "Didn't see anything that someone should consider objectionable. Was Z the one who didn't like it? Afraid some readers would move on because it wasn't vanilla?"

"Z was one of many," is all I'll confirm.

"Shrimp are ready." Ace removes the pot from the heat. He reaches into one bag and removes a container of feta cheese. He uses a knife to open the lid and dries a wedge of the cheese before crumbling it on the shrimp. "The heat of the shrimp, garlic and onions will soften the feta." He removes the top from the bulgur wheat, stirs the contents and then plates the wheat first gingerly placing the shrimp atop the small mound of wheat. He carries the plates over to my work table. I have to move my computer to make room for the dishes, but then scurry around to find silver and napkins, paper of course since I don't have any cloth ones in the apartment.

Ace comes behind me and helps me be seated before taking his own seat. "To fish and cheese, something Italians would never eat, but it's a great pairing."

I take a sample of the shrimp and wheat and find the salty cheese adds a dimension to the shrimp I'd never experienced before. The Brunello washes away the saltiness and brings out the sweetness of the shrimp. "This is excellent. Did you make up this recipe or did you borrow it from someone?"

"I've never had it in a restaurant, but I'm sure I'm not the only one who has come up with this combination of flavors. It's one of my favorites, though."

"You can make it for me again." I offer as a way to let him know I'm willing to see him again, but not to agree to anything more than that. There's something about the weird proposal that's still sticking in the back of my mind. He has to know it's too soon for me to move on from that. So, what's his end game tonight? Get me in bed so I'll see he's a tender lover and that will cause me to accept him? Not likely. He's not worked the meal prep the same way X did. Didn't get me involved in anything other than taking the shrimp tails off and pouring wine. X had our hands into bread dough together, touching each other and breaking down the barriers we put up. Opening up our senses so when we made love, we were open to anything that involved his body touching mine. I'm certainly not open in the same way tonight. This is a different game he's playing, but I'm at least willing to play along for a while now that Cindy's father isn't in my future bed.

Ace looks across the table, looks into my eyes as if he's trying to read my thoughts, which I know he can't do. Just the same, it's a bit unnerving. "Penny for your thoughts."

So, he can't read me and is even willing to pay for them. "I was just thinking I don't know where you're trying to go with our potential relationship. One minute I'm going to be a surrogate mother and the next you seem to be more interested in getting me into bed, but if you're sterile I'm not sure how that all works."

That same small nod, as if he's trying to remember all the defenses I'm using. Is this so he has a rehearsed response the next time, with someone else? "Cindy and I had a healthy sex life. I haven't been with anyone since, but I can still have an orgasm. It's just as if I'd had a vasectomy because there are no live sperm in the ejaculation."

Cold, clinical. As if he were the doctor describing his condition. "Nevertheless, we won't be checking out your apparatus tonight, if that's what you're hoping for."

"Not at all." Ace professes innocence. "Wasn't where I was going. After all, you brought it up. I was just hoping to clarify my earlier proposal and convince you to see me again. Making love will come when we both feel it's right. And not before."

FIGURE OUT

Maybe I was offended by his presumption that we would make love. I don't know. Whatever it was, I got up and asked him to leave my apartment and locked the door behind him. It seems we always part this way. I'm upset with him for one thing or another. Is he that insensitive or am I that hyper sensitive? I don't know but I'm not happy about the situation and I hope he isn't either. But then again, maybe he'll just give up on me and leave me to X.

I wouldn't be unhappy about that outcome.

And then I get the text I was expecting earlier when Ace showed up at my door.

J:

Ever heard of Senegal? Me neither but here I am. Chasing down the ultimate Akkra. Never heard of Akkra? Me neither until one of my writers suggested it. Said he'd had it in New York. Have you? Some kind of black-eyed pea fritter. Who on earth eats black eyed peas besides our friends from the south? And none of them born after 1980 I might add. So anyway, I suggest we pass on the Akkra, book a ticket to Azerbaijan only to find the local host's mother died and I'm without a local sponsor. So here I am in Senegal. Doing Mission Impossible where I'm supposed to explain why Akkra is a must have for all the elite diners in New York. By the way, thought your blog was balanced even if vague. But I'll take that.

X

I think about his blog for all of a second before responding.

X:

*Senegal? I mean could you find any place further from New York?
I miss your touch and the wonderful dishes you prepared for me.
There has to be a way we can share time together again. I know
your travel schedule doesn't favor it, but would you route yourself
this way before you head off to Amalfi and your new project? I
promise to make it worth your while.*

J

Not exactly what I wanted to say, but I'm afraid if I'm any more
vague he won't get the message. Why is it the smartest people tend to
be the least aware? I mean I could probably send him a picture with my
genitals circled and he still wouldn't understand what I'm suggesting.
This way maybe he'll think there's a possibility I'll write a really great
blog on his new venture. At least that might convince him to come this
way.

J:

*Already on this side of the world. Other than to see you no reason
to come back that way. Nonetheless, let me see what I can do about
pushing back the start date on my new adventure a week. That
would give me the time we need. And I truly sense that 'we' need
the time. I'm hopeful you can help me sort out what's going on in
my head. At the moment I'm confused about why I'm taking on
this new venture. Hoping to prove something to myself, but not
sure if that makes any sense. And worse yet, not sure it's
commercial if you know what I mean. Maybe you could help me
sort all that out.*

X

My heart leaps as he apparently thinks I can help him understand the opportunity and the downsides to it he is about to begin. Maybe I can help him avoid a disaster, or help him understand that his instincts and research were on target.

X:

You know where to find me. Waiting for you.

J

Probably more than I should have said, but too late now. Don't want to sound like he's all I have going on in my life, don't want to sound needy or dependent upon him in any way. Just want him to know I'm here for him if he needs me in whatever capacity. Not a good admission from a blogger who is supposed to be independent and objective about my subject matter. But I'm not and I readily admit it to myself. Now if Z were to ask that same question, he would get a different answer, although he would probably prefer that I have a closer relationship with X as it would ensure we get the full scoop.

Now that I've committed myself, I instantly regret that I have no more asking power with him. Can't inquire about his project further until or if he shows up here. Can't ask for anything from him period. I have to wait and see where things take themselves and hope he comes through New York. At that point I'll be able to get the answers I need for the next blog. But what this all means is my next one can't be about X or his project. Have to go find something else to discuss for the next few days. I'm not sure what that will be. I've frankly run out of ideas. But I'll have to think about it for a while and maybe something will come to me.

A text comes in I'm not expecting.

J:

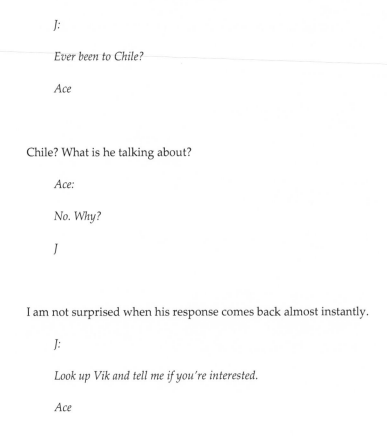

Ever been to Chile?

Ace

Chile? What is he talking about?

Ace:

No. Why?

J

I am not surprised when his response comes back almost instantly.

J:

Look up Vik and tell me if you're interested.

Ace

Vik? I have never heard of it. I pull up the website and find it is not just a wine, although a very good one, but a hotel and winery that is difficult to compare, since it's a twelve-thousand-acre estate. The hotel looks quite interesting. Each room decorated by a different artist. The winery underground with a stream running over the barrel room to maintain the desired temperature. Interesting. Could be a good story, but what is Ace asking? I have to assume he wants to know if I want to go there with him. Do I with all that he's pulled on me so far? I'm sure I won't get back without sleeping with him at least once, and more likely every night we're there. Am I willing to do that for a story until X comes back to New York? Am I really that easily bought?

And again, the response comes in barely a nanosecond, as if he were anticipating my question.

> *Ace:*
>
> *What are you proposing?*
>
> *J*

> *J:*
>
> *A weekend, a week. You tell me.*
>
> *Ace*

Now I'm faced with a decision. Clearly, I should just say no and get on with life. But here is a story that could be a good diversification for my blogs. Would he be willing to play it hands off?

> *Ace:*
>
> *What are your expectations? This can't be a quid pro quo.*
>
> *J*

This time his response takes a little longer. Guess he didn't expect me to phrase it quite that way.

> *J:*
>
> *No expectations. Just time to get to know each other. You want to cut it short my plane will take you home immediately.*
>
> *Ace*

As long as those are the ground rules this would solve a problem for me. Material for my blog and maybe more answers about Ace while I'm waiting to see if there is going to be any opportunities with X. I have to assume there will not be, although he at least opened the door that a visit with me could be beneficial to him. I have to take that as a hopeful sign, but I can't start expecting anything more than he's not coming back to New York. As soon as he raises that to his producers, I'm sure they will kill the idea and he'll be in Amalfi. If I want to see him, I'll have to go there. But is that such a bad idea? Maybe a week in Amalfi would be good for my blog because I'll at least be able to take some pictures. That would add more depth to my blogs and possibly bring more interest. Probably should do the same at Vik. Who is Vik anyway?

I google him and find out he's a billionaire. Not only is he a billionaire, but Forbes describes him as a fascinating character. Maybe I ought to look into the whole angle of why would a billionaire decide to create a high-quality wine in the wilds of Chile and open a hotel that only a small number of wealthy people would ever be able to visit?

Maybe there is more to this opportunity than it appears on the surface. And how did Ace know about it in the first place? Did he ever visit there with Cindy or her family? Is this one of those places that the rich go to because they know the other folks who come there have to be in the same social standing? If they weren't, they'd never be able to pay the daily rate? Maybe I'll meet some fascinating people while we're there. People who could be influential in driving eyeballs to my site. That would make Z happy.

Ace:

When?

J

Again, the response must have been thought out before he sent the text.

> J:
>
> *Meet me at LaGuardia at 5:00 pm*
>
> *Ace*

Tomorrow. I should have known he wouldn't give me time to think about it and possibly back out. But tomorrow? I'm sure it's only because there aren't earlier flights down to where would that be? Santiago? Probably the closest airport.

> *Ace:*
>
> *You going whether I come or not?*
>
> *J*

Again, an almost instant response.

> J:
>
> *Nope. So, don't make me pay for a reservation I'm not going to enjoy.*
>
> *Ace*

I have to play with him at least a little.

> *Ace:*
>
> *Why do you think this will be more enjoyable than our previous*

times together?

J

J:

Because I have you for ten hours on the flight down and ten hours on the return to make sure you know and understand me. Once you understand why you're so important to me I think everything will change.

Ace

Now what the hell does that mean? Understand he needs an heir and that he thinks it's all right for his father-in-law to fuck me to have a kid he will raise? I know he said that was just a test, but the way he said it originally, there has to be something to it. Maybe not exactly as he put it to me, but I've got to think life with him will not be all sunshine and roses.

Ace:

You can't tell me now why I'm so important to you?

J

And again, his answer must be thought out ahead of this conversation.

J:

We need something to talk about tomorrow or it will get to be a very long flight.

Ace

Smartass. Why does he always do that? Lure me back and then
send me away thinking I never want to see him again. And then he's
back with something that meets a need I have. Meets an emotional
need, I realize, although I doubt I could have verbalized it until just
now. X awoke something in me. A need for intimacy. X is flirting with
whether he will give it to me, but I have to assume that at the end of the
day he will not. Ace seems to be saying it's something that could result
from us spending time together. But there's no compulsion or even
assurances of anything. It's as if he's playing my emotions knowing that
I'll eventually give in to him because my needs will drive me to him. Is
that true? Is that what I've been reduced to? Someone who is that
predictable? Does that mean I'm just like a million other women?
Dependent upon some man who is certainly less than ideal to rescue me
from a life of singular loneliness?

Ace:

*That better not be the only thing we talk about or it will be a very
long flight.*

J

Now my question is whether he will answer that observation and
tacit agreement to come, or will he just assume he has me where he
wants me and just show up at the airport? I don't even know what
airline. Although if I go on line, I can probably figure it out.

J:

*Terminal B, gate C-14. 5:00 pm departure. You need to be there at
least an hour early and remember to bring your passport. You do
have one, don't you?*

Ace

Now he's just trying to piss me off.

Ace

Yes, do you?

J

Chile. I've never been to South America. I need to do some research so I know what I'm getting into. What is the language issues down there? Spanish everywhere except one country as I remember. Which one? Is it Chile that speaks something else? I could hope for English but somehow, I don't think that's how it works. Nobody down there speaks English as a native language, I think.

X was in Bolivia. Cooked something strange. What was it? Am I going to spend this whole trip thinking about X when I need to figure out what I'm doing with Ace?

ARRIVAL

Chee-lay. That's how Mauricio, who is our guide and driver pronounces the name of his home country. Chee-lay. Everyone I heard always just called it Chile like the peppers, although that's spelled differently. Mauricio is giving us the usual tour guide explanation of why Chee-lay is such a great country to live in. Mauricio clearly knows a lot about his country and is telling us things that are interesting. However, I'm sure I'll have forgotten much of what I've learned by the time I get back to New York.

The flight was awkward, to say the least. He wanted to kiss me when I met him at the airport, but I ducked the kiss. I want him to work for my affections and not just assume, even though I am going to be sharing a bed with him I'm sure. We really didn't talk much while we waited, although Ace told me a little more about the Vik Winery and what I can expect when we get there. I probably hurt his feelings when I asked him if he would summarize his comments and send them to me in an email so I could reference them for my blog. In response he wanted to know if my blog was going to mention who I am going with. I assured him of anonymity, but that I would be discussing the fact that I'm going to be here with someone, just not who.

The drive down from Santiago is a little over two hours. I probably should be taking notes of what Mauricio is saying, but I've already detected a pattern in that he repeats some things. I can hope he continues to do that, and I can pick up the relevant notes on the way back to Santiago. I can't believe I'm already thinking about leaving and we haven't even gotten to the place yet.

"Would you like to ride while we are here?" Ace asks. "I'll need to let them know which day and whether you want a morning or afternoon session. Do you have a preference of mounts?"

"Mounts?" I'm lost, ride what?

"As I remember, and Mauricio, you may want to chime in here, they have a variety of horses. Everything from pintos to mustangs. Do you want a docile horse or something that's going to be spirited and want to go?"

"I've never been on a horse before," I confess. "Need a beginner's horse, whatever that might be." I know that sounds pretty boring, so I ask, "I take it you ride a lot?"

"Actually, I've never been on a horse either, so this will be an opportunity for us to both experience something new together."

I'm not sure about what Ace is telling me is the truth. I assume he's been here before. Been a lot of places like the hotel we are staying at. Riding horses must be a common offering of such places. Why didn't he ever ride?

"If I've never ridden before you're probably wondering why I would want to do it now." Ace almost seems to be reading my mind. "Cindy was thrown by a horse when she was in her early teens. She never got on a horse again. Since I'd never ridden before I knew her, it just never became a part of any of our travels."

"People adjust to the people they are with." I observe. "Do things because the other person likes it or not do things they don't."

Ace stares out the window, reflecting on something he elects not to share. The silence grows and Mauricio decides to add some color commentary.

"Vik is an especial place in Chee-lay. The winery and grounds encompass most of the Millahue Valley. Millahue in Spanish means golden place. This valley has always been very fertile and is a great growing location. Before Vik many different orchards and gardens produced much of fruit and vegetables for this part of Chee-lay. When the property was sold the new owners went about planting grapes in the most suitable microclimates for that particular variety. You will see maps when you visit the winery."

"If you were staying at Vik for the first time, what would you say is the most important thing to do while you're there?" I ask since Mauricio has joined the conversation.

"Oh, there are so many things about Vik. It has spectacular views of the lake and vine covered hillsides. And the rooms. I enjoy just visiting the other rooms. Each one has totally different art styles. Each has a different view of the grounds. And they do wonderful food and wine pairings. The wine is always Vik wine, but they now have three different blends and you'll get to sample all three with your meals."

I look out on the countryside, and in the distance I see what appears to be a huge metal object sitting on the top of a hill. I point to it and ask, "What's that Mauricio?"

"That's Vik, or I should say the hotel at Vik. That's where you are going to be staying for the next few days"

I watch the object grow in size and definition as we get closer. "Almost looks like a flying saucer that landed on the hilltop." I say to no one in particular.

"The owners like modern art." Ace responds. "Flows into the architecture of the place."

Now I have to ask, "How many times have you been here?"

"First time to stay. I was here for lunch a few years ago. I told Mauricio then that I wanted to come back and stay here someday. Well, it's someday."

Interesting. He didn't return with his wife, but decided to bring me here instead. I wonder how what he's doing with me might be a reaction to the things he either did with his wife and therefore won't do with me, or are things he always wanted to do but somehow never convinced his wife to do. I've read about rebound relationships. Where someone loses someone important to them and they form a relationship with someone who is a transition person. They think this relationship will work, want this relationship to work, but because they rush into it there is no chance. Is that what I am? A rebound relationship for Ace. Someone so different from his wife that he hopes he can get over her sooner. If that's what this is, I should probably just enjoy the weekend here and chalk it up to a great experience but with no expectations that anything more will come of it. If that's the case, I should relax and put this whole trip into context.

"You've been quiet." Ace notes. "What are you thinking? Are you sorry you came?"

I shake my head in response, "Just thinking about the hotel. Now that I can see it sitting up there overlooking the valley, I'm starting to appreciate what you've been saying about the views."

"The views will be so much better for me when you're in frame of each one." Ace responds without thinking about how that would sound. I know what he's saying, but why did he put it that way? Almost like he's thinking of the picture more than the experience itself. Thinking of the memories he will have of our time together more than being here and just taking it all in. Is he fixated on memories because that's all he has of his wife now? The more I think about how Ace acts it seems he is almost totally consumed with memories and regret. The life he expected was cut short in a very abrupt way. No time to prepare for it. Difficulty in adjusting to a solo life when all he thought about was a duality. Accommodating someone else's desires, needs, wants and thoughts. Doing things that have meaning for two, because in many cases they are the result of compromises or building upon a concept of the other. I've never experienced that kind of life. I've always been alone in so many ways. And to see Ace alone after having that duality relationship is sad. But how do I help him make an adjustment? Help him find a new path for himself that may or may not include me? Maybe that's my role. A Sherpa if you will. A guide who carries the worst part of the burden to help the other get to the pinnacle of their goals.

"You didn't like that thought," Ace finally tries to engage me again since I'd drifted off into the questions this whole trip raise for me.

"Not the thought, but just the way you put it." I finally admit. "What do you think will happen here? Are you looking for a new experience or are you looking for more memories?"

Ace jerks his head as if he'd been slapped. "I don't need any more memories," comes across like he's carrying a weight and he has no idea how to unburden himself from it.

"Does that mean I'm someone you can forget as quickly as you met me?" I accuse him now.

"This hasn't been a quick process for me." Ace responds immediately. "I have known of you for years. You were a part of an almost daily conversation for a while. And you forget I've been reading your thoughts for a long time now. You are not someone I met in a bar and will not be calling again after one night together. I hope you can see I'm much more serious about a relationship with you than that kind."

"I guess we'll see about that this weekend, won't we?"

"We will." Ace responds in an almost curious tone. "Maybe I can convert you from a skeptic to a believer. Maybe I won't be able to. But when this time together is over, I know our relationship will be different. And at the very least your blogs will be different. I'll be interested in seeing how you capture this place in words for the rest of the world to comprehend."

I spend the rest of the short drive watching the golden building on the top of the hill get closer and closer, bigger and bigger and the definition of the place grows. Mauricio winds through the vineyards and up the steep drive to the entrance, pulling up in the circle where we are greeted by two young men who carry up our bags, and the hotel guide. The guide, Flavio, is responsible for our stay, not like a hotel manager, but as a personal assistant who will see that everything is arranged, and any new accommodations made.

"Did you want to do the horseback ride?" Ace asks me once Flavio has gone over our agenda.

"Can we decide on that once we see how our time is going?" I respond. "I'm not really sure how this will all fit together."

"She's not been on a horse before and isn't sure this should be the first time." Ace explains to Flavio.

"It will not be a problem. We can accommodate you, although we may not be able to guarantee a particular horse at a particular time."

"Fair enough." Ace responds for us both.

Flavio shows us to our room. It is a corner room with floor to ceiling windows in two directions. From one we can see the lake and vine covered hillsides. The other looks up the Millahue Valley and the flatlands that end at this point. The flatlands are not covered with vines as I had expected. I should have noticed that when we first saw views of the hotel. We passed a few vineyards, but much of the land appeared to be undeveloped. Room for expansion. But then I remember Mauricio saying that they planted specific microclimates ideal for the different varieties they produce. Does that mean the flatlands are not ideal in some way? Are they better suited to either table grapes or other fruit and vegetables as was the custom before the current owners bought the valley?

The room is mostly silver colored walls and what I would call impressionist paintings. The bath is gray tile and silver metal trim to the porcelain fixtures. A huge mirror over the sink reflects on the tub and separate shower.

"Very nice," I announce as Flavio nods apparently expecting my reaction. The bed has a white comforter and the wood floors bring a grounding to the silver walls and picture-perfect views. I can understand why Ace thought of the picture aspect of this visit. Everything is over the top in that nearly everything you see is a work of art. My first thought is this is a place for inspiration. There are so many touch points to creativity. In my research I learned that the co-owners work together as a team to design and chose the artists who were commissioned to create the art for each room. Each artist represents a totally different approach to art, to the representation of nature, relationships and concepts. "Could we see any of the other rooms?" I ask Flavio.

"Unfortunately, we are full this weekend, so each is occupied. Maybe on your next visit."

Flavio must have seen my reaction to his suggestion of a next trip. "There will be a next trip. I can almost guarantee it. Very few of our visitors do not come back, at least for a day visit. In fact, we have now built a separate restaurant and shop down by the winery to accommodate the day visitors. You will come back as there is no other place on earth that is quite like Vik."

"This is my second visit," Ace admits. "I was here for lunch before the new restaurant, so we ate on the terrace overlooking the edge pool that overlooks the lake."

"That is my favorite place." Flavio admits. "A spectacular view, with spectacular food and wine and lovely company such as your companion, surrounded by all of this phenomenal art."

"Everything is spectacular except the art?" I ask to kid Flavio on his choice of modifiers.

"Art is never spectacular." Flavio doesn't sound upset with my comment. "Art is bad, good, great or phenomenal. At least that's how I classify it. You may think of it differently. We all do."

"So, when is our next spectacular experience?" I respond looking at Ace who is rolling his eyes at my whole exchange.

"Lunch is in half an hour. Just enough time for you to wash up and rest a moment. Your schedule provides much time for you to soak in Vik, to relax and be with the art and the natural views. There are hiking trails you can follow around the hotel. You may wish to be directly in the natural world. That is the best way to experience the spectacular vistas of Vik."

"And they pay you to do this job and live here?" Ace asks.

OPHELIA

As we sit at lunch, I'm composing the blog in my head. The meal consists of a choice of six incredibly well-prepared gourmet main courses accompanied by two family style sides. I select a local fish dish with oysters and peas in a green liquid broth. It is tender, flavorful and plays with your tastes. Ace selects the raviolis with mushrooms. Each ravioli is emblazoned with the Vik symbol and smothered in tasty mushroom sauce that enables the meat to almost melt in your mouth. The family style sides are a quinoa salad and pureed carrots which are to die for. This all is accompanied by a bottle of La Piu Belle, the medium-priced Vik wine. I am curious that the wine is delivered in a bottle which is also a work of art in and of itself. The wine is a blend of the various varietals on the estate and proves to be the perfect pairing for the variety of main courses we sample.

"Are you ready for a nap?" Ace kids as we make our way out of the wine bottle lined dining room that sits directly behind the terrace where Ace had previously had lunch here.

"Need to walk off the wine." I respond. I'm not inebriated or anything, but I certainly know I've had more than a glass of wine, even though it was with a great meal.

"And start writing your first blog?" Ace seems to be reading my mind again. This reminds me of my earlier thoughts about how someone in a relationship starts to think of the other person's needs, wants, desires and interests. Ace is doing that to me. Anticipating what I will want to do next. Horseback riding? Blog writing? What do I want to do? There has been no discussion of what he wants to do while we are here. But then I realize he must have put the agenda together with

259

either Mauricio or Flavio before we got here. So, he would have made sure we are doing the things he is most interested in.

"What's on the top of your list of things to do while we're here?" I decide to ask.

"Let's take a walk." Ace points me towards the front entrance. The hotel itself is open except for the various rooms, so all the walkways constantly have a wind that blows through. Not a fast wind, but a cleansing wind that gives the hotel a natural clean feel.

Once on the trial Ace decides to answer my question. "The winery. Saw it last time, but it's the kind of place you want to share with others. Much like the hotel seems like a space ship, that theme continues on there. You'll see what I mean. They also do an interesting tasting, giving you just a sip of each of the component wines in the icon wine blend and then a taste of the icon wine itself. Helps you pull the individual grapes out."

"Didn't realize you were so into wines." I admit.

"I enjoy learning about them, thinking about how long it takes to produce a good wine. All that goes into it. The effects of the weather, how much sun the grapes are exposed to, how much rain and cold or warm temperatures. I just find it fascinating that something that's so central to the human race is really an uncontrolled experiment in the vagaries of nature, imposed upon a natural process. Any one element is different from one year to the next and the bouquet and taste can be totally different. A great wine this year can barely be a good wine next year, depending on those same uncontrolled factors."

"I've never thought about wine quite that way." I admit.

"Makes for good conversation when you're on a trip with someone you're just getting to know." Ace smiles that best smile he uses to show he's trying to be genuine and trustworthy. I'll bet he's practiced that smile a lot in the Real Estate development business. If people are going to invest with you or lend you millions or billions of dollars, they need to trust you are going to do everything humanly possible to repay the loans with full interest, and deliver the dividends and growth to the equity investors.

"So, you don't talk business with someone you're just trying to get to know." I wonder aloud.

"If they bring it up I'm happy to talk shop. But I'm a follower in that regard. I don't want to bore someone unless they're really interested in it."

"What are you going to do now that you're no longer family in a family business?"

"You've made an assumption. In my case my in-laws still consider me family, but only because Cindy chose me to be a part of her family. We have a cordial relationship, both professional at the business and personally as their son-in-law."

"Until such time as you replace Cindy with someone else." I point out.

Ace closes his eyes for a moment. Seems to be reflecting on something that must have been a difficult conversation somewhere in the not too distant past with his in-laws. "No one will replace Cindy, just as no one will ever replace your parents or siblings, if you have any. I have to make room in my heart and my life for someone new. Someone who will grow to have a special place, not the same place as Cindy, but a place that is as meaningful and important to me, just in a different way. Do you know what I'm saying? People have multiple spouses. Something happens between them and they decide not to continue as husband and wife. Some people have lots of different spouses. Each one has their own special place, not better, not worse and not more important than the others. Just different. Contributing in a different way to be a better person."

"You've apparently given the subject of where do you go from here a bit of thought." I suggest to see what he has to say.

261

"More hours than anything else I've had to consider since her death." The pain, sadness and regret are palpable. I see he tears up but quickly wipes away the moisture before I can see it on his face. He brings out a kerchief to wipe his forehead as a gesture to hide what he is really feeling.

"Let's say for the time being that I buy the whole premise that you want to start over, have relationships that are meaningful to you because that one key relationship is gone. Let's say I even think you might see me as someone who could be a new significant other for you. I still don't understand why you would think that, but let's set that aside. What is it you want in this new relationship? Someone who will challenge your thinking? Someone who will show you a different side of life? Someone who will bask in the glow of your genius? Someone who will run away with you, tour the world? Create a whole new set of memories so those that are so painful to you will recede and leave you in peace? Be careful how you answer this because if you get it wrong, I'll be asking for that private jet home to New York."

Ace takes my hand and squeezes it. "You didn't need to frame it quite so brutally." His voice is soft, hard to hear over the sounds of nature that have enveloped us. "But your honesty and questioning nature is what made me want to spend some time with you. That's the first part of your continuing quest to understand why you."

He has my attention now. I can tell by the tone of his voice that what he is telling me is hard for him. I have to think that means he is telling me what he actually believes. Whether that is the truth is a whole different matter. His erratic approach to me has pushed me to be a skeptic. This is his one moment to convert me and he apparently knows it.

"Now what were your categories? Someone who will challenge my thinking? You most certainly do that. What you write about. How you see the world. What you think about these chefs who are the best in their field, and yet you call them out regularly. Even though you were never a chef. You don't go after them because of their culinary skills,

262

but because they have lost sight of what food means in culture and tradition and to a family. I would expect that if we spend any time at all together you will continue to challenge my thinking just because that's who you are. You would never become a subservient member of a relationship. You will always have an opinion and you will always express it even when you are shown that there may be a different way of looking at a situation or issue or problem that may be as valid. I'm counting on you to be you."

He passed the first test.

"What was the second question? Someone who will show me a different side of life? You've already started that process for me. Reading your blogs, I've seen a widely divergent set of societies on this planet. You have taken me places I'd have never considered visiting. Did you know that after your blog on Chef X visiting Sicily and discussing how they prepare seafood that I went there and spent a week touring the island? I did that because of you and your blog. I didn't see Chef X's show on it, although I must admit that after I booked the trip, I did watch it. Thought you did just an incredible job of summarizing, painting word picture of that experience. You drove me to want to go there. Not X. You did that."

No. I had no idea my words could have that kind of effect on people. Z is only concerned on delivering eyeballs. He never goes to how many of those sets of eyeballs actually follow through and visit the places I describe. Here is Ace telling me that he is one who had done exactly that. So, what do I make of the effect of my words on Ace? Can the rest of me ever deliver what he's expecting, or will my intellect be enough for him? I thought I was at least adequate in bed. But after X's reaction I'm not so sure anymore. And here I am thinking about X when I'm trying to deal with Ace. Shit.

"The third thing you talked about. What was it? Something about basking?"

"In the glow of you genius." I finish the thought.

"Genius? In this room if there is one genius it's you. I'm good at one thing. Putting deals together, but only because Cindy's father was an excellent teacher. If he hadn't taken me under his wing and shown me over and over what to do, I'd have never gotten it. Yeah, I'm good at doing it now, but it took me a long time to change from being a professor to a real estate developer. No one could hope to bask in the glow of my genius. First of all because there is no glow, and second because I may have been a good academician once, but I'm not a freaking genius, or even close."

"I think you underestimate yourself." I respond gently, hoping to shore up a self-perception I can see is probably inaccurate.

"I must humbly disagree." Ace looks away from me at the valley beyond which is partially cast in sunlight and partially in cloud obscured shadows. But no matter how you look at that valley it's a spectacular vista, just as Flavio had described it. "I am a creature created on a false promise. I promised Cindy that I would love, cherish and obey her until death we would part. I never considered that Cindy would invoke that clause before I would. I was supposed to father her children and keep the family business prosperous until the next generation could take over. Unfortunately for Cindy she did not choose wisely. She didn't marry someone who could live up to his end of the bargain, to father children who would be the next generation to run the family business."

"Stop this right now," I insist. "We're not here to revisit the past. We're not here to lay blame. We're not here to assess what might have been. I get the picture. I get that you're feeling guilty you were chosen and now you haven't delivered on your part of the bargain. Water over the dam. What are you looking for? For the future and you and someone other than Cindy?"

"The day she…" Ace starts but hesitates as if he's not sure he can finish the thought. "I said to her that she was worthless. I didn't mean it literally, but I must have struck a chord I didn't know was there."

Now it all makes sense. Ace feels guilty for what he said. That his comment triggered his wife's actions. "Why did you say that to her?"

Ace can't look at me now, very quiet voice in response, "She was the chairperson for a charity dinner. But she had all these other people she really didn't know doing all the work. When something got screwed up all Cindy did was blame the poor woman who made a mistake. I asked why Cindy didn't help the woman rather than just let her fail. She told me that wasn't her responsibility. I just automatically responded that as Chairperson she was responsible and letting someone fail was her failure too. If she wasn't willing to be responsible, then she was worthless. I still don't know if I could have changed anything by not saying what I did."

"It's not your fault." I inform him gently. "If Cindy was so fragile that a single comment would send her over the edge…"

"How did you know that?" Ace flares at me. "No one knows…"

"Knows what?" I ask carefully and in a controlled voice.

"Cindy jumped to her death. I was standing next to her. One moment we were looking out over a valley and the next she was gone. I couldn't stop her. Had no idea what she was thinking at that moment. That was never reported anywhere. How did you know?"

I shake my head, "I was using a figure of speech. I didn't know."

Ace closes his eyes, drops his head, gently shakes it and is silent for a long moment. His eyes open and he looks at me differently. I can't fathom what he's thinking right now. "What was that last category?"

I have to think a moment, "Someone who will run away with you, tour the world. Create a whole new set of memories so those so painful to you will recede and leave you in peace."

Ace nods. "Peace. That's a word I've not heard in a bit. Peace. Run away and tour the world, much like we're doing at the moment? Guess you've passed that test. But your question is whether that's what I'm looking for. To answer your question, yes and no. Clearly travel is important in a relationship. I have the means that if we wanted to retire from the business my income would permit us to travel year-round, wherever we want to go. But that's not what I'm looking for. I'm not trying to cause my memories to recede. That will happen over time no matter what I do. So, the answer to your question is I am not looking for a transitional person who will distract me while I figure out a new purpose to my life."

How did he know what I'm thinking about being a transition person? Ace continues to hold my hand as we hike around the estate. He is gentle in his grasp, but firm if I seem to lose balance, showing strength when needed and gentle support when it is not. The more I get to know this guy the more I wonder how I ever got on his short list of candidates for life companion. "Okay. So, you answered a part of my continuing quest as to why me. You've given me honest reactions as to why I might fit what you're looking for, but at the end of the discussion I'm still puzzling on why me over all the other thousands of women who would have answered those same questions to your satisfaction."

"It's your blog." Ace responds simply.

"My blog." I'm not sure how that answers my question.

"In your blog you reveal your soul by how you frame questions and answer them. I already have insights about you it would take years to learn about anyone else.

"Nobody is going to want to be with me for the rest of their life based on what I write about. You've got to give me a better reason."

"Despite the fact you can now see I'm not the cold-hearted monster you thought I was when we first met."

"Not good enough." I'm still not sold. "You might be someone I'd be willing to have a drink with and compare notes about how we perceive life and all that goes with it. But someone to intimately share what no one ever sees?"

"Except O." Ace points out.

He got me there. She sees the good, bad and ugly for sure. "There are always exceptions," I agree.

"And if she keeps coming back, it can't be so horrible that you're an axe murderer or anything. I have a lot of respect for Ophelia. She seems to have a good head on her shoulders. And from what she's said at your Friday get togethers, your blogs would be shit without her fact checking you and giving you expert advice."

"Well, there's that." I agree. "O is a special person. Maybe you should date her."

SURPRISES

Dinner at Vik is also a special time. And again, as soon as I sit down at the table my mind is already going to blog mode. The evening feast is literally that. We never see the menu as Williamson, our waiter summarizes the evening's offerings, with the exception of dessert which he tells us is a chef's surprise. The first course consists of an octopus fillet on a melted feta cheese sauce covered by a razor thin beet. We are served both Milla Calla, the entry level Vik wine which literally means golden house for the hotel which casts a golden vision sitting atop the hill overlooking the Millahue lake, and Vik, the icon wine from this estate. Williamson repeats what Mauricio told us earlier, that Millahue means golden place in the indigenous language. The second course is sweetbreads, cooked to a tenderness that makes the dish appealing and yet different from most sweetbread dishes. The main course is a pork tenderloin encrusted with pecorino cheese and cooked in its own juices. The result is a dish that is moist, tender and flavorful all at the same time. The dessert, which was a chef secret until served proves to be mascarpone cheese rolled in crushed pistachios in a honey sauce.

All this and two bottles of wine? Each dish is a work of art both culinary and in presentation. They are a feast for the eye, the nose and the taste buds as each dish passes over the tongue. What else can I say other than I hope I remember all my thoughts long enough to write it all down? For tomorrow I'm going to need to bring a note pad with me just so I don't forget a thing. But I won't forget my visit to Vik, regardless of what happens in the relationship with Ace. He may have been here before, but I can have no hopes of ever returning, despite Flavio's insistence that I will. Maybe he will prove to be right. But at the moment I have no such hopes. I wonder if Ace does. Or will this turn into the place he brings each of the ladies he is courting to replace Cindy, even though he seems to have intellectually come to the conclusion that no one will replace her. Someone new will merely cause him to make a place for another to share at least a portion of his life. Is he saying he has come to the conclusion that nothing is assured? That what may look like a lifetime commitment may not prove to be such? If I'd lost a husband after only a few years I might feel the same way. But at the moment my limited experience only lets me feel it in an intellectual way. I hope I never have to feel it the way Ace is.

After dinner we go sit on the back terrace overlooking the lake and the vine covered hillsides. The moon is up and even though we can see much of this from our room we aren't ready to go back there just yet. Particularly since going back to the room would imply sleeping together and since we haven't yet worked out what sleeping together will mean better to put that encounter off just a bit longer. Create a mood. Enjoy the experience, the Chee-layan winds blowing through the hotel passageways, blowing through our minds and souls to help us come to terms with the ghosts that are haunting both of us.

"Not a menu I would have expected." I observe to Ace.

"That's what's so great about this place. Pure inspiration. Nothing is the expected. Nothing stands alone, but is part of a woven artistic expression."

"Writing my blog for me?" I kid Ace, but I have to admit he has chosen words that resonate for me about this experience we are sharing.

"I wouldn't assume I could ever do that. Would be too hard for me to express things quite the way you do. I'm way too private a person for that."

"But you're being open with me." I respond a little confused by what he's trying to say.

"Yes, but this is a highly unusual set of circumstances for me. How long have I been coming to your Friday night events?"

"Been what? Two or three months?" I try to remember when he first showed up.

"Almost six months," he clarifies for me. "For the first several months I said so little you hardly knew I was there. Even last week, with one date, if you want to call it that, you still hardly knew me. I hope this trip is changing your perceptions about me, for the better. But I don't think anyone else who attends those Friday nights has a real feeling for me or who I am or what drives me."

"That's deliberate." I seek to clarify.

Ace nods, takes my hand and gently kisses it before resting it on his left leg, but continuing to hold it. "This is magical. I wish I'd come here earlier, but I'm glad we're sharing it now. Glad you can write a blog about it to educate more about what this place stands for."

"Will you come back as Flavio has foreseen?"

Ace considers my question for a moment, "Yes. I think we will come back here at some point. Not right away because there is so much of the world for me to show you and for us to experience together. There's not enough time to sit back and say we'll do it later. So many things intervene between now and then. So, coming back to your criteria of what I'm looking for. Traveling companion is one of them, not all the time. But several times a year for sure. What about you? Is that something you're looking for?"

I smile at Ace because he clearly hasn't lived on the lower East Side recently, even though he told me he was born close to there. "I'm hoping to one day have a relationship with someone who can share some of the bills. That might give me enough money to go out and splurge once in a while. But travelling companion? That's never been on my radar. For me going from my apartment to meet you at Washington Square Park is a major trip. And by being here, I can see you don't live in that world anymore."

"But I did until I went off to college, on a full scholarship I might remind you."

"Not going back to those days." I surmise aloud.

Ace looks around, muses a moment, "I could if all the money disappeared." He looks closer at me. "Those things happen, you know. If I were to get overleveraged on my properties, there was a crash of the markets and tenants bailed from my buildings or there was a change in the nature of our government and we had broad nationalization of private assets. Any of those were to happen and I'd be right back in the poverty streets. So nothing is forever. Just because we haven't known those kinds of dramatic changes in our lifetimes, our parents and their parents did. So never say forever, because that's not going to be the case either."

"A bit fatalistic?" I poke at him.

"When you have nothing, you don't worry about losing it all. Not a big change in your life. But when you have a lot. Then you constantly worry about what could happen. What bad choices could I make that would bring down the house of cards my life is built on. I'm depending on literally thousands of other businessmen, just like me to make prudent decisions that will grow and enhance their businesses. But that's not realistic. You take a thousand people and put them in a room. Not all of them will make the best decision every time. Bad decisions will lead to reversals. Reversals lead to vacancies in my buildings. So, no matter what I do, I can't put space between me and those who will guarantee, or not, my continued success."

"For me, it's depending on Z to publish what I write, and the thousands of readers, like you, thank you, who advertisers are willing to pay to expose their products and services to. Without either of those sources of income I'm on Poverty Street as well. I'm good as long as I keep writing interesting and relevant blogs. That stops and the paychecks stop."

"See." Ace seems happy. "We're not so different. We each have

271

different masters, but without them we go back to living on gardens we grow in the back yard and our ability to sell what we don't consume to those who can't grow enough to live."

"If I have to grow anything, I'm in big trouble." I hold up my left hand, "See no green thumb. You've seen my apartment. Do you remember one green living thing?"

Ace considers for a moment, apparently trying to recall what he did see when he prepared dinner for me. "You're right. Nothing green."

"It's not because I haven't tried. I just don't have what it takes to nurture a plant to old age. They just don't like the environment in which I thrive."

Ace considers my thought. "Are you really thriving there? I mean it's all sterile and functional. But what kind of environment is that? Look around. This place was designed to inspire, to overload your senses so everything you see, eat, drink, feel is linked somehow to art. It's almost the antithesis of your everyday habitat."

He has me there. No art in my apartment. Nothing to stimulate my creative juices. Will I write better here or there? This could be the ultimate test for me. If my best blogs ever are a result of working in this environment, then I know I have to do something about bringing art in to where I work. But at the moment I can't afford to do that. So why am I even worrying about it? I'm not ready to make the leap into this world. I live in another. One where everyday people struggle to make a living, hoping they won't get behind on their bills because the chances of ever catching up recede by the moment in a world increasingly embracing the new and discarding as useless the old. And I'm not old, but can already see those younger than me, hungrier than me, who are trying to break in. They would seize on any mistake I make to replace me. And in a nanosecond, I'm history. I'm last year's blogs. I'm not what people want to read so why would anyone value what I have to say? And maybe that's why Vik is so important to my future. If I can come out of here with a series of blogs that catch the attention of a wider audience than I've had in the past, then I've validated my value. The ability to find new sets of eyes. The ability to bring increasing numbers to the advertisers. That's all they want. But I want more. I want to be good, to be valued, to be credible and capable and wanted all at the same time. I want an audience. Every actor wants an audience. But Ace doesn't. He just told me that. He would rather remain in the shadows and make money the old-fashioned way. Provide something in short supply but that everyone needs. A home. An office. A place to buy things they can't find on the internet, or where they want to try it on, or see it and feel it before they buy. And even the number of stores are quickly declining. So that portion of Ace's empire is quickly crumbling. Having a diversified portfolio becomes essential when social trends obsolete what has until now provided dependable earnings.

I have to shift back to his question about thriving. "I've done all right where I am."

"You have. But what does that say about you? That you're able to do well in a sterile place, devoid of inspiration other than what is in your head. Just think, if you were writing from here for a week. What kind of new creative juices would be unleashed? How much could you grow your audience? Especially since, as you noted, not everyone will have the opportunity to come be a part of this. It's a special place for a special group of people and it doesn't expect to find people without means of ever coming to visit them or buy their wine or follow them on whatever media they prefer?"

"What are you suggesting? That I move here and do all my work surrounded by incredible works of art? I couldn't afford that and probably you couldn't either." Although I'm making an assumption on that last point.

Ace rises still holding my hand, but he looks down at me. "I think it's time we make some decisions. The world of 'what if?' will always be there. But we're going around in circles at the moment. I want to bring you into a world where creativity and innovation are everyday parts of what you do. For some unfathomable reason you have chosen to remain in a sterile and uninspiring environment. Why you think that helps you perform at your best, I don't understand. I would offer you more than you have probably ever imagined. And I have to underline offer. You could take advantage of my offer, come and be with me, but still wish to work in a sterile environment. If that's what works best for you, who am I to argue with success? But as a result of being a part of art and innovation and creativity, if that doesn't propel you to greater levels of achievement then I have seriously misread you and a whole bunch of other creative types. I've seriously misread what makes someone perform at their highest levels."

I resist the tug on my hand as he wants me to get up. But this terrace is just so magical, the sun setting and casting long shadows as day turns into night. The stars appearing where moments before only day light illuminated the sky with blue colors and white clouds. And now I'm being pulled towards a moment of decision. Will I give in to his charms and sorrow and insights into me and the world around him, or will I continue to resist? He's made the decision a hard one. Made me peer into my soul and my values and everything I've taken for granted for the last... I don't even know how long I've held these beliefs about myself and the people I work with and the people who read my blogs, including Ace.

I take one more long look at the stars over the lake and the vine covered hills beyond. Ace tugs again and I find myself rising to my feet and following him back to our room. 'Our room.' I hadn't thought of it in those terms until just now. That instantly reminds me of the time I spent with X and how we made love. Reminds me that I thought of that as 'our' experience even though X clearly didn't. Is that what will happen tonight? Will I have a breakthrough sexual experience that Ace wakes up and pronounces as just average? Will I be the one to walk away disappointed that my perceptions are so misaligned with reality, or at least the reality of my partner for the night? I don't know. And that is the nagging question I'm trying to answer as we reach our room door. We are in the front of the hotel, facing the Millahue Valley. The wind is in my face, the air is clean, and it helps clear my wine intermediated brain. I am very likely to have a sexual experience tonight and my senses are dulled by the wine, as opposed to my night with X where it seemed everything was enhanced by his touch, our co-creation of the meal we both ate and then the way I reacted to his touch in bed that night. Reacted to what I thought he was trying to communicate to me. That I was someone important to him. Someone worthy of his time, attention and shared experiences. I was wrong, it appears, based on his comments subsequently. But that was still a magical night for me. So how can tonight even begin to compare when I'm nowhere near as open to Ace, where I'm nowhere near as turned on, where I'm nowhere near as blending my soul with his, at least in my mind.

Ace closes the door and follows me into the room. No blinds on the windows obscure our view which I remember from being in the room when it was still light out. Home lights dot the valley, but there is not much in the way of civilization out there, just orchards and gardens and vineyards. Low hills frame the valley, but it is quiet and distant and calming. Ace approaches me from behind as I look out the windows, putting his arms around me and his chin on my shoulder. "As beautiful as you," he whispers in my ear.

"Bullshit," I respond. "I know I'm not beautiful. Actresses are beautiful."

"Beauty is inside, whether your mind or your heart. Your beauty is all three. You are a beautiful woman to look at, you are a beautiful woman with an intellect that is the equal of anyone and you are beautiful because you care about others, even those you've never met."

He spins me slowly to face him. Those tender lips grace mine in the same fleeting way. No pressure, no tension, nothing that would suggest anything other than tenderness and patience. Is that who he is? Someone who is both tender and patient? Someone who would let me thrive in my own areas of expertise. Someone who would be my biggest cheerleader while ensuring we have what we need to persist with those things that are most important to us? Why have I never thought of these things before? Why have I always thought I would be alone? Why have

I never considered an alternative existence to my tiny apartment near the Hudson River? I did once. But that died when I was maybe ten. When my parents lost their business and we were poor once again. Having gone through that cycle several times I guess I just resolved that I would always be poor and make the best of it. And that is exactly what I do. Make the best of whatever situation I find myself in, whether at work or with people. Make the best of it.

Ace slips my shawl off my shoulders. Lets it fall to the floor. The seduction has begun. The tender kiss continues as he gently rubs his hands over my back, coming around over my arms. Tenderly, oh so gently. His hands gently press me towards him, making contact in a hug that is not forceful, but brings me to him.

What do I want to do? Go along, resist or take control and make love on my terms? I've never done that before, but I've never been in Chee-lay before. I decide the time has come for me to see if Ace is serious about a relationship.

I push him away, far enough that I can push his jacket off his shoulders, pull up his shirt and reach for his belt. My aggression is in contrast to his gentle approach. How will he handle this? He begins to unbutton my blouse as I pull down his pants.

Ace slowly pulls down my skirt, trying to slow me down. I step out of it. Now down on my knee I reach into his underpants and find he has come to attention. This will be fast unless I find a means of slowing things down. Maybe that's what he's been trying to tell me without any words. I take him in my hand and squeeze, feeling him shrink almost immediately.

"Why did you do that?" Ace seems surprised at my action.

"So I can catch up. You're way ahead of me at the moment."

Ace nods and slowly continues his undressing of me. He is no longer stiff, but remains extended. His posture seems to relax as he steps out of his shoes and removes his own socks. I help him with his shirt and now we are naked, standing only inches apart. Ace seems to take me all in for the first time, seeing me as few have seen me.

Ace carries me to the bed, laying down next to me, He has an amused expression.

"What's so funny?" I have to ask.

"I have to admit you're full of surprises," he responds as I get on top of him.

TRY ME

Our days at Vik flew by. Ace admitted he had never been on the bottom before. It was a whole new experience for him, although he also mentioned in passing that the loss of control was somewhat disorienting to him. I discovered I have nothing to fear about being the aggressor in our lovemaking. In fact, I actually enjoy setting the pace and making the decisions rather than just reacting to what Ace decides. This is very different from what I've experienced before, including with X, which I was convinced was the ultimate orgasm for me. I've now found that's not necessarily the case. Making love doesn't have to be a dominant person in charge. With Ace the lovemaking flowed from one to the other and back, with each of us at different times slowing ourselves to allow the other to catch up, or search out stimulations that brought each of us along faster, but still at our own pace. I'm not confident yet that I've found a new me in all of this give and take, but I've definitely found a voice I didn't know I had.

Maybe I let myself find a new voice because I felt I had absolutely nothing to lose with Ace. I expected when the trip was over I'd probably never hear from him again. He would have gotten what he wanted, although I'm still not sure exactly what that is. He would have erased whatever demons drove him to Vik in the first place. And then he would go on to find the next person who could bring joy and happiness into his life. I've tried to do that on this trip, but I am still waiting to see him let go and laugh from his gut as people do when someone is totally free to express joy. Maybe I've just not been playful enough with him to evoke such an emotion. I know I'm a reserved person and for me to have let go as I have on this trip is a whole new experience. A baby step, but still I have to believe a step in the right direction. A step where I'll be able to express emotions, characterize observations, and directly communicate thoughts I've held back when they may have been more beneficial if expressed.

How would things have gone with X if I'd been this free with him? Probably not well. I let him guide me through an opening of my senses as we cooked together. And he took advantage of every open sense to create sensations in me that he then shared. A different way of making love, but one he seemed very comfortable with. And that was his gift to me. The ability to experience a shared awakening of my senses and a heightening of the experience through skilled stimulation of every cell of my being until a magical release brought us together as one on the summit of our shared pleasure.

So here I am on the flight back to New York. Ace is asleep in the seat next to mine. And I can't sleep. So, I'm reflecting on the days in Chee-lay, reflecting on what I discovered and reflecting on what I want to do with all that I've learned. Most of it can't be the subject of a blog, but I think my blogs will reflect insights I've not been willing to express before. Will that make me a better writer? Will that attract more eyeballs? Will Z finally acknowledge he's not going to fire me and hire someone half my age who barely reads and can't spell, but knows all the buzz words her friends have invented so their parents will have no idea when they're talking about sex? I know he will hire several bloggers half my age, but only in hopes of attracting a new generation of readers. More eyeballs. But I suspect Z will have to change some of his expectations. That generation doesn't read. A six-hundred-word blog would be like asking me to read War and Peace in an afternoon. But Z has a business to build and he may find a format that attracts those eyeballs. My guess is he will have to find someone who can communicate essential information in twelve words or less. Yes, that's what we're coming to. A world of surface level information from which opinions are formed and buying habits established. And that world will be fine with Z. Just keep the eyeballs tuned in.

I decide to draft a summary blog about Vik since I have several more hours before we land in New York.

PURE INSPIRATION

I have never before been in an environment where you are immersed in art, innovation, creativity and the best of everything. But such a place exists in the Millahue Valley of Chile. *(Oops, almost wrote Chee-lay)*. The Vik Winery Estate is twelve hundred acres of some of the most fertile and perfect growing conditions for grapes in all of South America. On the other side of the mountain that frames the Hotel and Winery is Clos Apalta, a wine estate owned by Casa LaPostolle. The 2005 vintage from the Clos Apalta estate was voted number one in the world by Wine Spectator. A rare and very prestigious honor. So, you know growing conditions anywhere close by should be nearly ideal. But that's not always the case. Microclimates abound. Each climate dictates a terroir and a wholly different bouquet and taste experience. Each expression of this place will blend differently with different dishes created by talented chefs for the guests at the Vik hotel, among other chefs world-wide.

The dining experience is not to be missed. Two different restaurants serve guests, one at the hotel for those staying on the property and one at the winery for the day guests who come for the wine tour and tasting alone. Both are served from the same kitchen and prepared by the same gourmet chefs. So each meal is a work of art in the presentation, in the flavors you experience in your mouth and in the pairing with a Vik wine. Even the bottle the La Piu Belle wine comes in is eye catching in the original graphic depiction of a beautiful young woman – the most beautiful, as the name suggests.

The beauty of the Millahue Valley is undeniable when viewed from the floor-to-ceiling windows of the hotel rooms, framed by works of art commissioned individually for each and every room in the hotel. Each room is totally different and named after the artist who created the in-room experience for the guests who select their room. If you wish to stay at Vik, I strongly suggest you communicate with your guest guide, currently Flavio, discuss your preferences in art, and he will ensure you are engulfed in a resonant environment during your stay.

The immersion does not stop with your room. Everything you encounter at Vik is a work of art in and of itself. Whether finding the Vik logo emblazoned upon the raviolis at lunch or the lobby filled with wall art, furniture art, and multimedia sculpture, art is everywhere, art is everything and you are now a part of that art experience. Even the terrace on the back of the hotel, overlooks an edge pool that overlooks a lake framed by the mountains and vine covered hillsides. Layer upon layer of art, beauty, inspiration and all built upon a winemaking tradition among the best in the world.

The result is pure inspiration. No one can visit Vik without being inspired about what is possible, what is motivational, what is essential to feed the soul. A hike around the estate communicates a sense of solace, of nature embracing you and guiding you towards inner revelations. Riding horseback through the massive estate enables an understanding of the early days of the Chilean experience, when horseback was the only means of transportation. In fact, we were told that the owners rode across the estate before purchasing it to select the areas they would develop into the hotel and winery. This choice of transportation resulted from the rugged terrain where any other means would have been much more difficult. Thus, Vik is modern, Vik is built upon tradition, and Vik is intended to inspire any and all who would venture into the heartland of Chile to find themselves, find inspiration and find the wellsprings of their own creativity.

After rewriting a few times, I become bored with the project. Ace stirs and opens one eye to gaze upon me, almost like he's checking to see if we are still together, whether this experience ever happened, and whether he would find a smile on my face or a grim expression of expectation with the real-world looming just a few more hours away.

"Writing your blogs?" he asks as he pulls himself up in his seat.

I nod but don't vocalize a response.

"Mind if I read?"

I hand him the laptop and discover I'm holding my breath. I've never watched someone read one of my blogs, never heard their instant review. What will Ace think? Especially since he shared this particular experience with me. I see him close one eye, as if he doesn't agree with something I wrote, but I'm afraid to ask him, afraid to interrupt his reading of my work. Afraid he won't like it and will tell me exactly what he does think of it.

He glances at me and then hands the laptop back over the seat with no expression.

"You can't get away with that!" I exclaim thinking he's not going to tell me anything.

"I was hoping for at least a passing reference to your handsome companion," Ace teases.

"I referenced you when I mentioned we were told about the owners riding their horses to find the location of the hotel and winery."

"Pretty weak." Ace turns away. But then he continues, "Actually I like it better than most you've written. More inspiring, if I can borrow one of the terms you used at least a dozen times in what? Six hundred words? You really think it's an inspiring place? I guess it is for someone who appreciates art like you clearly do."

"You didn't think it was inspirational?" I'm amazed.

"If you like art, yeah, I guess." The sly grin that had appeared has disappeared again.

"You saying you don't like art?" What's he saying to me?

"Did you see any at my apartment when you visited?" he challenges me.

I shake my head as he continues, "I didn't see any at your place either. That was what got me to thinking about Vik. As you say in your blog. Art encompasses everything there. I was hopeful it would stimulate you to think differently. From reading the blog, it appears I succeeded at least a little."

I nod that he succeeded at least a little, but then he continues.

"But the question that remains for me is whether or not you will consciously try to elevate your art, having had an experience like Vik?"

I hadn't realized what he was doing with this visit. He was trying to make me better. I had no idea. I knew he read my blogs, but had not thought he would deliberately try to help me see that I can be better, I can elevate my work, my art. But then I get angry, "Is this what you do? You go around observing people who could be doing something better. Then you give them an all-expense paid experience to help them realize the deficiencies in what they're doing? Is that what the idle rich do? Take pity on the poor and take on a charity case? Do you go to your exclusive clubs and swap stories about how you found a semi-literate blogger and helped her become at least intelligently readable? Is that what you're going to tell all your friends about me next Tuesday?"

And Ace starts laughing. That full belly laugh I've been waiting for the last several days. The laugh I never thought I'd ever be able to get him to let go with. Only I don't know what I said that is so funny to him. How am I ever going to be able to get him to enjoy life if invoking a belly laugh is something I can only do accidently and without a clue as to how I did it?

"What?" I finally ask as he gets his laughter under control.

"Is that what you really think?" Ace shakes his head. "That I'm a snobbish do-gooder who is only in it for bragging rights?" He laughs again at the very thought of being a do-gooder.

"Well, aren't you?" I try to convey a cross expression, but his laughter has made that real hard. "You just said you took me to Vik after seeing my working environment. Clearly you thought I needed help."

"Well, don't you?" Ace comes right back at me, the laughter over; the serious Ace back in control. "I'm not trying to do anything that will change you the way I might want you to change. Art is way too personal. What one person thinks is a majestic sunset another just thinks of another night arriving. One person sees the sun, another the darkness after the sun sets. I can't make you better. Only you can do that. Yes, I hope I gave you a chance to think differently. But you can choose to ignore all that Vik stands for. You can choose to never change in your approach to your art. You can choose to spend the rest of your life in your lower west side apartment and never come out to see the sun. Those are all choices available to you. But only you can decide which of those choices you will make. You may choose never to respond to any of my texts, or answer my calls. Or you may want to spend the rest of your life with me. And if I don't choose you, then your choices are more limited. But when it comes to your art. That choice is yours and yours alone."

I'm overwhelmed but then one sentence settles in. "Did you just propose to me?"

"I don't think so." Ace looks puzzled.

"You just said something about me wanting to spend the rest of my life with you."

"I did." The puzzled expression passes. "That wasn't a question. It was an observation of what you may want."

"I didn't know that was an option," I clarify.

Ace tries to sit up straighter, but has to bring his seat up to do so. "We both have options. But there's a big difference between a few days together in an extreme world and life together in a world of responsibilities, deadlines and changing consumer and corporate tastes, desires, wants, needs and expectations."

"You're saying life together would be very different than the few days we just shared." I clarify.

"It would be. Very different. And at this point I don't think you can appreciate exactly how different."

"Try me."

BORGO SAN MARCO

I'm still trying to get my head around the last week when of course a text comes in.

J:

Best blog ever. Glad you went on your little get-away. I'm expecting a new blog on some aspect of your Chilean adventure each day for the next week. You clearly must have come back with enough material. I've also decided that if you need to do select travel to inspire you I think the added eyeballs you generated will justify it. Not suggesting you get on the next plane and just go somewhere. But if you have a great potential topic I won't have a problem with you going.

Great work, Z

Great work? Even Ace wasn't that enthusiastic. But if I pulled a new high on eyeballs I can see where Z would relax on expenses a bit. Particularly since Chile didn't cost him a dime and I'm sure he'll be looking for me to get Ace to take me someplace else.

Six more blogs on Chee-lay. If they were only twelve words each that would be easy. But six hundred each, with increasingly inspired language and message? That's going to be a little harder. Ace pointed out that I needed inspiration to bring out the best of me. And I'm still not sure if he was talking about my writing or me in bed with him. We did it twice a day and sometimes it lasted for hours. I have probably more time in the sack with Ace than I do on airplanes, now that Z has raised that option. And now that we're back it almost seems like it never happened other than in my mind. Ace has gone back to manage his property development projects. I'm back writing blogs about Chee-lay for the next few days and then what? Blogs on the new restaurants opening in major cities around the country? Wine tastings of some of the creative new blends coming out of Slovakia and Croatia that can only be purchased in those countries because they make such small quantities? Do a little travel blog with it to convince people to go visit Dubrovnik so they can try some of these imaginative new wines? I'm sure any and all of them would suit Z. Probably attract new eyeballs, at least from people who have heard about Slovakia and Croatia but have never been. And I have to sleep alone tonight. Something I probably need to get used to again. Back to managing my expectations. Back to being alone.

Is that what's bugging me? That I discovered a whole sexual side I didn't know existed, that I got to explore it for a few days and now I'm back in solo mode? Yeah, that's it. I could always invite Ace back for a reprise, but he made that little speech about if he didn't choose me that my options are more limited. Yeah, I caught that although I never brought it back up to him. I didn't want to put him on the spot or have him confirm that he wouldn't chose me for ever after. But he chose me for a few days. I have to lower my expectations again. I'm the transition girlfriend. I mean there are so many women in this city. He has as many choices as he wants while I basically have none. And there's still that whole thing out there. It never came up on the trip, but the whole heir thing he used to spook me or test me or whatever that was. It's still hanging out there as a caution I have to keep in mind if I do get together with him again. If he does decide on me from among the millions who are better suited to his lifestyle, to his social standing, to his place in the world. I have to know I don't. So why am I obsessing about him when before the trip I had so many questions, doubts, so many concerns?

Another text:

J:

You can't hide under a rock. How was the trip and what's the deal with Ace? Is he around or was this a very expensive one nighter?

O

Of course, O wants the whole scoop. I really don't feel ready to go through it right now. Probably because I have so many questions about what really happened there. What was the real motivation for taking me in the first place? And where does this whole sexual awakening thing leave me. O will really want to know all about the sex. Was he good, was he as gentle as I indicated he seemed to be based on that first kiss. How do I explain to her that I was the one who turned that all upside down?

Of course, the phone rings. O won't let me ignore her.

"I get it." Yup, it's O. "No digital trail. Not going to text me with anything someone will be able to use in court against you. No problem. We can meet at Starbucks. You chose which one. Any Starbucks in Manhattan will work for me and if you're afraid of being recognized by one of your readers we can always go to Staten Island. I don't think anyone there reads food blogs. You eaten over there recently? Seems to me the last generation of chefs went through there as punishment. See how bad food can be so they'll work harder, you know? If you're forced to make bland food you eventually yearn for something more, something better. And that's when they move over to Brooklyn as a sous chef. Learn a little about sauces. See what they can do for the main course. Spice things up and not with ketchup and mustard or bell peppers."

"I guess you missed having someone to talk to while I was away." I respond. "Must mean no Damien yet."

O's voice drops lower and quieter. "Correctomundo on both

accounts. I never knew how hard it was going to be to get a guy into my bed. Particularly one with big hands like Damien."

I realize telling her about Ace and our shared experience is going to be hard. Will have to gloss over some details I normally would have given some further explanation about. Damien?"

"I think he's seeing someone. No confirmation on that. Rumor has always had it that he was one never to turn down an invitation. So, either the rumors were wrong or something changed in his life."

I shake my head. Something isn't adding up here. "If he were with someone exclusively, I don't think we'd be seeing him on Fridays. He'd be with her right after work. Something else going on. Who does he talk to the most when he's with us?"

"Z." O responds without thinking.

"And who else is always sitting right there?" I wonder aloud, probably making an inaccurate connection.

"Janelle." O connects the same mental image I have of Friday night.

"Z's admin." I complete the thought. "You see her there, but you don't see her since she's sitting right next to her boss. Makes sense because we all know Z's not banging her. His wife would have his balls for lunch."

"You sound like you're more afraid of Alicia than you are of Z."

"His wife... well, you know what I mean." I can't even think of the words to describe Z's wife Alicia. Her family had the money to start the business. They keep Z on a short leash. I can't imagine he would do anything that could cause his whole life to disappear in an instant. And without her family's money, Z wouldn't be able to stay in the game.

"So, you think Damien is banging Janelle." O pronounces the

obvious conclusion.

"Not important what I think. You're the one who's disappointed he hasn't made the move you so expected by bringing him to Friday night."

"Guess it's time to move on." O decides aloud. "So, speaking of moving on, what happened to you in Chee-lay."

I had texted O about the different way to pronounce it early in the trip, but then hadn't sent any more communications. Probably was a mistake.

"You read the blogs." I put out there to lure her away, but she won't bite.

"That's all about where you were, not what happened to you while you were there."

"Sure, they are. All about inspiration. All about immersing yourself in art. That's what happened to me. I discovered I needed to become inspired in my writing because it had become somewhat predictable. Pedestrian. Less than interesting."

"You're pretty hard on yourself, but I think you're wrong. Sure, your new blog was at a whole new level for you. Don't know if you can maintain that. Would be incredible if you can. But your blog was one of your best. The fact you took it up a notch? Great. A result of being in a new environment? Yeah, I can see that. But what does all that have to do with you and Ace?"

"Ace told me he noticed I needed inspiration and that's why he took me to Vik. Said there was no more inspiring place he knew of. Said he was hopeful I'd figure out how to make the linkages between art and food."

"You telling me you went to Chee-lay with Ace and all you did was eat and drink in an art gallery? You could have done that here by taking a Hershey bar into the Guggenheim Museum. I don't buy it. What really happened down there?"

"We talked about him, mostly. About what it was like to lose someone who was the center of his whole life. I can't begin to imagine what it was like for him to ..." I have to stop myself before I say what Ace said hadn't appeared anywhere. "But he's trying to heal. Trying to find new meaning in life. Find a new center to his universe."

"Are you it?" O zeros in on something I didn't want to discuss, but here we are.

"The new center of his universe?" I narrow her focus. "Not hardly. He has a million women to choose from in this city alone. We had a massive argument on the way back about his attempt to make me a better blogger. But he tried to convince me it had nothing to do with making me anything. He wants me to believe he only wanted to show me a different side of life so I could make decisions on my own that may take me to a different place. A place where I'm contributing more to my art in whatever way I decide to go."

"Did you have separate rooms?" O isn't going to let me off.

"No." I confirm.

"Twin beds?"

"King."

"So, you slept with him."

"Price of admission." I decide may be one way of putting it to get me out of the box I feel I'm in since she's not sleeping with Damien. If she hadn't confirmed Damien was occupied elsewhere, I probably would have been more truthful, but now I just don't want her to feel badly that I'm getting mine and she's not getting hers.

"Well, how was he? And don't give me any bullshit about

obligatory sex. If things weren't working out, you would have been on the next plane back. So, it had to be good. Had to be good enough that you did it more than once."

"He's not X." I try to say so she'll get the impression that he wasn't as good as X.

"Obviously. But, how was he? As tender as his kiss?"

I did tell her about that. Probably should have waited to see if it went anywhere before discussing how his kiss was. "Not completely." I'm still trying to limit this so she doesn't get upset.

"Did he hit you?" O takes my response to the extreme.

"No." I protest so she won't spread inaccurate information about him.

"So, tell me and stop making me ask all these questions."

"Obviously I didn't write home about it." I'm still not willing to tell her.

"You know you really piss me off sometimes." O tries to decide what to say next, instead she simply hangs up.

I quickly replay that conversation and decide I'll give her the details when she's over Damien, which will probably be Monday. Not all that much invested in him since they never slept together. Then a text comes in.

> J:
>
> *I think I made a huge mistake with my new project. Not working out the way I thought. You can find me at Borgo San Marco in Positano. I need someone to talk with. I'm sorry I didn't come through New York. I regret so many things.*
>
> X

THE FAMILY

J:

Didn't think you'd take me up on my offer quite so soon or quite so expensively. Better be a great story for what this is going to cost me. Good Luck.

Z

New York to Rome is only eight hours, the train to Naples is two and the Circumvesuviana train around Mt. Vesuvius another hour to get to Sorrento. Then it's another forty-five minutes by Uber to Positano. I would have taken Uber from Rome until I figured out how expensive a three-hour ride would have been. So even though I'm costing Z a mint, I'm trying to be conservative in my expenses as best I can.

I check into the Borgo San Marco which sits just above the beach with broad ocean views. However, I had to carry my bag down several flights of stairs to find the place. I thought the driver would help me, but he dropped my bag and was gone. Guess Asian women aren't his thing. Anyway, as I descended the stairs, I was certainly glad I packed light since I only expect to be here two to three days. Anything longer and I'll have to wash out underwear for the flight back. Z would never let me buy clothes here just because I misjudged how long it would take. I don't have enough extra money to buy a pack of gum at the moment.

I ask about the restaurant and discover it is the balcony on top of the hotel. The kitchen is one floor lower and the wait staff is constantly running up and down stairs to serve the patrons. Not an ideal situation, but when you're in Italy and most of your patrons are visitors from who knows where in the world and the view is as important as the food, well, that excuses an inefficient layout.

A brief stop in the room to shower and change clothes and I'm wandering the halls of the hotel to find the kitchen. I push through the swinging doors and find a small kitchen with five staff members at their stations preparing the night's meal. The sous chef is X. The chef is not someone I recognize. So, I am instantly confused. How could a chef as famous as X be working in a tiny kitchen in a resort community as the sous chef? This doesn't make any sense to me until I see the camera and sound men huddled in the storage room. They must have rigged up a fixed mount for the camera and microphone. The cameraman apparently has a remote that lets him move the camera around the room to pick up the action. They probably have mics around the kitchen so they can pick up what the Chef and other members of the staff have to say about anything in particular.

They are apparently filming at the moment. I hang back so as not to interrupt. But the Chef notices me and comes over to shoo me out, I'm sure. I read his name on his chef coat as he gets near, 'Chef Luigi Libretto.'

"You not come in. This a close kitchen. Dining room, she open at seven. And that's for you tourists. No self-respecting Italian eats before eight."

"Please Chef Libretto, I'm here to see X." I point in the direction of the chef on camera.

"Everyone want see X. Not today. You see him not cooking. Go."

X apparently hears the conversation. He looks over to see me looking helpless in the face of an upset chef. He takes his chef hat off and comes over to me, gives me a bear hug and then turns to Chef Luigi

Libretto. "An old friend and critic. Please let her stay until we finish the tape." He nods to the camera and sound men. "She sit with crew in storage room."

Chef Luigi Libretto clearly would rather have me gone. There are enough strangers in his kitchen, enough interruptions to the flow of food preparation. But he relents. I need to ask X how he knows Chef Libretto and why this chef is tolerating X. I can understand the publicity this will give Borgo San Marco, but at the same time it will expose secrets they may not want out. Show the personalities of those who are preparing the food their guests will experience. Will that be a good thing or not? From the text from X, I would have to say the jury is still out on settling that argument.

"Did you just get here?" X asks me as he escorts me to the storage room. "You're staying here at the Borgo, aren't you? I'm so glad you came. After our last conversation I wasn't sure you would."

"Of course, I came. That was never a consideration." Although until Z's note about traveling it was really never a consideration. I'm looking around the compact kitchen, looking at the faces of the other members of the kitchen staff. "So, this is your new project."

"Yes. I'll explain everything, but I need to get back to my station. We're holding up shooting for you."

The camera and sound men make room for me, offer the chair the soundman had been sitting in, but I nod thanks and remain standing. The sound and cameramen get back to work as X returns to his station.

"Every sauce has secret ingredients that reflect both the imagination of the person who is making it, whether a grandmother, mother, daughter or son who is learning, helping in the kitchen and over time mastering both the ingredient selection and the special techniques their family elders use to create that wonderful smell, wonderful and unique taste." X unleashes his rambling narrative which has been a trademark of his programs. "Cooking in Italy is a tradition.

But it is also a part of the culture. Every grandmother and mother is the focal point of the family food foundation that organizes the daily discussions amongst the family members, friends and relatives who stop by. It's almost forbidden to have a conversation without offering something to eat. And if you eat, you must sample a wine that will complete the experience, the exchange of information, the discussions of matters both large and small, but of ultimate concern to those having that conversation. It is this nexus of food, family, friends and fundamental presence that makes Italy unique. But what I have learned in my travels, is that no matter where you go, who you talk to, what culture you are examining, it is all the same fundamentals. It is all about how food is the center of the experience. Food brings people together. Food is the centerpiece of the exchange that takes place because food is the constant. Created from family recipes. Handed down from generation-to-generation. Something familiar. Something that assures you everything will be all right, regardless of the nature of the crisis of the moment. And in every family there is always a crisis. Some are monumental. Some are small. But food reassures us that this too shall pass. As a family we will see the dawn. As a family we will emerge from the current situation stronger, smarter and better able to cope with the next emergency."

The cameraman moves the camera to bring the pot X is stirring into frame.

"This ragu is typical of the Libretto family traditions. The meat is a blend of ground lamb, beef and pork. While many ragus have similar blends of meat, the Libretto family has a particular affection for duck. So, there is also a small amount of ground duck breast mixed in. That may not sound so exotic. May not seem like a reason to fly half way around the world to Positano to try Chef Libretto's creation. But there are other secrets that bring about layers of flavor that may or may not be unique to his family. But they are secrets that in tasting the ragu you might miss until you pair it with a Super Tuscan or a Salice Salentino, maybe even an Aglianico wine from the Puglia region which is not so far from here.

"I have spoken with Chefs all around the world. One constant I hear is that the more local the ingredients, the more the flavors blend. One chef explained that when everything comes from the same terroir, the same soils conditions, the same weather that year, the same pollination from the local bees, the same fertilizers that the ingredients blend better. The flavors don't compete, they harmonize. Now I know that may sound like a different way of expressing what happens in an Italian kitchen, but I think it is a harmony more than flavors that complement each other. They exist together and create flavor stacks that build on each other. This may be a hard concept to convey, but I think it's fundamental to food anywhere in the world. I think it's also part of the reason that food in some countries has become dissociated from family, dissociated from life.

"Food in some places is an obligation in order to not die. Food is not a fundamental building block of the social fabric. In Italy people live to eat and in other places people eat to live. I've heard that expression used many times. But when you work in a kitchen, whether in your home or in a restaurant, you see food differently. You see the passion that goes into the creation. One of my critics recently wrote a blog about food as art and how art pervades life. That the most creative places on earth are where art blends with life and all that life entails. I hadn't thought about that until I read her blog. I can tell you from my own experience what she observed is true. Most people don't see it. But I have seen it first hand, anywhere in the world I have traveled. Life is a work of art. Art is in each of us. It is the expression of that art, whether in food, words, paintings, sculptures, furniture, or just how you arrange your space that reveals who you are. Displays what makes you unique in the world. Gives you something to talk with others about as you try to comprehend their art.

"We may think of famous artists as the pinnacle of art in the world, but I don't believe that's true. I think the true artists are those who create a life and guide it to adulthood and then release it into the wild to see what it will make of itself. They are the ones who create something so spectacular that only those who really watch for it can see it. Hidden magic if you will. There but not seen by anyone who doesn't know where to look. And that new life will never disappoint. It will take a road less travelled. In almost every case not the road the creator would have chosen. But that's what makes the new life art. The ability to blaze a path, to imagine a difference from what they have known. To simply be different."

I'm amazed at how wide-ranging X's comments are. Of course, I'm flattered that he mentioned my blog and what I had to say. But he has taken a much more global perspective about his subject than I've seen him take in the past. Is that what this new project is all about? Demonstrating that food is more than a collection of meats, vegetables and spices thrown together in a million different ways, but at the end of the day it is all just meat, vegetables and spices so no reason to get all excited. I'm not really sure what this program is all about. Is he working in this kitchen? Or is he just using it as a studio to illustrate the points he wants to make? And did he just exhaust all the points in one speech? If so, where does he go from here? I'm not sure, but either he's gathering his thoughts to launch off in another direction or he's just resting for a moment.

Chef Luigi Libretto approaches X. "Chef learned every recipe in this kitchen from his Nona. Who is Nona?"

Chef Luigi responds, "Nona in Italy is grandmother. In my case my family is not so old between mother and daughter. So, my Nona is actually my grandmother's mother. She is almost a hundred years now. But she cook from age ten when she learn from her Nona. So, the recipes I prepare have been in family six generations, maybe more. No one has been able to tell who my Nona's Nona learned from. It may be many more generations, I not know."

"And the other members of your kitchen staff?" X gestures to the others in the kitchen.

"Roberto is the son of my sister Sophia. He prepares our breads and makes our pastas. Fresh every day. Roberto went to USA. To culinary institute. Near New York. He graduate top his class. Fancy restaurants there ask him come cook for them. He say no, return to Positano. To family. He could be big chef like you. But family more important."

"Family or a girl?" X seeks to clarify.

"Roberto marry her when he return. She likes Positano. Not so happy New York when she visit. Little Roberto come soon."

"So, Roberto gave up a promising career for a girl." X pushes Luigi Libretto to confirm.

"Life is compromise when life is about family. Some people not care family." Luigi gestures like pushing away. "They all about me. I all important. They are ones who not cook. Food about sharing. It about family. It about giving to others you special talent. Something you create to make family and friends happy, content, and relaxed. Feel all is good and tomorrow will be good too."

"So, Roberto gave up what would have made him successful to be with those he loves."

X is still trying to bring out the point about family. I see that, but why is he going back to it again and again?

"Roberto not give up. Roberto chose life he want. We have all done that. Family comes first. Food connects us. So, food becomes natural part of each of us. Those who chose to carry the recipes from generation to generation become chefs or Nona's. It all same."

"Who else do we have on your kitchen staff?" X finally got the comment he wanted. I wonder how much of that discussion will end up on his program.

"Isabella holds secrets our ragu. You talked meats in sauce. Isabella knows all ingredients, how much, which are perfecto. She very patient. Ragu takes much time to bring flavors just right. She and

Roberto come early to prepare."

"And who is Isabella related to?"

"Isabella my daughter, second wife. First wife no have children. She tired waiting for me come home from restaurant. Go Naples with butcher. Eh. What can you do? Isabella mother first wife sister. She not so unhappy I never home. She makes beautiful dresses and sells them stores here and here." Chef Luigi gestures toward nearby stores.

"So, I'm doing Isabella's job today." X confirms.

"Isabella also make dolce. Best Tiramisu and Lemoncello cake I eat." Chef Luigi pats his more than ample stomach.

X nods to the other member of the kitchen staff.

"Lorenzo my brother. He prepare all secondi piatti. The fish, the seafood, the lamb chops, steaks, veal. He plates dishes. Hands off to wait staff. Ensure everything perfecto."

X muses a moment probably for effect. "You keep everything in the family."

SORRY

I go back up to my room after a while because X continues to shoot his new project. I've had a sample of it, believe it will be interesting, but wonder if the focus is too restricted. He seems obsessed about how the family and food seem to be bound together somehow. That's a great theme for an episode. Maybe you could make a series of it going around the globe showing how food plays that central role in the lives of individuals. But he also touched on the fact that some people have dissociated food from family. Dissociated themselves from family and therefore the whole nexus he's describing has disappeared. Is that what he's really trying to explore in this project? How people get lost when they disconnect from the traditions, expectations and social bonds of a family?

I can see where that might be a worthwhile project. But I'm not sure if it would hold an audience once he's shown the linkages in three to five different cultures. Why would I want to watch an exploration of the same theme for a whole season? What makes his last program so compelling is you never knew from one show to the next what he was going to talk about. You didn't watch because you were interested in Hong Kong street food, even if that was what he featured that episode. You watched because he was exploring some aspect of food and how it is prepared or how it is paired with something you never would have thought about.

He makes dining out interesting because he provides provocative insights about how different cuisine is prepared, how it is paired and what the ritualistic aspects of the food might be. Things you would seldom or ever take the time to consider. And when confronted with the dish you've seen on his show, you suddenly have understandings you didn't before. You have insight that makes the whole experience more interesting. It gives you something to discuss with the others with whom you are dining that night.

Somehow, I'm starting to see why X is concerned that he may have made a mistake with this new project. Will people react to it in the same way they do with his current show? Should he have stayed with the tried and true formula? Sometimes staying on the cutting edge requires you to blow up what you've so carefully constructed. But if you do it too early or too late you may lose the audience you built up over time, lose the good will and expectations that people have about you.

About nine pm a knock on my door leads me to open it finding X standing there, still wearing his kitchen jacket, but no hat. Tomato stains are evident from the ragu he made for the show. He looks tired, exhausted really. I put my arm around his shoulder and lead him into my room. "That the first episode?" I ask to see what he wants to talk about.

He shakes his head but says nothing as I deliver him to the bed, where he sits down, head down, looking at his shoes, or so it seems to me.

"What's wrong?" I try to get him to talk to me.

"I've tried... but I just don't know."

"Want to get something to eat and talk about it?"

He glances up and barely smiles at me, "You were listening."

"Of course. You're trying to explore a difficult subject. Hoping you can hit us on the head with a two-by-four because so many are blithely going about a life that has little meaning, is disconnected from everything that has mattered for centuries, and somehow we think the world will be better for it."

X frowns, "I don't know about that last part. I don't think most people think about the world. So, whether it will be better because they have unhooked from the umbilical cord doesn't really matter to them. They're self-absorbed. They're the only thing that matters and they don't amount to much so if you look at it from that point of view, they don't really matter either. If they aren't here, no one will care."

I nod, knowing what he's talking about. I see people every day on the streets of New York, going to work, coming home from work. Going to the store, buying clothes or whatever. They seem on autopilot. Not much phases them, but few engage them either. They are living out a life, but what is the meaning of it? "What made you decide to explore this topic?"

"I feel it too." X responds. "I thought if I came to where food, family and creativity intersect I might find the connections I was feeling the loss of."

"And you're not." I surmise underlies his near panic and evident depression.

"I thought I could just slide into Luigi's kitchen and become a part of the whole thing. Luigi doesn't know that my cameraman speaks fluent Italian. He listens to everything and tells me over dinner what the others are saying about me. They're trying to accept me, but I'm not in the flow of the family. They have all known each other their whole lives. They have all learned from Roberto going to the Culinary Institute, but they decide what they want to use and what doesn't fit their technique, their tradition, their family terroir, if you will. I really think there is something to that. A family terroir. The more a family gets spread out the more the whole terroir breaks down. I don't know. I guess I thought Luigi's family would accept me if anyone would. I've known him and his whole family since I was a kid. In fact, he was the first person to notice I seemed to have a knack for cooking simple things. I was always trying to make bread. Now what kid makes bread when you can buy it at the grocery store and that's what everyone's mom sends in with your peanut butter and jelly? I never liked air, or what I thought was mostly air. So, I went to a local bakery and asked them how they made bread.

The owner took me under his wing and talked to my parents. Said he would teach me how to make bread if they would let me come to the bakery at three-thirty in the morning before I went in to school. I was just fascinated by the whole process. How adding yeast to dough makes it rise. How adding different ingredients can change it so radically. To make it sweet or savory. To make it dense and full of seeds or airy like a challah. I don't know why I identified with bread as a kid when no one I knew cared about anything other than Wonder bread and baloney."

"It led you to become one of the most recognized chefs in the world." I offer to make him realize he shouldn't be depressed. "You can still make your project into something important. You're on to something here. Whether it's a series or a segment of a larger series I'm not sure. But you can learn from this and so can your audience."

X seems to refocus on me for a moment, thinks about my comment. "You missed my point. And if you missed it how can I expect my audience to understand what I'm feeling? But maybe the answer to that is maybe I shouldn't want them to understand what I'm feeling."

"Feeling?" I zero in on the word that had eluded me previously. "What is it you want us to feel?"

"Hope," comes as his single word reply.

"Hope that those who have dissociated from family and society can reconnect?" I try to clarify.

"It's more than reconnect." X reflects. "It's more like reintegrate. Reignite a flame, a passion, a set of desires. Become part of that which they walked away from. And that's not so easy. If you put time and distance between you and those who are a part of you, they may no longer care about you, want you to be a part of the traditions and family events that are important to them. And when you don't value food and the connections that food represent, you don't experience the same familiar comforts that make all the turmoil in your life melt away."

"Are you saying you want to go home but don't know how to get

304

there?" I extract from his rambling discourse.

"I can't," is his simple response. "I have no home. I've wandered the world for so long there is no anchor holding me anywhere."

"What about your family?"

"My parents passed when I was twelve. Raised by my grandparents who passes when I was thirty. No brothers, no sisters. No one to connect to. And besides, I was adopted. So, I have no family traditions, no Nona recipes, no roots and no family tree."

"But you know people all over the world." I point out. "How can you feel alone when you are recognized anywhere you go?"

"You still don't get it. You of all people who probably knows me better than anyone else I can think of. You who dissect my soul, show my superficial analysis, point out when I miss the whole point of the presentation I'm trying to make. You're my Jiminy Cricket. You're the one who keeps me honest, keeps me focused on delivering a quality program that will entertain and interest a diverse audience. Without you my show would have disappeared years ago. And if you don't get it, is there any hope that anyone else could?"

"Tell me what I'm missing." I throw back at him.

X rises and walks over to look out the window on the blue Mediterranean Sea only a few hundred yards from my window. An incredible view on an ancient body of water than has seen the rise and fall of civilizations for thousands of years. Waters that remember the first men venturing beyond their own shores. Exploring what lies beyond. And building empires, destroying empires and building a modern society that clearly hasn't connected everyone to the fundamentals of human emotional needs. "It may be as simple as you."

"Me?"

"Making a connection, a lasting connection. You tried to point out to me that I ignored your needs when we were last together. I was self-absorbed. You were the one who tried to connect with me. I didn't think about connections that night. I thought only about pleasing me and hope you were pleased as well. You would have positive thoughts about me and hopefully continue to feed me the criticism and support I need to keep going. You've held up your end of that deal. I'm the one who disconnected from you even though you kept offering to keep that connection alive and even build on it. The way I've treated you I don't deserve what you've so freely given. For that I'm sorry."

"Why are you dwelling on the past when your issue seems to be what lies ahead?" I try to refocus him on something that I hope to steer to be more responsive to his needs.

"I am what I am because of the past and that past is limiting my options going forward," sounds rehearsed. As if he's thought about this moment at least a dozen times. Why?

"Hold on. You're famous. People know who you are and like what you do. That's a franchise for the future. You bring insights to situations that people value. That is the basis for a valuable future for you and your audience. And speaking of audience, with the work you're doing now you have a great opportunity to grow that audience. Touch new lives. Extend your franchise to a whole new generation and group of people who are looking for insights and meaning in their own lives. You bring that. Do you have any idea how many people would die for the opportunity to live your life? To visit exotic places around the world. To meet fascinating people. To try foods no one has ever heard of outside a tiny community? People envy you, not because you're disconnected, but because you're connected to the very things you were talking about on your program today. You have those insights. You have the ability to make people all over the world think about subjects and issues no one else is introducing into their thoughts. Don't you see that?"

"Superficial." X responds.

"What do you mean superficial? The thickness of the crust on a Crème Brule is superficial. Making people think is not superficial. It brings meaning to lives. Maybe not the art you were speaking about in being a parent, but you still have that option. If you think what you're doing isn't so important in the greater scheme of things, then maybe you ought to have a kid or better yet a half dozen kids so you can create your own kitchen staff that consists of friends and relatives. Your family. The idea of connections doesn't have to only be retrospective. Not just those who came before and are your contemporaries. You can start a whole new generation of your family. You can mold them, support them, and give them all the connections they need to succeed. And I'm not just talking about family connections. Being in the business the way you are, you have connections that would ensure your family can be anything it wants to be anywhere it wants to be. Don't you see what a great advantage that is? An advantage few have. A pathway to success few have. You can almost ensure that your family contributes more to society than any of the rest of us."

"That's nonsense. You contribute with your blog. You contribute to me, shape what I do, make me better. You can do the same and yet you don't have a family of your own either. Why not? Why aren't we talking about you in this conversation? Why am I the only one feeling this way?"

"Is it because you travel the world and have no home to speak of? But you established that as your chosen path in life. You gave up the restaurant life for the travel life. You could have been home every night. Maybe late. But you could have come snuggle with that one most important person in your life. But you chose a different path, one that would bring you to global attention. You became larger than the life you ever could have had in one restaurant, in one city making one menu per season. That was a deliberate choice on your part. I can't tell you how many millions of people are glad you made that choice. Because you have entertained, educated and informed people about food, culture and civilization the world over in a way that is personal and important. So, let's stop this discussion about how your life has no meaning. You just need to look at things differently. Make the connections you feel you are lacking and get on with the life you were destined to live."

X shakes his head. "You're connected directly with people all over the world. My connections are indirect at best. This is no life for anyone, I'm sorry you don't see that."

ASPIRATION

X decides to break the tension between us. "The final episode is about to air."

"Final episode?" I apparently didn't take the same turn his mind did.

"My travel series. You should enjoy this one."

I turn on the television and find the English language channel broadcasting his show. "Hi everyone. Thanks for joining me for my final installment of X marks the spot. Tonight, we are in Boston joining Chef Wendell Holmes at the Great Dissent. For those of you who aren't familiar with this particular eating establishment, Chef Holmes is a direct descendent of a prominent Boston family. In fact, one of his ancestors sat upon the Supreme Court where he was known as the Great Dissenter. He was also known for a quote often repeated in Boston, 'A mind that is stretched by a new experience can never go back to its old dimensions.'

"So, Chef Holmes has taken that thought in a new direction." X continues. "The specialty of his restaurant is a variation on a Barefoot Contessa pork tenderloin recipe."

The camera zooms in to a tray on the preparation table in the restaurant kitchen. X and Chef Holmes approach the table and the meat on that tray. "Could you describe how you prepare this particular dish for us Chef Holmes?"

"Absolutely, X." Chef Holmes goes through the steps, demonstrating what he is discussing as he describes it. "The preparation begins with washing down the tenderloins and patting them dry, laying them on paper towels to absorb any excess water or moisture. Next, we strip rosemary and thyme leaves from their stems and chop them up into fine pieces, placing them in a bowl when complete and then mixing with a teaspoon of course pepper and a tablespoon of course sea salt. When this mixture is ready, we add the secret ingredient, which is finely chopped marijuana seeds."

X stops him here, "Marijuana seeds. Finely chopped."

"Yes. A tablespoon is about the right amount, but you can vary that according to taste or your objectives for destressing in this meal. We mix it in thoroughly. Now is the interesting part. We cover the tenderloins with an unflavored olive oil, then spread the herb and spice mixture over the oil-covered tenderloins. Finally, we wrap each loin in prosciutto, wrapping around the loin such that the entire loin is encased with the thinly sliced dried ham. I like to let this sit for a few minutes to make sure it is at room temperature and then bake in a hot oven, set for 350 degrees for about twenty-five minutes. This is served with an apple chutney. There are hundreds of apple chutney recipes, so I won't suggest that one is better than another. It should be a matter of taste preference."

"What wine do you generally recommend?" X asks, knowing he's setting Wendell Holmes up on this question.

"Generally, a wine is not required to pair with this dish. It has the effect of creating the same end state from the herb rub mixture."

"If someone wanted a pairing anyway?" X persists.

"In my experience a nice Cab Franc is always excellent with Pork Tenderloin." Chef Holmes muses before issuing a cautionary warning. "But I'd also recommend the diner go easy on the wine when consuming this dish. The effects are not only unexpected in the mouth but in the general response to the dish."

"How popular is this dish in your restaurant?"

"It's our specialty, so it outsells everything else on the menu by quite a margin."

"What else do you spice in this manner?" X wishes to show that The Great Dissent is not a one trick menu restaurant.

"We have an extensive array of dishes that incorporate cannabis in the spices. "Chef Holmes responds enthusiastically. "They include chicken, duck, lamb, roasts… even prime rib can be prepared with the appropriate seasoning to have an effect on the diner."

"Would you consider this a recreational or medicinal use of cannabis?"

"Neither really. This is incorporation of a spice or herb in food preparation. Does anyone regulate the application of basil or oregano? What's the difference between dill weed and weed? If you're using it to season or add spice to the flavor of food who should care? I mean marijuana brownies have been a staple in many homes for decades."

"There has been a tradition in your family for nearly two centuries of stimulating debate, examining new ideas and challenging established precedent. Is that what you're hoping will happen amongst your patrons or are you simply trying to create a national debate about the many potential uses of cannabis?" An unusual question for X, but this is an unusual show for X. Normally he stays clear of anything that might have a political overtone.

"Both, really," Chef Holmes responds with a considered look into the distance. "This is Boston, the birthplace of our nation. Where the first shots of the revolution were fired. Maybe the Great Dissent is firing the first shots of a food revolution. Just think if every chef in the world simply included cannabis amongst his or her spices. What would be the effect upon mankind if it were just another ingredient in what we eat every day? I would say, none, other than some people with certain allergies might find themselves less sensitive to them. Conversations might be more relaxed. Debate more civilized. People might be more willing to listen to each other. What if people were willing to consider an alternative position to the one they have formulated, not by considered exploration of all of the facts, but because someone they know or consider an expert rattles on about it. I'm not saying that incorporation of cannabis in food preparation will have that kind of transformative effect upon our society, but someone needs to experiment, try it to see what kind of effect it may have. I for one believe in trial and error. I think it's okay to try something. If it fails? Well, I've learned something. If it succeeds in delivering the desired results? That's great. And if it ends up resulting in something unexpected? Then we reconsider based on whether it's a good or not so good result."

"You get a fair number of politicians in here." X wants to continue exploring the non-cuisine aspects of this food experiment. "What's been their response so far?"

"We decided to do a general disclosure on the menu rather than calling it out on every dish. We inform our patrons that cannabis is an ingredient in certain rubs and spice packages we use. If anyone is concerned or interested in knowing about which dishes are inclusive of this use, they should ask their server."

"And?" X pushes the question for more specifics.

"Some ask and some don't. Of those who ask I think there have been a few who have declined the dish, but on balance I think there are many more who have enjoyed it than have declined it."

"Has anyone else in Boston followed your lead?" X looks around as if he were perusing the streets around the restaurant, although he clearly can't see them.

"No other restaurant has chosen to advertise cannabis on their menu." Chef Holmes states carefully.

"What about nationally? Anyone else you know of or are you the sole practitioner of 'higher' grade steaks and chops?"

Chef Holmes laughs. "I'll have to remember that. Great play on words. To answer your question, I'm not aware of anyone who is doing it quite the way we are, although I've spoken to a number of chefs who are experimenting with cannabis. None have confirmed actually serving it to the public, incidentally. I don't understand the trepidation, personally. It's not unlawful where recreational use is permitted. It's a natural substance as opposed to all the pills people take for one thing or another. I think of it as just another spice on my spice rack."

"Do you see yourself carrying on the tradition of your ancestor? Stretching the mind with a new experience?"

Chef Holmes laughs again. "Quite literally. That was one of the guiding principles we had when we decided to open a restaurant serving traditional fare but prepared in a different way. As you noted, our pork tenderloin is based on a Barefoot Contessa recipe. I mean how much more mainstream can you get. Probably half of the women in America who cook at home have tried at least one of her recipes. And cannabis is not the only twist we have incorporated, but I'd prefer to invite your viewers to stop by and learn more about these twists. You see, we talk to our patrons. I know that's a bit unusual in the restaurant industry. Stock recipes all prepared exactly the same for every patron tends to be the norm. And when you're looking for consistency that approach works well. However, in the grand Boston tradition, we recognized that while all Americans are equal under the law, not all Americans have the same palate. Some people like spice and heat. Others want bland and protein. Some want charcoal coating and others want you to pass a steak over the flames as quickly as possible, just to sear in the juice. Everyone is slightly different. So, we talk to our customers about our standard fare. We ask questions about how we can make it suit their tastes more precisely than the standard preparation. Does that make sense?"

"Steak houses will ask do you like rare, medium or well done with a number of variations within that range." X pushes back.

"A recognition that not all tastes are the same, but we go beyond the number of calories burned to raise the temperature of the meat. We want to know what is the best meal they ever had. Describe it. And in describing that best meal we get insights into how we can prepare this meal to suit their taste. A step beyond, if you will."

"Push the palate pleasing approach to an extreme." X notes. "That creates more work for your team in the kitchen. Makes you focus on nuance and how to prepare a meal in the gray areas between the well-established zones of traditional preparation."

Chef Holmes smiles enigmatically. "If we don't learn how to elevate our skills, our insights our creativity, we have to rely on others to do so for us. What is to be learned by asking others to do what we should? Not everyone needs to be the frontier of food nuances. But some of us do. If we don't create them, it's not likely that others will."

"The frontier of food nuance. What a great description of your approach to cuisine. You've led us into an unexplored territory and are proving that there is nothing to worry about. No hostile natives waiting to try to reclaim what was once their exclusive province. So, what's the next frontier of food nuance? What's next for Chef Wendell Holmes?"

Chef Holmes glances at X curiously. "I would see those two questions as requiring different answers. The next great frontier for cuisine is reducing calories and keeping taste. Every attempt at that has been a compromise. There must be a way to make tasteful foods not contribute to obesity. Now for Chef Wendell Holmes? That's a different question. I'm not a food scientist so I'm not on that eternal quest for calorie-free taste. I'm looking for an opportunity where I can bring my family values and traditions and at the same time awaken memories of family comfort in fine dining."

The episode ends with X appearing on screen alone and without a chef jacket. Instead he is dressed in a fitted Italian suit with contrasting handkerchief in his jacket pocket. "My next adventure reflects the desires of Chef Holmes. To find the roots of family comfort in fine dining, but even more fundamental, to create an understanding of the central role of food in all the meaningful social discourse everywhere. I hope you'll join me in this next exploration. And until then, remember, X marks the spot for our next adventure, together."

I click off the television. "Very nicely done. A great way to close out that phase of your life. Leave a legacy of showing how we are all moving beyond our prejudices, learning from our past and remaining optimistic about a future where we can accept differences, and celebrate enlightened understanding."

X frowns at me even though we are sitting side-by-side on the end of my bed. "Did you watch the same program I just did?"

"Absolutely." I affirm. "What about what I just said do you not agree with?"

"Everything. I thought it was a terrible way to end a career. We talked about one ingredient, not about a new way of preparing wild boar, a new way of rolling pinci pasta to make it thinner, or the latest expensive kitchen gadget for all the women to decorate their kitchen since so few of them actually cook or even prepare meals at home. Nothing of substance from what my audience has come to expect of me."

It's clear to me that X knows it was a great episode, meaningful on so many levels. He's mocking all those who have copied him who specialize in preparation methods over the whole dish, focus on appliances rather than what is made by those appliances. The new gee-whiz attachment that will automatically make paper-thin pasta. Just load it up and it will deliver perfection every time without you having to do a thing.

"You know what I've come to realize?" X asks.

I shake my head not sure where he intends to go next.

"Your thought about me creating my own restaurant and staffing the kitchen with my kids. There is some appeal to your suggestion. But the more I think about it, I've come to the conclusion it wouldn't work."

"I don't understand. Why not?"

"A family has to be rooted in history. A time, a place. Rooted in the land, the family terroir, like I described before. Without that terroir, without Nona recipes, without all the generations of tradition, conversations, solving problems together, persevering through the bad times and celebrating the good, there is no life to the food. No art, as you so rightly pointed out. Food and art are inseparable, but both require inspiration that only comes from all that has gone before, all that has contributed to the DNA of the family that exists here today. They are one and inseparable."

"Okay. So, what's the problem?"

"I don't have any of that history. I don't belong anywhere. I have no distinct terroir. So, any food I create will have no distinction. It won't be special to anyone, most importantly it won't be distinctive to me. It won't comfort anyone. It will be food to live and that's all. And from everything you learned at Vik, that's not a life. That's not contributing. That is only existing in a world of sameness. And that's not something I aspire to."

ENDS AND BEGINNINGS

Of course, X stayed the night. I tried as best I could to comfort him. To make him see the corner he painted himself into in his mind is only in his mind. It doesn't exist in the mind of his audience. It doesn't exist for me. It took a long time to get him aroused and focused on making love. Even when we finally did, I know he was less engaged with me than when he came to my apartment and we made love after cooking together. When he finally fell asleep, I felt I'd let him down somehow. As if I'd not been able to bring him back from some dark place he is staring into. He came to me for help. Said he needed someone to talk to about the disaster he was creating. At least he thought it might become a disaster. Watching him shoot the episode, it was interesting, engaging in many respects. But I could understand his trepidation. I had difficulty understanding how he was going to come up with new material to get through an entire season from just one kitchen. But then I'd not sat through all the meetings to define the project, line up the backers and convince the network to guarantee to air the episodes. If it bombed, there was no way they would. But X's instincts are good. I'm sure he's already planning on changes to the format to ensure its audience and success.

I fell asleep with those thoughts running through my mind, listening to X's heavy breathing. It seemed to me that he was both mentally and physically exhausted. So, I cuddled up behind him, with my arm around him, hoping he would feel my attempt to comfort him, feel the assurance I wanted him to have that everything would be all right. But then I feared I had not delivered the comfort food to him that would reassure him that not only will he get through this period of uncertainty successfully, but that he would learn from it. That he would become stronger and be better prepared for the next challenge that he would face. And somewhere I knew the issue will be that he will continue to face these challenges alone because he feels disconnected from the people who matter most to him. His audience.

I must have slept fitfully for I awaken to find myself turned away from X. I don't feel him behind me and realize the day has begun. Does that mean he got up and went up for breakfast without me? Probably thought it would take me too long to shower and get myself made up for the day, even though I think of myself as pretty low maintenance that way. Not into a lot of cosmetics to highlight my best features. I seldom go out with people so no sense using eyeliner when no one is going to be staring into my eyes. Although X might be later, so I need to consider some makeup today.

I roll over and see X standing on the end of the bed, looking away from me. Why would he be doing that? And then I see the thin rope strung over the fan that comes around his neck causing his head to fall forward. The image slowly burns into my mind, slowly raising a voice in my head saying that something is terribly wrong. But I can't believe what my eyes are telling me. It can't be. It's not possible.

I leap up, working my way across the bed until I bring my arms around him. In the process I push his legs forward. He is hanging there. And the effect of my push is the fan comes down from the ceiling on top of me as I land on top of X.

"No! X! What have you done? This can't be. You can't have possibly…" I'm crying as I try to revive him, not even having noticed that the ceiling fan has risen a bump on the back of my head where it landed on me. I don't feel the pain in my head. I don't feel anything except the horror of the moment.

I don't know when I finally called the office. All I know is at some point others are in the room. Photographers, policemen, hotel staff. I don't even know who most of them are or why they are there. All I know is X is gone. Forever. And I couldn't save him.

A week later I write my next blog. It has taken me a week to realize I have to say something about X since the rest of the media has now had its say.

A NEW BEGINNING

Chef Xavier Francis pushed the boundaries of what we know about cuisine on every level that matters. And in doing so he made us wonder about a world in a way no one else has. We owe him a debt of gratitude for making us more aware, more introspective and more focused on what it means to create in the one sphere that is most essential in our lives.

Two weeks ago, I wrote about the interplay between art, life, food and creativity/inspiration. I put creativity and inspiration together because in my mind they are inseparable. One leads to the other and the other enables the first. Chef X taught us many lessons, but on his last day he told me he had learned one from me. That lesson was all life is art. Wherever you go, whatever you do, however you do it, you are contributing art to the world. In his last show and the first under a new format he was developing, he talked about how the most important art is your progeny. You create something unique in the world. No matter what role that individual takes as her or his alone, that person is contributing something new to the world. And how they contribute it is art. A form of expression. A work of beauty that maybe only a few will view, understand or appreciate. But that individual is the most important source of art in the world.

On his last day Chef X also talked about a family terroir. How important it is to have roots upon which you can build an environment for yourself and your family that will allow you all to be comfortable, safe and inspired. To enable you to conceive of the art that you will bring into the world, whether food, paintings, furniture, a building design, a more effective sales approach, a clean office building or a research paper for a university class. Everything you produce is art and builds upon the art of those around you. The mission we each carry with us is to elevate our art. To bring our creative abilities to a higher plane. To deliver something we never considered possible.

Chef X was at a turning point in his career. He was gambling that a new format would enable him to reach a higher plane with is art, to reach new people, to inspire more discussion about the meaning of food in a world, the meaning of art in life and the meaning of life as the capsule holding all that is important to each of us and our families.

On that last day, Chef X lamented that we have failed many people in our world. That we have allowed individuals to disconnect from family and the family terroir. To dissociate themselves from the art that their family has built upon for generations. To live a life that is barren of connection. Bereft of meaning. Contributing art that does not inspire, does not enable either themselves or others to explore new areas of our existence. Chef X talked about how such people feed themselves with meaningless nutrients, that do not comfort them, that do not connect them, do not energize or enable them to do anything other than exist. Chef X lamented this fate of so many and that those of us who remain connected have allowed so many to dissociate to the detriment of all.

Underlying all of my discussions with Chef X on his last day was his despair that so many have lost hope of achievement, lost hope of reconnecting with family and lost hope that their contributions will inspire themselves, family, friends or strangers also looking to contribute their own art while reaching a higher plane and audiences.

An hour after I sent that blog, I received a text:

J:

You have elevated all of us with your blog. We are all mourning the loss of X.

Z

I couldn't find the words to respond. The next text came shortly thereafter.

J:

I'm here for you when you're ready to talk.

O

The third was the one I didn't expect and have the most difficulty reconciling.

J:

You have become my inspiration. Art is in you, surrounds you even if you only see it in your mind's eye. You elevate all of us through your words. What can I do to help you now that we have all lost X?

Ace

I decide I have to think about his question. But then the only response I could give enters my mind:

Ace:

Teach me to cook.

J

The End

About the Author

dhtreichler toured the global garden spots as a defense contractor executive for fifteen years. His assignments covered intelligence, training and battlefield systems integrating state of the art technology to keep Americans safe. During this time he authored seven novels exploring the role of increasingly sophisticated technology in transforming our lives and how men and women establish relationships in a mediated world.

Keep up with all of dhtreichler's latest work and essays at www.dhtreichler.com.

Also by dhtreichler

Emergence

Barely Human

The Ghost in the Machine: a novel

World Without Work

The Great American Cat Novel

My Life as a Frog

Life After

The Tragic Flaw

Succession

The End Game

I Believe in You

Rik's

The Illustrated Bearmas Reader – Ralph's Ordeals

The First Bearmas